THE SEQUINED STALKER
SPEAKS . . .

I feel good tonight. Very good, indeed. I think I might finally be rid of Doctor. The look on his face was soooooo satisfying this time. The best yet. He hurt more. Surprise on his dumb face.

I told the reporter I didn't ''stalk.'' Didn't like the name. Suggested a better one. That was a laugh. Now she calls me a *monster*. Little does she know. It's all in the eye of the beholder. I must speak to her again. Set her straight. Scare her a little.

I had to go out after I read the paper. Everything took place as I predicted. I am *attuned*. *Attuned* to what people might do. That's what made it so easy. That's why no one will ever catch me.

Books by Anne Reed Rooth

FATAL STRANGER
EYE OF THE BEHOLDER

EYE OF THE
BEHOLDER

ANNE REED ROOTH

CHARTER BOOKS, NEW YORK

**Dedicated to my family, my support,
my fans, my life**

EYE OF THE BEHOLDER

A Charter Book/published by arrangement with
the author

PRINTING HISTORY
Charter edition/February 1990

ISBN: 1-55773-314-7

Charter Books are published by The Berkley Publishing Group,
200 Madison Avenue, New York, New York 10016.
The name ''CHARTER'' and the ''C'' logo
are trademarks belonging to Charter Communications, Inc.

PRINTED IN THE UNITED STATES OF AMERICA

10 9 8 7 6 5 4 3 2 1

Prologue

They rode in silence to the fifth floor, glancing alternately at each other, then quickly averting their eyes to the flashing dials ticking off the numbers. He was having a hard time remembering her name. At this point it would appear rude to ask her again. Her expensive perfume filled the elevator, reminding him of Christmas visits to a department store cosmetic counter. She would have looked good in anything, but the white beaded dress and the feather boa thrown casually over her milky shoulder put her in a category he could only classify as smashing. Yet he thought she could have done without the small cocktail hat.

The elevator opened with a soft whish. Holding the door, he stepped out first and looked from side to side, relieved that the hall was deserted.

"Here we go," he said, still a touch apprehensive.

"Thanks," she answered in the throaty contralto that had attracted him in the first place. And the smile. Vermilion lips. Pure white teeth. Fire and ice.

The hall was dim except for the crystal sconces casting eerie arcs of light on the walls. They walked side by side, her small feet in satin pumps, quiet on the thick carpeting. From the window at the end of the hall he could see that mean gray cataracts scummed the evening sky. There was still time to call it off, but he was fast approaching the point of no return. Just a few more steps and they'd reach his hotel room. Now was the time to decide.

He hesitated ever so briefly and she caught it right off.

"Anything wrong?"

"No, no," he answered, fumbling with the key. He pretended to be a little drunker than he actually was. Somehow it put the situation in a better light. An excuse for tomorrow. Balm for guilt.

She smiled at him patiently as he worked on the lock. He looked up. Her eyes were a gray-violet and reflected the light in pinpoints of purple. The points of light seemed to fly like sparks. She was either a trusting soul or a reckless one, to go off with a stranger, he thought. Reckless abandon. The term spurred him on, high anticipation with him now. He would proceed as planned and no one would ever be the wiser.

He opened the door, stood aside for her to enter, then stepped in and closed it behind them. They stood for a moment, exchanging glances, the silence awkward. Then came her seductive smile, putting him at ease.

He moved to embrace his conquest. With lightning speed and expert aim, she made a startling move. Stunned, he looked down at the small red splotch widening on his best white shirt. Then back at her face. Her small ears were set far back, which, coupled with the wide-set eyes, gave her the dangerous look of a wild horse. She suddenly brayed like one.

Clutching his chest, trying to stifle the pain, he slumped to the floor. She bent down and deftly removed the sharp object that had pierced his heart.

With a white-gloved hand, she opened the door and left. A remnant of her hasty departure fluttered through the air. Just as he closed his eyes for the last time, he watched the single white feather from the boa float down and settle on the carpet.

1

Hawk Sullivan slouched in a lounge chair on the patio of his Spanish-style bungalow, admiring the spray of red bougainvillea hanging over the fence. Clusters of palm trees dotting the wide green lawn stretched toward the sky, swaying slightly in the breeze off the glistening Pacific Ocean visible in the distance. From a side table he picked up a sweating glass of vodka and tonic and sipped slowly, wondering what the man who had called wanted. Marshall Meyers, he'd said his name was, sounding vague.

When Sullivan and Manuel Castro formed the detective agency, there was an idle period when clients were few and far between. But they'd hustled their butts until their reputation took root, and now things, if not sailing along, were hobbling in the right direction.

Since he and Castro were longtime friends, the partnership terms were loose and amiable, like the two who entered into the agreement. Sullivan was an ex-FBI agent booted out of the service because he preferred to bend rules rather than follow them, and Castro, a San Diego police sergeant on suspension. Working out of Sullivan's house to provide him a tax deduction, they allocated fifty percent of fees from any case to maintain agency expenses, the other fifty deposited into the pocket of the one handling the case. When pressed, each felt welcome to dip into the till. They alternated taking assignments, but if someone requested one person in particular, they did their utmost to comply.

Castro was just finalizing a nasty divorce case, their least favorite endeavor, which put Sullivan up at bat. He needed extra money badly for an overhaul payment on the thirty-foot ketch he couldn't comfortably afford, but irrationally couldn't part with. He'd traded in his old Peugeot, called the Chug, for a sleek black Porsche he named Felix after his favorite childhood comic strip. That debt needed servicing also. He'd always said money was only as good as the use to which it was put. His two possessions made him feel he'd achieved some status, despite the maintenance strain. He figured the object of life was to gratify oneself without getting arrested. Besides, unlike Castro, he didn't have anyone to save it for.

The idea brought a certain emptiness as his mind drifted to Evelyn Casey. A most unusual lady. Unpretentious, industrious, even though she was a wealthy oil heiress, the widow of the legendary Andrew Casey. When her husband was alive, Evelyn had rebelled at being a rich man's satellite and had gone back to college for a master's degree. She was tenacious almost to a fault. At a time when Sullivan hadn't cared about life in general or himself in particular, she had dogged him to find her sister's murderer because she was dissatisfied with the San Diego Police Department. Reluctantly he agreed, and with her background in psychology, they joined forces, albeit shakily. She had infused new life into him.

Their bond had been forged under extreme adversity, and Sullivan was anxious to test the relationship in normal circumstances. He knew he would see Evelyn again, but had no idea when. Her sister's case had ended with an unexpected turn that put their association in limbo.

The doorbell brought Sullivan to his feet. He had intended to change, but time had slipped away. Castro, always a vision of sartorial splendor, would disapprove of his faded Izod, worn chinos and Top Siders. He figured if "clothes make the man" his local haberdasher would be President instead of hawking shirts behind a counter. Evelyn Casey once said he had an air of rumpled elegance about him. He liked that.

Passing through the den, Sullivan bent his rangy frame forward to glance in the mirror over the Chinese chest. He raked his hands through his sandy sun-bleached hair and inspected his teeth. His eyes, green as the underside of a four-leaf clover, were alert; the whites, shot with coral threads, a tell-tale trace of too much communion at Jack Daniels' altar the night before. Tributaries, he liked to think experience had etched, fanned over his temples. So much for self-evaluation, he thought, opening the front door.

"Mr. Sullivan, Marshall Meyers," the man said, and extended his hand, his eyes almost as colorless as ice.

Sullivan nodded, accepting the man's strong grip. "Come on in, Mr. Meyers." He stepped back to allow the well-dressed man to enter. The dark suit screamed money. The closely cropped blond hair and the militaristic stance vaguely suggested a Wehrmacht officer out of uniform.

"Nice place you have here," Mr. Marshall Meyers said, his eyes ranging over Sullivan's den.

"Well, thanks." Sullivan was proud of the place. Cluttered, informal, furnished with memories, it revealed a chunk of his history, each piece a fine one, bargained for in some foreign bazaar.

"Quite a collection of books. You must read a lot. And records." He gestured toward Sullivan's bookcase crammed with leather-bound editions of his favorites:

Dickens, Melville, Trollope, Lewis Carroll, and detective novels, from Agatha Christie to John D. MacDonald and Lawrence Sanders. Record albums Sullivan had intended to put away littered the floor.

Sullivan shrugged. "What's a day without Mozart? And, yes, I find that reading passes the time nicely. The old need to live vicariously." He smiled.

"I wouldn't think a man like you would find it necessary to live vicariously." Meyers' eyes strayed to Sullivan's English desk.

"You'd be surprised." As Sullivan predicted, Marshall Meyers was dancing around the reason for his presence. Best put him at ease and get to the point, Sullivan decided. "Well, the sun is over the yardarm. Join me?" He lumbered across the room and semicircled behind the bar.

Meyers looked relieved. "A scotch. Rocks, please." His hand edged the silver frame on the desk. "Your wife?"

Sullivan glanced up from mixing, his eyes holding on the photograph. "Yes." Karin was so lovely that summer before she became ill. Life was lovely. "She's dead." He was able to say the word now. It still hurt, but he could say it. Evelyn Casey had taught him how to live again.

"I'm sorry."

"Me, too." Sullivan handed Meyers his drink and motioned for him to sit down. Sullivan sank into his favorite easy chair, propped his feet on the ottoman and lit a cigarette. He'd been trying to evaluate Meyers' accent. Southern, Georgia maybe, but a heritage he was trying to disguise by careful pronunciation of vowels. "Where are you from?"

"Los Angeles."

"Lived there long?"

Meyers grinned. "Long enough." Meyers crossed his legs, running his thumb and forefinger down the crease of his trousers. "You've got quite a reputation, you know. I read about the South American–based executives who were kidnapped and the ransom you were hired to negotiate.

Instead, you tracked down where they were being held, busted in under heavy security and rescued them.'' Meyers clucked his tongue in approval. ''Walked them clear across the border into Bolivia.''

Sullivan grimaced. ''I got lucky.'' That case was yesterday's mashed potatoes; much more current was the serial killer he and Evelyn Casey had tracked like hellhounds and finally captured. Sullivan wondered if the man knew about that one, the case that had changed his life.

''I heard your luck came close to running out recently. I understand you were hurt in the process of catching the serial killer who murdered the sister of the Dallas oil heiress, Evelyn Casey.''

Sullivan lifted his eyebrows, ignoring the reference to his injury. ''Let's just say Charlie Christmas' luck ran out first.''

''Are you okay now . . . physically, I mean?''

''Last time I checked,'' Sullivan shot back.

''Must have been something being face-to-face with a serial killer,'' the man said, clearly awed by the prospect.

''Being face-to-face with any kind of killer is not your basic fun.'' Sullivan thought how the public was especially intrigued by serial killings, drinking in every word the press wrote about them. And now serial killing had reached its all-time fame, if it could·be called that, with the first woman serial killer in police history on the loose in Dallas. Intrigued as the next, he himself was following the newspaper accounts carefully as headlines screamed across the country.

Sullivan saw that the man was staring at him.

''So, Mr. Meyers, what's up?''

Meyers swigged down a large slug of scotch, then cleared his throat. ''My aunt has recently died and left an estate in excess of five million dollars. Her will left everything to her son, Matt, my cousin. I have reason to believe he's dead.''

''Reason?'' Sullivan asked, blowing a smoke ring.

Meyers leaned forward, his stare intense. "About six months ago Matt got into cocaine. Really hooked. Auntie threatened to commit him to a drug center. Matt ran off to South America. São Paulo, Brazil. She got a letter from him saying that he'd straighten out on his own, then come back. Matt kept writing for money. I knew he would buy coke with it, but Auntie felt she had to send it in case he needed it to live on. Then he wrote and said he needed to move on. Was going to Brasília, because he'd gotten into a little trouble in São Paulo and wanted more money. She sent it but he never cashed the check. He hasn't been heard from since. I think Matt's trouble caused her heart attack."

"What happens to your aunt's estate if your cousin *is* dead?" Sullivan watched Meyers stiffen slightly.

"If he predeceases me, the inheritance goes to me."

Sullivan took a drag off his cigarette, then crushed it out in an already overflowing ashtray. "Let me nutshell it. You want me to try and prove he's dead so you won't have to wait seven years to collect your inheritance?"

"That's about it," Meyers answered, greedy eyes casting into the future.

It helped to like a client, but something about Meyers turned Sullivan off, the set of his jaw, the glint of greed in his eyes. It wasn't fair to judge someone by appearance, though he was often guilty of the act. However, the idea of going to South America appealed to him enough. "You'd want me to go right away, I take it."

"Tomorrow, if possible." Meyers reached into his breast pocket. "Here's Matt's picture. I've written down everything about him, description, last place he was staying, everything that might help you. I know from the caliber of your past cases that your fee must come high." Meyers whipped out a cashier's check. Standing, he handed it to Sullivan. "This should cover it."

Sullivan looked at the check. Fifty thousand dollars, U.S. Frowning, he laid it on the end table. He picked up his drink and took a swallow, then glanced up at the man before him. "Mr. Meyers, this is way too much. If you get that inheritance, you won't have it long if you continue to be so willing to part with your money."

Meyers face was tight with restraint. "It's worth it to me in view of what I stand to receive. Everything is relative, I figure."

Sullivan struck a stick match on the underside of the table and lit another cigarette. So Meyers was already wealthy, but obviously it wasn't enough. "I don't charge what the traffic will bear. Twenty-five and expenses will do it."

"The check's already made out." Meyers laid a business card on the table. "You can reach me at my office in Los Angeles to let me know about your progress. I'm staying overnight here in San Diego at the Westgate. Call me when your reservations are made. You'll leave immediately?"

Sullivan pushed up from the chair to walk Meyers to the door. "Yeah, I'll leave tomorrow. All my travel documents are current and in order."

"Fine," Meyers answered, obviously pleased with the outcome of the meeting.

Sullivan opened the door for Meyers and held on to the edge for a moment as Meyers went out. "Mr. Meyers?"

He turned back. "Yes?"

Sullivan hesitated, then asked: "What if I find your cousin alive?"

The question lifted Meyers' eyebrows before he settled into an assured expression. "I don't think you will, Mr. Sullivan. But, if you do . . . well, that's the breaks. As they say where you're going, *buenos días*." He smiled, lips only, wheeled around and hurried to the car parked in front of Sullivan's house.

"They speak mostly Portuguese in Brazil, Mr. Meyers," Sullivan said under his breath.

He strolled back to his chair, reviewing the discussion.

He started to sit down and attend to his unfinished drink, then decided to clear his thoughts by jogging on the beach instead. Heading for the bedroom to get his running shoes, he stopped by the stereo and put on Beethoven's Fifth. Music to tie your shoes by, he thought, moseying down the hall. Music to pay your bills by was even better. Half of that check went into his shallow pockets, the other into the agency coffer. A good deal all around.

Rummaging around on the cluttered closet floor, Sullivan finally located his shoes and started back to the living room. Sometimes that was as far as he got. This time he would make himself go. But it was so easy just to sit in his chair, have a drink and procrastinate.

He sat down, allowed himself one swallow, then laced up his shoes. He decided on a last cigarette, just to hold him, when Castro came wheeling in. He was a study in sky blue, from shirt to socks.

"Christ, man! Are you deaf?" Castro sauntered over to the stereo to turn down the volume, his movements fluid as if his joints had ball bearings. "Can't hear a thing."

"I could hear the music," Sullivan said, lighting a cigarette.

"Who was that I saw leaving?" Castro's voice held a slight trace of a Spanish accent.

"A client," Sullivan answered, looking at the check Meyers left. He glanced up at Castro. "I changed right after he left. I'm going jogging." He smiled pleasantly and handed Castro the check. "Eyeball this."

Castro took the check, his face cracking into an expression of supreme delight. He gave Sullivan a "high five" and sank down in the chair facing him, chocolate-brown eyes dancing. He had a solid muscular build Sullivan envied when he thought about it, a nose with a suggestion it had been broken innumerable times and a wispy moustache. With judo Castro could ground any two fistfighters before they knew what happened.

Sullivan explained what Meyers wanted him to do. "I didn't much like the fellow."

Castro gestured with his hands. "So you didn't like him. You're not looking for another best friend. You've got me. Besides, his money is as good as anybody else's. And we haven't got that much of anybody else's."

Sullivan gave him a look. A look from Sullivan was never a casual thing. "I'll be off tomorrow. I suppose you can manage without me here."

Castro grinned, showing the slight chip in his front tooth. "Well, I'll try. Just about got my case wrapped up. Maybe somebody'll boogie in with a fat check for me like Meyers did." He stood. "I came by to get some papers out of the files. You want to go with Olga and me to La Maison for dinner."

Sullivan pushed up. "Thanks, but I don't like to leave a place trying to figure out what I ate."

Castro cocked his head. "What you cook is not the stuff the American Heart Association dreams of."

Sullivan waved him off, then went out the patio door. He squatted by his patch of anemic herbs, examining the plants. He wondered if he'd fed them too much fertilizer or not enough. Karin had always tended the herb garden while he handled the gourmet cooking. A nice combination, he thought wistfully. Now he had to rely on dried weeds from a bottle. Pulling up a sprig of parsley, he stuck it in his mouth, straightened and headed toward the beach.

Before he reached the sand, he heard Castro call. Turning, Sullivan saw Castro high up on his balcony, his hand fashioned into a fist and held next to his ear, signaling a phone call.

"Who is it?" Sullivan yelled over the ocean's roar.

"From Dallas," Castro answered, as if mouthing to a lip-reader.

Sullivan chugged back up the rocks, his heart pounding, but not from exertion. Things came when you least expected them. He had finally stopped calling Evelyn Casey, making a concerted effort to be patient with her. Now, striding across the patio, he pictured her, that silky blonde he cared so much for. The laugh he liked to hear, the face he liked to look at. The aquamarine eyes that sparkled with intelligence. The sassy way she talked that amused him. But the trouble had taken it all away. Maybe, just maybe, she had finally put it behind her.

Racing across the den, he picked up the receiver before Castro could speak. "Evelyn, how are you?" He motioned for Castro to hand him a cigarette. "Pardon?" He was suddenly alerted.

"This is Captain Roger Chandler, chief of Homicide in Dallas, Texas," the voice fifteen hundred miles away repeated. "Am I speaking with Hawkins Sullivan?"

"You are." He felt a surge of trepidation. Dallas Homicide? Did the call have any connection to Evelyn Casey?

"I'd like to talk to you about the serial killer case we have here."

Lighting the cigarette, Sullivan turned his back to Castro and settled down to listen. As Chandler spoke, Sullivan's interest grew by leaps and bounds.

After a five-minute spiel from Chandler and several mutters on the other end, Sullivan said, "No, I'm not *that* busy right now, but I'd have to know more about the case before I could commit." Sullivan sensed the chief was at his wit's end, but gave Chandler no indication of his interest, thereby reserving some bargaining power. "I guess I could rearrange my schedule to be in Dallas by noon tomorrow to discuss the case." He hung up and turned in his chair, a broad smile on his lips.

It was Castro's turn for a look. "You're a smooth liar."

Sullivan shrugged. "I try to be good at whatever I do."

"Well, what was that all about other than blowing off fifty grand?" Castro paused. "Sullivan, you need that money. *We* need that money."

"Captain Chandler wants me to work with Dallas Homicide on that lady serial killer case."

"The Sequined Stalker?"

Sullivan nodded. "He's got an allotment from the city manager to hire any extra help the special task force needs."

"From the city manager? It can't be much money. You didn't even ask how much it is."

"Didn't think of it. I'm just going to *discuss* it with him."

"I know you. You've already decided you're going to do it, but you let him think you're on the fence."

Sullivan tried out his best innocent look. He knew Castro didn't buy it.

"It's really Evelyn Casey, not the case. If you ask my opinion . . ."

"I didn't," Sullivan cut him off. "Listen, no harm done. You're finishing up, you take Meyers' case. Since you're the token minority in this agency, you should get a break. You'll love South America. A fellow like you would blend right in. Take Olga with you. Meyers is loose with money. I'll call and tell him that you're going to take my place. After all, you can do what he wants as well as I can, so what does it matter who goes?"

"Is that how you look at the situation?"

"I'm not looking at it. You are. I've got to pack and make some phone calls." Sullivan walked out with a spring in his step. His desire to see Evelyn Casey was intense, to say nothing of his anticipation regarding the case.

2

Hawk Sullivan took in Captain Roger Chandler's office with one sweep. He'd expected drab surroundings and standard institutional battered furniture, the typical domain of most homicide chiefs. Instead, Chandler's setting reminded Sullivan of a furniture showroom's close-out sale. The desk was dark wood, not metal, the chairs and couch upholstered in nubby brown material made to last. Chandler had personalized the place with mementoes and plaques, and on his desk was a silver framed photograph of a plain-looking woman people probably called sweet and two clean-cut teenage children.

"Welcome to Dallas," Chandler said. The pleasant country face with the wind and sun of Texas etched on it cracked into a smile. His twang was not offensive, but left no doubt about his origin. "I appreciate your coming."

Hawk Sullivan shook hands with the captain and felt calluses in his palm. Chandler, a man big enough to have played college ball, knew what work was. Sullivan settled in a chair when Chandler rounded his desk.

As they exchanged pleasantries Chandler continued to eye Sullivan as if memorizing his face for a police line-up. Sullivan had been sized up before and didn't mind. Chandler was just evaluating the commodity he'd heard so much about and had the power to purchase. Sullivan had played his old game of picturing someone before he met them and graded himself A on Chandler, though he hadn't expected to be so immediately impressed by his presence and self-confidence.

Sullivan lit a cigarette before he saw the No Smoking sign on Chandler's desk. He glanced around for a place to put it. Chandler opened a drawer and pushed an ashtray across to him.

"A leftover from the old days. Be my guest. I don't really mind all that much."

Sullivan took the ashtray. He'd finish the cigarette but wouldn't smoke another in Chandler's presence. Already he had a hearty respect for the man.

Chandler leaned back in his chair, bridged hands across his chest. "You've had recent firsthand experience with a serial killer, Mr. Sullivan, and I frankly need all the help I can get. You were once the FBI agent in charge at the Dallas office, so you know the city. You came immediately to mind as a 'fit' with this case." Chandler rubbed his forehead as if to wipe away the wrinkles. "This country's had Ted Bundy, John Wayne Gacy, William Bonin and many more, but *never* a woman serial killer. We can't even get a profile of the killer from the FBI Behavorial Science Unit in Quantico. Nothing to base it on, only professional guesswork. So we have no idea what kind of monster we're dealing with here. The media is having a field day with this Sequined Stalker, as they've named her. In the mean-time, everybody from the commander to the police chief and mayor wants my scalp. The entire situation is at a boiling point. The press and public are making jokes about the police force like they did when Kennedy was killed here."

Sullivan knew how Chandler felt. He glanced out the window. The Dallas skyline hung like a backdrop, sparkling copper and silver buildings shining as if freshly scrubbed by a giant steel-wool pad. "I've kept up with what was in the San Diego papers. Five murder victims in a span of about four months, the latest day before yesterday. All five were out-of-town doctors attending medical conventions and were murdered in their hotel rooms."

Chandler nodded. "Dallas is a big convention center. The city depends on the revenue. Organizations are starting to cancel, moving to other cities. The city officials are demanding results to end the exodus. I just want to end the killings."

Sullivan stubbed out his cigarette. "Obviously this killer has a thing for doctors. All killed in their own hotel rooms by an obvious pickup who was actually luring *them* to their rooms. Brief me on the rest of the facts. What about the weapon? The papers said it was some sharp object that hadn't been identified. They hinted at an ice pick."

Chandler shook his head. "Not an ice pick. The murder weapon has not yet been satisfactorily established. It's a thin but sharp-pointed object, long and strong enough to pierce the heart. Could possibly be a type of syringe used to draw fluid from the chest cavity. To be right on target each time . . . one single thrust to the heart . . . the killer had to have some medical knowledge and better than the average woman's strength."

Sullivan frowned, mumbling to himself. "An athletic woman with medical knowledge." He met Chandler's eyes. "Any signs of struggle?"

"No. No skin fragments found under the victims' fingernails. No human hair strands other than the victims', but we picked up long blond hairs from an expensive wig."

"Any victims have connections to each other, aside from being doctors?"

"None." Chandler exhaled as if suddenly weary. "Their ages ranged from forty-four to sixty-eight. None of them knew each other. No prints at any scene except the victims' or hotel employees'. At the third crime scene the ID technician found a couple of silver sequins. Then came the media tab, 'the Sequined Stalker.' ''

Sullivan leaned forward. "So you're saying that at the first two crime scenes nothing was found?"

"That's correct. At the fifth scene ID found a white feather. I think our girl is getting careless. I know something of the nature of serial killers, men anyway. They think they're omnipotent and do get careless eventually."

Sullivan cocked his head to one side, his mind shifting gears. "Maybe not this one. Maybe she wasn't at all careless. Maybe she wanted publicity, a handle to be put to her. She probably revels in the name, the Sequined Stalker. Serial killers like recognition. Some start playing games with the police, calling, giving clues, mocking their inability to catch them."

Chandler blinked, absorbing what Sullivan had said. "Families of victims all checked out." Chandler patted a stack of files. "All of the interviews are in here. Each victim attended a convention cocktail party before he was killed. All those present were questioned. Computer checks of recently released criminally inclined female mental patients proved nothing. Same with convicted murder parolees from Huntsville. We hauled them all in and questioned them. ID Section search for known offenders proved nothing. We made use of the FBI Latent Descriptor Index in the Identification Section, but no results."

Sullivan realized how many new aids had been developed since he'd left the FBI, but he was familiar with the Latent Descriptor Index. Their computer compared the characteristics of a crime under investigation to the known proclivities of criminals on file. When it found pronounced similarities, it suggested suspects and produced their fingerprints. "Computer cops," Sullivan mumbled under his breath.

"Beg pardon?"

Sullivan waved his hand. "Nothing. Thinking out loud. Please go on."

"We've had the usual confessions. Sixteen in all. Complete cranks. We have only one thing. A room service waiter got a partial view from the other end of the hall of a blond woman leaving the last victim's room. He said the woman wore a small hat."

"Not much help," Sullivan added. "There's always that chance we could get lucky. Nine times out of ten a killer is caught because he makes a stupid mistake, parks his car near the murder scene, gets a ticket which shows up on the computer, something like that. We've done nothing but fill in the blanks."

Chandler sat straight in his chair. "You said 'we.' That mean you're signing on?"

"If the deal includes my partner, Manuel Castro." When Sullivan called Marshall Meyers and explained that his partner would take the case in South America, the man had balked. He didn't want a Mexican cop on suspension working for him. Sullivan told Marshall Meyers where he could put his inheritance so that it would be fertilized and grow to bigger proportions. "I work better with him around to help. He's a good man to have on the team." Sullivan touched his breast pocket for his cigarettes, but didn't take one.

Chandler glanced at the ashtray. "Go ahead and have a smoke." He watched as Sullivan lit up, then continued. "The allotment from the city manager is not much, I'm afraid. Certainly not for two people." Chandler looked embarrassed. "I was hoping to snare your interest with the case before we talked money. I wanted you to meet the two heads of the task force I've formed, read the files, go to the latest crime scene while it's still fresh."

Sullivan leaned back in the chair and crossed his legs. He saw that he had on one black sock and one blue one. "Let's say I'm sufficiently snared."

"Ten thousand."

"We've shared less before." He'd give Castro a razzle-dazzle about how much experience the job would offer, the publicity it would garner for their agency if they caught the first lady serial killer. Tell him to think of the future.

Chandler's smile was that of a small boy at his own birthday party. Now he'd gotten two gifts when he expected one. "Deal." He pushed the files toward Sullivan. "Get familiar with these. Find a place to stay. I want to know where you are twenty-four hours a day and what you're doing. I'll arrange for some special identification so you won't have any problems with your investigation." Chandler focused hard on Sullivan. "I want to warn you that any evidence in a homicide case has to be collected properly, reported and filed or it becomes inadmissible. We are not going to blow this."

Sullivan kept a straight face. Obviously Chandler knew of his propensity for bending rules. "Absolutely."

"I've read your FBI profile. It said you make extensive use of personal initiative, tend to improvise. That was just for openers. The list goes on. Well, that's fine on occasion, but it can also spell rogue. I will not tolerate any unorthodox shit. I want that clear. You have a gun with you?"

He had brought a gun. "A .357 Magnum."

"Is it registered?"

Sullivan had to think. Some of his guns were and some weren't. "Certainly."

Chandler punched his intercom. "Tell Gilbert and Day to come in here." He leaned back in his chair. "These are the two lieutenants who head up the task force. Each one has a team. A sergeant and three investigators on each."

Sullivan turned as two men entered the room. Both eyed him with curiosity, then glanced in unison from his cigarette to the ashtray and on to the captain. Chandler made the introductions. "Mr. Hawkins Sullivan is going to be working with us here and I expect every cooperation. He'll be the liaison between the two teams.''

Sullivan shook hands with the lieutenants and asked them and the captain to call him Hawk. The name Hawkins grated on him even though it was his mother's maiden name. Sullivan's eyes swept over the two men. Blond with closely cropped hair, Lieutenant Ross Day was stocky, biceps bulging through double-knit, his complexion ruddy and slightly pockmarked. Polyester checked shirt open at the neck. By contrast, Wayne Gilbert was as handsome as any man Sullivan had ever seen, dressed in the trendy manner to which Castro would like to become more accustomed. Tall, slim; jet-black hair combed neatly back. His smile a flash of white perfect teeth against the dark complexion. His eyes onyx and just as hard. A spark shot between him and Sullivan, suspicion and dislike.

''Heard a lot about you,'' Lieutenant Gilbert said, an innuendo in his voice.

Chandler caught it, stood and said: ''Just a word on the issue here. Sometimes there's rivalry about who makes a collar on a perp and that can make a gap that criminals slip through. I won't stand for any of that here. I don't give a damn who makes the collar so long as somebody does before more people get killed. I couldn't care less if this bitch killer drops dead or gets run over by a garbage truck. Just so she's stopped. This is what it's all about.''

Sullivan thought Chandler could have been a CEO addressing his sales force. He hoped the two lieutenants were mollified and wouldn't hoard leads. After Chandler told them to meet Sullivan at the Meridan Hotel at three to show him the crime scene, they marched out, Gilbert more stiffly than Day. Sullivan tried to understand Gilbert's resentment. Not only was an outsider encroaching on his territory, Sullivan's presence made him look incompetent.

Chandler checked his stainless-steel watch. ''You've got two hours to get settled before you meet Day and Gilbert. There's a medical convention here next week and we've got to make security plans." He handed Sullivan the thick files to study. "What'd you say your partner's name was?"

"Manuel Castro. Manny."

"You can call him in San Diego and have him fly to Dallas. He can start tomorrow."

"That won't be necessary," Sullivan answered, without change of expression.

Chandler stopped in his tracks. "Beg pardon?"

Sullivan got to his feet. "I'll introduce you to him now. He's just outside the door."

Chandler gave him a look of bemused astonishment. Sullivan was sure it wouldn't be his last.

3

Evelyn Casey sat on her terrace overlooking the Olympic-size swimming pool. The tennis court lay just beyond a row of tall hedges, and to the left was her guesthouse. The rose garden she'd instructed the gardener to leave to her careful tending suffered from lack of attention. She took no joy in it now.

She picked up the morning paper, her eyes holding on the blazing headlines, then reread the latest story Carole Wheeler had written about the Sequined Stalker. Carole was making a name for herself in journalism circles. After covering the serial killer case that Evelyn and Hawk had been involved in, the cub reporter from San Diego had accepted a position with the *Dallas Morning News*. When the news broke that the first lady serial killer in history was on the loose in Dallas, Carole was right on top of it.

Evelyn dropped the paper, her hand shaking slightly. She had a feeling Hawk Sullivan's trip to Dallas had something to do with the case. He'd said he was coming to see the homicide chief, nothing more. She longed to see Sullivan again, even though she was trying desperately to divorce herself from the past that he was part of. She clung to the idea that time was her greatest and possibly only ally in helping to fade the dark burden that stained her soul.

She reflected on the circumstances surrounding her introduction to Hawk Sullivan. Though only months had passed, it seemed long ago. The last time she'd seen her sister alive was when she dropped Sara off at the airport to fly to San Diego for her tenth college reunion. Her sister, as it turned out, had been cleverly manipulated into a conversation by a prowling serial killer during the flight. Sara was later found murdered in her hotel room.

Dissatisfied with the progress of the case, Evelyn flew to San Diego. There she was offered little civility and no encouragement from the chief of Homicide, the archetypal television law enforcement officer, minus only tinted sunglasses. When she vowed to hire someone on her own, a sympathetic sergeant on the force, Manuel Castro, recommended an old friend he'd lost touch with, Hawk Sullivan, an ex-FBI agent.

On first meeting, the daring renegade whom Castro had described seemed anything but that. Soured by his wife's premature death from cancer and hobbled financially by the expense of long illness, Hawk Sullivan appeared little more than a drunken derelict. Banking on Castro's confidence in Sullivan, Evelyn decided to hire him. Besides, something about him inspired Evelyn to give him a chance.

Savvy enough to view the case as his last chance, Sullivan struggled to become the ace he once was. Stage by stage, Evelyn watched his progressive revitalization, happy in the knowledge that she'd assisted in that very worthy person's rebound.

Blinking, Evelyn returned to the present. She got up, walked across the yard, picked up a hose with the fertilizer attachment and halfheartedly sprayed the roses. The jeans and denim shirt felt not only damp against her skin but loose and baggy. She was blessed with a figure she didn't have to work at, but in the last few months eating seemed to take more energy than she had to spare. For a period she'd even stopped getting dressed.

Evelyn glanced at the tennis court, dreading the game she'd promised Carole Wheeler. Her psychologist had suggested exercise and she'd made the mistake of telling Carole, who now had taken on the role of coach, forcing her to swim laps and hit balls. Carole could barely play tennis, didn't understand the rules and couldn't swim at all. Wearing a straw hat to keep the sun off that buttermilk skin peppered with freckles, Carole always sat on the pool's edge and kicked her feet in the water. Evelyn knew the kooky reporter was only trying to help.

Shielding her eyes from the sun, Evelyn looked back at her house. She had to go in and put on a tennis dress. She could remember the time when she awoke each morning, anticipating what the day might bring, even examining the previous one to determine if she'd made the most of it. But no more. A day was something to get through before facing the night.

"Hey, look at you," Carole Wheeler yelled, appearing on the terrace. "You're not dressed for tennis."

And neither are you, Evelyn thought, laughing at the sight before her. Carole Wheeler had braided her carrot-colored hair into a mass of pigtails that stood straight up. She wore high-top tennis shoes and green knee socks that met flaired-leg white tennis shorts. Her T-shirt looked as if paint had been thrown on it, and around her shoulders was something posing as a jacket, never mind the heat. Coming down the stone stairs, colors flashing in the sun, she looked like a kaleidoscope that had broken free from the cylinder.

"Your doorbell doesn't work. I banged on the door for Mary to let me in, but I guess she was gabbing like always on the phone. Listen, we've got to get in our game before ole Hawkeye gets here. What time is he coming by? I can't wait to see him.'' Carole was an ardent fan of Sullivan's ever since he gave her a stiff lecture on the difference between exploitive journalism and responsible reporting. After the lecture he gave her the prized inside track on the serial killer, Charlie Christmas, which finally brought her the recognition she deserved. ''Bet he's here about the Sequined Stalker,'' Carole said, continuing her staccato delivery. ''He didn't say anything about it?'' She nodded. ''Yep. Bet you. Bringing that handsome devil Castro, too.'' She rolled her eyes. ''Go on.'' She made a pushing gesture. ''Get dressed. I'll just warm up on the backboard.''

On the terrace, Evelyn turned back. Carole swatted the ball hard, but it missed the backboard altogether. ''Carole, Quinn's coming by with some papers for me to sign. Tell him I'll be right down, okay?''

''Hope he and Hawkeye don't run into each other,'' Carole yelled back, taking another slug at the ball.

Evelyn hoped so, too. Her husband's sudden heart attack three years ago had left her the majority stockholder of Cougar Oil and Quinn Stewart, Andrew Casey's former second-in-command, at the company's helm. When Quinn and Hawk met during the course of the investigation of her sister's murder, their dislike for each other was instant and permanent. Looking after what he thought were her best interests, Quinn figured the detective had his tentacles wrapped around Evelyn merely for monetary purposes. A meeting between the two was equal to lighting a match to a stick of dynamite. Once Sullivan was rubbed the wrong way, he stayed rubbed.

''When you come back I've got something really weird to tell you that happened this morning.'' Carole glanced at the drugstore Timex she always wore. ''Hurry! I was saving it to tell you and Hawkeye at the same time, but I don't think I can wait.''

Evelyn noticed how a slight Texas accent had crept into Carole's voice. The reporter was originally from Oklahoma, her mother a full-blooded Cherokee, her father an Irishman, which accounted for her coloring and her aversion to "fire water." Her journalism education was acquired at NYU along with her machine-gun manner of speaking, which, mixed with her new accent, gave her voice an almost comical tone.

Evelyn slowly climbed the winding stairs to her bedroom. For months now she had secluded herself there, taking refuge like some wounded animal looking for a place to curl up and hide. Quinn had tried many times to take her to dinner, but she wasn't ready for an appearance at the country club with judging eyes fastened on her, minds imagining what it had been like. Soon after the incident she'd found some people too embarrassed to talk to her. Others wanted to pull her into their circle of friends like an exhibit or trophy. With so many refusals, Sullivan, unlike Quinn, would have probably told her to go to hell. She knew she made too many comparisons between them. No two people could be more different.

Evelyn sat at her dressing table and stared at her reflection. Her hair was a blond tangle. She doubted the society columns would refer to her now as striking, a term she didn't particularly like but one frequently used to describe her. Her cheeks had hollowed, the aquamarine eyes she considered her best feature, dulled and haunted. Bracing her elbow on the table, she rested her forehead in her palm. The thought of seeing Sullivan was bringing back all she'd tried to forget.

Shaking, she dropped her hands in her lap. You didn't kill another human without a blistering blow to the psyche. People might think killing is easy, like blowing away someone on television. Pick up the newspaper, see how common it is. Evelyn now knew that killers didn't walk away without being maimed inside no matter what the circumstances. She had once in confidence asked Carole if she could kill another human being and have no qualms about it. Carole said yes, that in Evelyn's circumstance

she could have done it. Deep down Evelyn had expected
that answer. Everyone would have said the same thing, but
when you had actually done it, things changed, you looked
at it differently. She closed her eyes, remembering the moment three months ago when she deliberately took aim and
pulled the trigger.

"Miz Casey? Mr. Quinn is here," she heard Mary yell
from the landing.

"Be right down," Evelyn answered. Quinn's early arrival might be excuse enough to cancel the tennis game.
She went downstairs and walked into her den where Quinn
Stewart waited. Quinn was a formal kind of man, rarely
out of a dark pinstripe, and today was no exception.

"Morning." He glanced toward the French window. "I
see your friend out there is trying to kill the ball. She
asked if I had come over to see Hawk Sullivan."

Evelyn flinched. That sounded typical of Carole. "I was
going to play tennis with her, but I've decided not to. You
have the papers for me to sign? It won't take long, will
it?"

Quinn opened his briefcase, pulled out a sheaf of papers
and laid them on her desk. "I've checked where you're to
sign, but I want to explain a few things to you first."

Quinn sometimes treated words as if they were money
and it was necessary to economize, then on some subjects
he'd pontificate until she wanted to scream. With time short
she wanted to change before Sullivan arrived, try to look
her best. Plus, the thought of Sullivan and Quinn meeting
made her uneasy.

Finding it hard to renew any interest in the company
business, she glanced around the room as Quinn launched
into his spiel. The den was her favorite room in the house,
a place where she felt safest. Each piece of furniture, each
object, had been chosen by her and arranged with care.
The coromandel screen, the deep couches covered in
cream silk, soft matching rugs over in-laid hardwood
floors. Bookcases lined with leather-bound volumes. Tall

Chinese vases filled with armfuls of gladiolas. Antique cane-backed chairs on either side of the Louis Quatorze desk where she sat. The only thing that looked out of place was the inexpensive brown glass fluted dish on the coffee table, the type of prize people won at carnivals. It was the only article she possessed from her mother's house. She treasured the dish she remembered from childhood.

Quinn leaned over the desk. "You can sign now. I'm satisfied things will go smoothly."

She trusted his judgment and scribbled her name as quickly as possible in the marked spots. When she finished, he returned the contracts to his briefcase and sat across from her as if he planned to stay awhile. She felt herself grow nervous.

"Have any idea why Sullivan is in town?"

"He didn't say."

Quinn reached out and laid his hand on hers. "Let's have dinner at the club tonight. It's time you were getting out."

He looked so hopeful that she hated to turn him down, but even if Sullivan's presence was unsettling to her, she still wanted to leave the evening free to be with him, if he was staying overnight. With a man as mercurial as Sullivan you never knew when his plans might change. "Not tonight. I planned to stay in," she added as courtesy, but the remark sounded stupid. She stayed in every night.

"Maybe over the weekend," Quinn suggested.

"I'll see how I feel." She didn't enjoy being evasive. Quinn was attractive, his ice-blue eyes wise and kind. Wheat-colored hair and a cleft in his chin deep enough to hold a dime. A man any woman would want. Even when Andrew was alive, there had been a strong but unacknowledged attraction between Evelyn and Quinn Stewart, but out of loyalty both to Andrew and to Stewart's wife, nothing came of it.

Quinn and his wife separated two years after Andrew's death, but by that time Evelyn had met Hawk Sullivan, and even under the bizarre circumstances that brought them together they had segued into what could have been an important relationship. Then one gunshot put everything on hold.

"Is playing tennis alone something like masturbating?" Carole stood in the doorway.

Quinn gave a forced little chuckle. Evelyn knew that off-color remarks didn't amuse him, especially ones from Carole.

Carole plopped on the couch, drawing her legs up in a yoga position. She focused on Evelyn, her eyes shining a little too brightly. "I told you that something weird happened this morning. I got a phone call."

Evelyn looked at her, sensing this was no ordinary call. "Who from?"

"The Sequined Stalker."

"Oh, come on," Quinn huffed. "Had to be a crank."

Carole shook her head. "Wasn't."

"How do you know it wasn't a crank?" Evelyn asked.

Carole unfolded herself and leaned forward. "The voice was eerie, throaty. She said she didn't like my name for her, said she didn't stalk."

Evelyn shivered at the mere thought of contact with a serial killer.

"I can't wait to tell Hawkeye about this. I know that's what he's come about. Few police ever get the chance to deal with a serial killer and the Dallas police certainly haven't. Sullivan has experience. But nobody *ever* had a woman serial killer. That she's starting to talk to someone is a break. It happens sometimes. It's started now. And with *me*." Her expression showed a mixture of excitement and apprehension.

"I don't like hearing any of this and I'm sure neither does Evelyn." Quinn fumbled with a cigar, the wrapper sticking to his finger. He waved his hand, trying to free it from the clinging cellophane. Carole reached over and yanked it off. He lit the cheroot and blew a plume of smoke through the air. "I don't want Evelyn mixed up with any of this. You saw what happened the last time. Hawk Sullivan is trouble. To say nothing about dabbling around in serial killings. The police can handle it without him. They're very efficient.

Not always, Evelyn thought.

"Think Mary has any coffee left from breakfast?" Quinn asked, puffing on his cigar.

"I could use a Perrier," Carole said. "Caffeine will kill you." She glanced at Quinn.

"So will getting chummy with serial killers," he answered.

Evelyn gave up on dressing. No one was making any move to leave. Sullivan would have to see her as she was. She dreaded his confrontation with Quinn.

"However"—Quinn waved his hand—"I'm sure that call you had was a crank. I read in the paper how many crank confessions the police have had. You probably wrote the article. The world is full of cranks."

"This one wasn't a crank," Carole insisted.

"How can you be so certain?" Evelyn asked.

"I'll tell you when Hawkeye gets here. He'll appreciate it."

4

Sullivan and Castro left the Dallas Police and Courts Building. Leaning into the wind, they crossed the street and headed toward the parking lot. The dry Texas air seemed to have teeth in it, enough to bite one's lungs. The concrete radiated heat. Already Sullivan missed the California weather and wondered how people could live without the sight of palm trees. But Dallas was where Evelyn Casey was and that's where he wanted to be. Temporarily, anyway.

''Chandler seems like an okay guy,'' Castro said, opening the passenger door.

Sullivan slid carefully into the stifling interior of the rented Buick and lowered the window. He agreed with Castro, but also had the impression that Chandler was a tough taskmaster, as he well should be. Lieutenant Gilbert was another subject, one that could spell trouble. Sullivan wiped his sunglasses on his shirt, lifted them to see if any smudges remained, then put them on and drove through the tollgate.

Leaving downtown behind, they headed north on the Central Expressway where the city was having a tug-of-war between industrial and residential. They sped by out-of-favor fast-food restaurants, boarded-up service stations and run-down houses. Small stores, an old movie theater and a bowling alley were on their deathbeds. Expanded shopping centers moved inexorably toward the area, swallowing the outdated, spitting out upgraded versions of what was already there. For Sullivan's tastes, Dallas had too many malls, banks, hospitals, realtors, and condos with names like Chateau Camelot, Garden Gables and Valley Views. He liked the Dallas of the old days, a large country town, not the sprawling metroplex it had become. Castro rubbernecked like a tourist from the sticks. Sullivan barely noticed the scenery, his mind on Evelyn Casey.

Castro rubbed his hands together. "I'm anxious to get going on the case, but the money . . . it's puny."

"Don't start." Sullivan figured he'd motivated Castro on the merits of handling the case and it was settled. "Look at it this way. Ten thousand a week isn't bad."

Castro whirled around. "It's not a week and you know it. Ten thou for the whole case."

Sullivan turned off on an exit. "It's ten thousand a week if we solve it in a week."

"What brand are you smoking? You and I both know that won't happen. You could call it ten thousand a day if we solve it today."

Sullivan grinned. "Now you've got it."

They drove along a street where mansions bordered Turtle Creek. Sullivan pulled up to a pair of ornate wrought-iron gates and waited for them to part. Evelyn's estate was surrounded by eight feet of stone wall topped with gold arrowlike finials. They cruised down a winding driveway lined with trees so thick they met at the top and formed a tunnel of greenery. The columned two-story beige brick mansion loomed before them. The oversize double front doors were flanked by bronze urns holding

pyramid-shaped plants. Old carriage lamps Evelyn had
bought at an auction graced the walls.

Pulling to a stop, Sullivan watched Castro drink in the
setting, clearly impressed. "Some place!" he said to Sullivan. "And Evelyn's not the least affected by it."

Neither was Sullivan. The opulent surroundings could
have intimidated him, but Sullivan would never let them.
Intellect, not money, was the only thing that ever came
close to daunting Sullivan. "Let's go in." The moment to
see Evelyn had almost arrived and the thought filled Sullivan with anticipation.

They climbed the stone steps, rang the bell and waited.
Castro peered through the leaded-glass door. Sullivan rang
again, then knocked. He saw Mary, Evelyn's maid, padding down the hall.

She opened the door and gave no sign she recognized
him. "Doorbell's not working."

"Tell Mrs. Casey that Hawk Sullivan is here."

"Wait here," she answered, walking away, leaving them
standing like door-to-door salesmen. Sullivan suspected
she blamed him for Evelyn's state of mind.

Sullivan stuffed his hands in his pockets and glanced
around. Floors of black and white marble checks gave
over to walls covered in hand-painted linen. Twin entry
commodes were French, wiped with a subtle beige finish.
Overhead pinpoints lit Impressionist paintings of vibrant
flowers. Giant porcelain pots held lush green plants. Despite the grandeur, the statement of big money spent, Sullivan knew she had strived to make the place speak of
personal warmth and taste. Many of the items he would
have chosen for himself if he had the money.

"Jesus! This entry hall is as big as my whole house."

"But not nearly as comfortable," Sullivan replied,
glancing up the stairs toward the room where he once
stayed overnight. He had known he was headed back here
almost as certainly as a skyward arrow eventually plunges
back to earth. He saw the scene with yesterday's eyes.

Evelyn had surprised him by coming into his room after he went to bed. They spent a magnificent night together, one he'd played over many times in his mind. It was a beginning for both, a final release from the past.

He hoped to see her again now as she once was, a woman of good humor, blazing with intelligence, full of quirky insight and sly wit, a woman keenly interested in him. It was always as if there was a spotlight somewhere on her. In a crowd she was the only person he saw.

"Hawk!"

Sullivan looked down the hall when he heard her. This was the time he had waited for. He had a good feeling he hoped wouldn't go away. Most times the best ones did.

She started toward him, followed, to his disappointment, by Quinn Stewart. Then Carole Wheeler popped out of the den and trailed them to the entry. Sullivan and Castro moved forward to meet them.

Evelyn watched Sullivan walk toward her. He moved as always, like a hip-hung jungle cat, and as deliberately. She felt her heart lurch at the sight of him. His face was stamped with experience, some the wrong kind. Even properly attired, he managed to look as uncomfortable as a tough little boy dressed for Sunday school in hand-me-downs. He stopped, his eyes focused on her alone.

Everyone met in the center of the room. For a moment they all stood on the black-and-white-checked marble floor like chess pieces on a board. Then everyone started to talk at once.

"Hawk, I'm so glad you're here," Evelyn said, her manner tentative, without the verve that was so much a part of her. He always said that she didn't just enter a room, she invaded it. Clearly she hadn't shucked her trauma as he'd hoped. She was much too thin, fragile-looking. The aquamarine eyes were direct, but without the sparkle he remembered. It shook him to see her that way.

Sullivan shook hands with Quinn Stewart, who eyed him as if he were the type to hang around school playgrounds.

Sullivan would bet the man had his ties ironed. He looked like a clothes ad. Carole threw her arms around Hawk's waist and hugged him while Evelyn introduced Castro to Quinn Stewart. Suddenly Evelyn and Hawk were facing each other again.

Not knowing what else to do, he took both her hands, then leaned in close, giving her a ghost of a kiss. Out of the corner of his eye he saw Stewart stiffen.

"You've been on my mind," Sullivan said, then distanced himself from her. He started to ask her how she was, but could see for himself. He felt as if a hand had squeezed his heart.

Evelyn felt self-conscious. She knew those lazy green eyes missed absolutely nothing. "I'm getting much better," she said. "I still don't sleep well . . ."

Sullivan shrugged. He himself never slept more than five hours at a stretch. He glanced at Stewart, then back at Evelyn. "That's not so bad. A person who sleeps all night wastes too much of life."

"Ain't it so," Carole added.

Evelyn smiled at this man who had spent a long period of time wasting his life. A thought burst into her mind. The loss of a loved one had caused his deterioration. In her case, that wasn't the root of the depression. Suddenly her attitude didn't make sense.

"Are you going to be in town long?" Stewart asked him.

Sullivan pursed his lips. "As they say, just riding through."

"You're here about the Sequined Stalker, I just know it," Carole said.

Sullivan's eyes darted to Castro. "Well, since we have some experience on the subject, we're going to help out if we can."

"I've got a flash for you nobody knows yet." Carole glanced around to make sure the attention was all hers.

"She called me this morning . . . the Sequined Stalker. I named her, you know."

"Had to be a crank," Stewart put in.

Carole whipped around. "It wasn't. I know." She turned to Hawk, looking up at him.

Sullivan frowned slightly, his expression serious. "Go on."

"She said she didn't like what I'd named her. She didn't stalk. She had a better name for herself, wanted me to change it to 'the Fine-feathered Femme.' You know, like fine-feathered friend. Sounded more graceful."

"So tell me how you know it was the killer," Sullivan said.

"Because," Carole answered, carefully pronouncing each syllable, "at the last murder scene a feather was found. I have my sources. When I called Captain Chandler and said I knew about it, he asked me to hold the print on it. Could produce something by withholding some evidence now and then. It was not in any paper. So she had to be the killer to know about it." Carole smiled and lifted her chin, which Sullivan playfully socked.

"There's another doctors' convention next week," Sullivan said.

Carole Wheeler looked just past him into space. "I know. I hope somebody stops the killer before she does it again."

"About that call. It should be reported right away," Sullivan said. "It's an important turn in the situation . . . that she's starting to talk."

Stewart appeared agitated. "This whole situation is troublesome, to say nothing about dangerous. It's good that you're here to help, but I have to ask you to distance yourself and your work from Evelyn and myself. We live in another kind of world and can't in any way be involved in yours."

Sullivan fought to control his temper. "We all live in the same world. Unfortunately, one with a serial killer."

"Quinn," Evelyn said quickly, "hadn't you better get those papers back to the office and get them Fed Exed."

"Actually yes," he answered. "I'll get my briefcase in the den." He hurried down the hall.

"I've got to get going, too," Carole said. "I'm moving in with another reporter from the *News*. She's got a great place, and paying rent all alone was a drag on my budget. She's from Mississippi and what an accent she has. If I can stop her from saying 'y'all' when she's speaking to only one person, we'll get along fine." She looked from Castro to Sullivan, affection in her eyes. "I'm really glad to see you guys. We'll be running into each other since you're going to be working with Homicide. I've been going out with Lieutenant Wayne Gilbert." She put her hand over her heart. "He's better looking than Adolph Valentino."

"Rudolph," Sullivan answered, not especially pleased. On top of many things, Gilbert gave him the impression he was a real ladies' man. Sullivan hated the type.

"That was before my time," Carole said. "Hawkeye, I want to do an article on you, a profile. Say how you've come to assist in the case. Okay?"

Sullivan shifted his eyes to Castro, then back to Carole. "I guess it would be good press for our agency. Do I get story approval?"

Carole made a face. "You ought to trust me by now. I still remember the reaming you gave me."

Sullivan grinned. "So long as you don't call me Hawkeye in the article. Don't step on anyone's toes, either."

"Okay," Carole promised, prancing out the door. "See you."

Quinn appeared with his briefcase. "Well, I'm sure you three want to visit for a little while." He placed emphasis on "little." "I'll call you later, Evelyn."

"Could I use your ca—bathroom?" Castro said, catching himself before he said "can."

Evelyn motioned with her head. "Third door on the

right. Hawk and I will be in the den at the end of the hall. Want some lunch?''

"We had something on the plane," Sullivan said. "We've got to go to the latest crime scene this afternoon at the Meridan. Besides, I don't want to spoil dinner. They've got some pretty good restaurants here. Would you join Castro and me?''

"Why don't you both have dinner here?''

Sullivan rolled his eyes, as if considering the offer. "Only if you let me buy the groceries and cook.''

"Deal.'' Evelyn recognized the navy blazer she'd talked him into buying when they were involved in her sister's case. She remembered the ropes of muscles in his forearms, the slick look of bronzed skin, the breadth of his shoulders. She wondered what the scar from his stab wound looked like. Just seeing him made her feel better. His mere presence set a certain vibration in motion. "Do you remember the night when you stayed here?''

"I think I recall it.'' He smiled. "Back in the days when dinosaurs roamed the earth.''

They went into the den and sat side by side on the couch, leaning forward, both anxious to communicate, wary of how to begin. Sullivan decided to plunge in. "You just can't shake it, can you? Charlie Christmas is still a monkey on your back.''

Evelyn had a flash of Hawk Sullivan pinned to the deck like a specimen butterfly, the killer's knife through his shoulder, herself instantly glowing white-hot with panic. With Sullivan down, the man they had tracked for so many weeks rose to his feet, shouting at her, ready to escape over Sullivan's balcony. Able to push emotions temporarily aside, she recovered Sullivan's gun and fired. Again she saw Charlie Christmas' chest exploding into confetti, felt the first sting of reality that she'd taken a human life. "But he was getting away. I could have just let him go.''

"No way.'' Sullivan was firm and final.

Evelyn hesitated. "I didn't have to kill him.''

Sullivan saw Castro in the doorway and gave him a look that indicated he wanted no interruption. Castro remained still. "Christmas had threatened to come back for you one day when you least expected it. How could you have existed under such circumstances? Besides, you very likely saved others' lives by killing him. I'll bet you those other victims' families would have liked to have a crack at him. I'll bet you they even consider you lucky that you had the opportunity to kill him."

Evelyn glanced away from Sullivan, toying with imaginary lint on her jeans. Lucky, he'd said. And no doubt if the killer had lived he would have gone on to take other lives, probably her own. As the Bible mentioned, maybe she was due her eye-for-an-eye.

Sullivan saw her expression lighten. "That's the way to look at it. The only way." He nodded for Castro to come in.

"Guess we'd better be mushing on," Castro said. "We've got to find a place to call home, then get over to the Meridan."

Evelyn glanced from Castro to Sullivan. Suddenly she was hungry for an audience, especially Sullivan's. He really listened to the other person instead of thinking what he was going to say next, as most did. She said the first thing that came to mind. "Why don't you stay here . . . in my guesthouse?"

"We couldn't do that," Castro answered.

Evelyn knew if they were being employed by the city their fee couldn't be much, and certainly no expense account was included. "I'd enjoy having you around. Please stay."

"If Sullivan isn't reading half the night, he's snoring the rest of it. We'd better get a place with our own rooms." Castro eyed Sullivan, who wasn't offering any excuses.

Evelyn smiled. "The guesthouse has two bedrooms and two baths, as well as a sitting room. You're covered. It also has a kitchenette, but I expect Hawk would rather do his cooking in my big kitchen. How about it?'' Quinn would abhor the arrangements. As her financial advisor and trustee, he would always be an integral part of her life and she wanted them on the best of terms, but . . . it was her house.

"We'll unload our bags," Sullivan said, rising. He never liked to impose, but this time he felt his presence mandatory. He would take on not only the lady serial killer case but Evelyn's rejuvenation as well. He had an idea that might pique her interest. He'd broach the subject that night over dinner. She had helped him once. Now it was his turn.

5

Sullivan and Castro met Day and Gilbert in the opulent but nearly deserted lobby of the Meridan Hotel. Gilbert delivered the special police identification ordered by Chandler, eyeing Castro as he had Sullivan.

"Why don't you try it out?" Lieutenant Wayne Gilbert said, goading Sullivan. "The room we want to see is five-six-five. Capt'n Chandler hasn't allowed the possessions to be removed yet. So you can have at it."

"Everything's been dusted, of course," Lieutenant Ross Day added, cracking his knuckles.

Sullivan took the piece of paper and walked to the desk, Gilbert following. He presented the credentials to the clerk. "We'd like the key to five-six-five. Official police crime scene." Gilbert stood too close to Sullivan, his cologne overpowering.

"Here." The clerk slammed the key on the marble counter. "The whole floor is empty. The manager figured nobody wanted to stay on that floor with all that yellow police tape around the door. Our occupancy has dropped off all of a sudden. People canceling, afraid of this place. A shame how this murder has ruined our business.''

"A shame," Sullivan parroted. "Ruined Dr. Alfred Alexander's business, too.'' Sullivan had already started on the files and was becoming familiar with the murder victim. He figured he'd begin with the most recent killing and work back.

He and Gilbert, accompanied by Castro and Day, waited before the bank of elevators. One opened and the quartet stepped in. Sullivan glanced around, wondering if it was the same one Dr. Alexander and the killer had taken. He saw Gilbert admiring himself in the mirror, slicking back his hair with a palm. Sullivan purposely stared at Gilbert until he caught his eye. Gilbert straightened, dropped his hand to his side and licked the smile off his lips.

"I understand you know Carole Wheeler," Sullivan said to Gilbert as they ascended.

Gilbert grinned. "Cute chick."

"She's a real pal of ours," Sullivan answered, and let the statement hang between them, then lit a cigarette, knowing it was against the city ordinance to smoke in an elevator.

Huffing out a smoke ring, he said: "Carole told me this morning that the Sequin called her. I think . . .''

"Carole called me. I've already told the capt'n," Gilbert cut him off. "We've installed a monitor on her phone at the paper and on the one in her apartment, but that one's unlisted so the Stalker can't get that number.''

Day cracked his knuckles, a habit Sullivan was fast finding irritating. "It's a good sign the killer's starting to talk. Might give herself away somehow. I feel sure she's smart enough not to talk long enough for us to trace. We might be able to do something with the voice patterns, although she probably disguises her voice.''

Knuckles or not, Day had a few brain cells, Sullivan mused.

"The capt'n is willing to try anything," Gilbert said, his hard eyes on Sullivan. "He even called in a psychic."

Sullivan wondered if Gilbert lumped him into that category and imagined he did. "Those people have had some success. Especially at locating missing persons."

"I've never worked on a serial killer case before like you," Day stated. He unwrapped a piece of chewing gum, folded it double, then popped it into his mouth. "Must be something to catch such a sumbitch." Sullivan saw some admiration in Day's eyes.

"I hear the lady who hired you had to shoot him," Gilbert said, a smile playing on his lips.

Sullivan had to fight to control his temper. Gilbert resented his presence and wasn't going to make the situation easy. Any nasty confrontation might force Captain Chandler to stand up for his own man and send Sullivan packing to San Diego. Sullivan couldn't allow that. "She's got expert aim."

Castro, who had been studying the floor, looked up. "You ought to know. You taught her how to shoot."

They filed out on the fifth floor and Sullivan saw the room cordoned off by the familiar yellow tape, denoting a crime scene. Pulling the tape back, Sullivan unlocked the door and entered the room, staring at the heavy chalk outline of the body drawn on the carpet.

He stood very still in the center of the hotel room. There was to him a feeling of energy, of violence, as if the killer left a pattern in the air, the sense of evil in the place like dark air currents. They weren't the kind of thing a policeman would give much credence to, so he didn't mention it. Sullivan already hated the animal who had perpetrated such a crime.

While the two lieutenants sat in chairs, Sullivan and Castro poked around the room. Fingerprint dust was everywhere. Sullivan opened the closet and looked at the doctor's clothes, running his fingers through the pockets of a sport jacket. The doctor had probably been wearing a suit when he was killed, since he'd attended a cocktail party and there wasn't one in the closet.

He knelt and looked at the loafers. Poor devil wore Odor Eaters in his shoes, and the heels had lifts for added height. The doctor had been somewhat vain, concerned with his appearance.

Sullivan had trouble, as always, putting himself into the mind of the killer. This time it would be doubly hard. Sullivan was all too familiar with stories of investigators who could in a sense "become" the perpetrator, who could from the death scene interpret the events from the killer's perspective. For him, it was the opposite: he experienced the overwhelming fright of the victims, their last thoughts of what the circumstances surrounding their deaths would mean to their families. This rarely helped him glean any facts, although it greatly motivated him.

"He was a short sumbitch with stinking feet," Gilbert said, watching Sullivan holding the dead man's shoe.

On all fours, Sullivan turned to eye Gilbert, then straightened up and walked into the bathroom, Castro following in his tracks. He plundered through the doctor's toilet articles. A toothbrush, paste, deodorant, razor, comb, Grecian Formula to camouflage gray, men's hair spray. He picked up the bottle of cologne and was tempted to ask Gilbert if it was his brand. He studied a pill bottle, recognizing the prescription for high blood pressure. There was a pack of condoms. Sex was premeditated.

"With his condition, a good fuck might have killed the old fart if the Sequin hadn't got 'im," Gilbert said from the open door.

Sullivan didn't turn around, but felt Gilbert's eyes on him. The messy business of murder had a way of uncovering people's private lives, a way of peeling down to the core the victim and leaving exposed all those private places people spend a lifetime concealing. With no time to bury these secrets, a murder victim was left unmasked, vulnerable and all too human. Every article of the dead man's would have to be returned to his family. The five victims left those behind with shattered illusions of ones they loved and trusted. Sullivan had the urge to slip the condoms in his pocket, but knew he couldn't.

"Let's get out of here," Sullivan said to Castro.

"Seen enough? I knew there wasn't anything to find. We've been over this place with a microscope," Day said.

"I didn't expect to find anything," Sullivan said. "Just wanted to get a feel before I got started." Like an athlete warming up before striking into a run, he wanted to explain, but didn't want to make the comparison to himself. "I've got a novelist friend in San Diego who doesn't plow right into writing each morning until he's read the chapter he wrote the day before. Sort of gets him in the mood."

Day looked puzzled, but in Gilbert's eyes Sullivan saw a flash of understanding. Sullivan suspected Gilbert was a quick study, whereas Day was more a journeyman.

Gilbert checked his gold watch and glanced at Day. "Time to knock off. The team's gonna meet at the Palm for a drink. You ready to go, Ross baby?"

Sullivan caught the intended slight that he and Castro were excluded from the fraternity. "With the convention of ophthalmologists at the Hyatt next Tuesday, I think we ought to talk about precautions. Give the group a discreet warning about picking up women. Can't insult them, but they've got to be cautioned. Have one of your team in every elevator. Some staked out in the bars and lobby. Some at the cocktail parties and banquets."

"Good ideas," Gilbert answered, his first stab at sincerity. "We'll all meet at the station Monday and make our plans. I'll expect you both there. I guess you two are settled by now. I know you're going to read through the files and do some investigating on your own. But in case Day or I need to reach you, give us your hotel and room number." Gilbert whipped out a pad.

Sullivan knew Evelyn's number by heart. He'd called enough. When he gave the address on Beverly Drive, Gilbert stared at him. "There's no hotel or motel on that street. It's residential, a swanky one."

"It's a residence," Sullivan said. "Mrs. Evelyn Casey's."

Day and Gilbert exchanged glances.

They were silent on the elevator ride to the lobby. As they pushed through the revolving glass doors, Sullivan saw a patrolman in the process of ticketing his rental car in a No Parking zone. He sauntered over and whipped out his credentials. The officer looked puzzled by the document until Gilbert showed his badge and explained the situation.

"The capt'n is gonna issue you an unmarked car. Wants you to have a radio." Gilbert turned from Sullivan to Day. "That little piece on your team, Sergeant Gray, gonna be at the Palm? She cranks up my engine." He winked at Day. "Wish I was her boss. See you guys," he said to Sullivan and Castro.

Sullivan heaved himself into the car, thinking about Carole Wheeler involved with a man like Gilbert. She was in for a rough ride if she chose a whirl on his merry-go-round. He treated himself to some positive resentment, then drove away, telling Castro about Simon David, the gourmet grocery store, and what he planned for dinner.

Mainly he looked forward to time with Evelyn. He felt his breath catch at the thought of her and wondered if she felt the same about him. Her mind was still in a fragile state and he'd let their personal situation take a natural course, not rush it. He smiled to himself, picturing Quinn Stewart's face when he learned who was occupying Evelyn's guesthouse.

By six o'clock, Sullivan was dressed in a sport shirt, khakis, sockless in moccasins, and in command of Evelyn's shining stainless-steel kitchen. Stationed by the island in the middle, he stirred his tomato and basil-laced pasta sauce as the Mozart tape he'd put on blared through the ceiling speakers. He'd told Mary to vamoose, watch some television in her room, and he'd handle the culinary chores. He would, however, allow her back for the ever-important privilege of washing dishes. Castro was still in the guesthouse, dressing, and trying to reach Olga to tell her where they were staying. Evelyn was upstairs, changing for dinner.

Sullivan had spent as long as time allowed on the files and planned to finish later if it took the better part of the night. Already he was impressed with Gilbert's concise reports, his incisive summations and direct conclusions. Gilbert had potential if his personality didn't interfere. On the other hand, Day's reports seemed solid but labored, almost childlike when compared to Gilbert's. A plodder teamed with a whiz.

Sullivan slugged his Jack Daniel's on the rocks and broke the salad greens he'd selected into a large wooden bowl. The homemade dressing was chilling in the refrigerator. For dessert he'd bought Amaretto cookies and fresh raspberries, which were soaking in Cointreau. Had there been time, he could have made the pasta from scratch with Evelyn's well-equipped kitchen. He couldn't resist the veal chops at the meat counter and planned to serve them with a sausage and mushroom stuffing the following evening. He liked to plan ahead. And cooking allowed him to relax and think.

As the music swelled to a crescendo, Sullivan stepped to his right, then danced to the left, happier than he'd been in months. The doorbell stopped him and he went to answer, thinking someone must have repaired it that afternoon. Opening the door, he stared at Carole Wheeler. She was a wondrous sight, festooned rather than dressed. Around her carrot curls a black headband sprouted a huge black rose. Her dress was a black tent covered by a black cape. Witchy-toed black high heels on her feet, dark hose, she smiled at him.

"Guess who's coming to dinner? I was going out with Wayne tonight, but he had to work. Evelyn invited me over since my plans got canceled." As she walked down the hall, cape billowing, Sullivan was reminded of a bird trying to gain altitude. "San Diego was so casual. I like being in Dallas where you can really dress."

Sullivan poured her a Perrier in the den bar, replenished his glass and fixed a drink for Evelyn's arrival. They went into the kitchen, where Carole perched on the counter, swinging her legs.

"Don't you think Wayne is divine?" she asked.

Sullivan added the browned beef to his sauce, not looking up. "That's not an adjective I use much."

Carole rummaged in her black tote bag. "Here's some adjectives you might like." She handed him a newspaper. "It's the morning edition but it's already on the stands."

Sullivan was pleased by the article she'd written about him riding into town to assist with the Sequined Stalker case. He liked her writing style, choice of words, and most of all, the context was slanted so that it cast no disparaging light on the homicide chief or his task force. She briefly mentioned his FBI tenure, but gave no details. Sullivan folded the paper, remembering the disappointment in his father's face after his graduation from law school and the announcement that he was planning to join the FBI, his heroes from boyhood days in Washington. He never could please the old man no matter how hard he tried and was glad his father had not lived to see his son booted out of the service he hadn't wanted him to enter in the first place.

"That smell would lure a leopard out of the jungle," Evelyn said, coming into the kitchen. Looking rested and less intense than she had when Sullivan arrived, she wore a simple aqua silk blouse and skirt that matched her eyes, blond hair brushed away from her face and cascading to her shoulders. Small gold loops hung on her ears.

"I always say that a drink is like makeup. Makes everything look better." Sullivan's crooked grin was back. "Yours is waiting." He motioned to the squat glass on the counter, a vodka with a wedge of lemon. Knowing a choice without asking was an intimate gesture, one that passed between two people familiar with the other's habits.

"Thanks." Evelyn smiled and sat on a kitchen stool. Sullivan took the one next to her, the bright light beaming down on them as if they were on a stage set, the only ones on scene.

His large hand wrapped around the glass, Sullivan moved his fingers over the moisture. He had carefully chosen the words he thought might strike home. "Evelyn, I'm just getting into the case and I need your help. When I'm finished with them, I'll give you all the files to study. You're a woman. The killer is a woman. Putting what you know to use, I want you to think about the psychological aspects that might be present." He leaned forward. "I want you to make me a profile of the killer." He knew if the FBI Behavorial Science Unit couldn't adapt their information, there was little chance Evelyn could find anything positive, but the exercise would push the past from her mind, engage her in something useful and make her feel involved.

Sullivan watched her eyes widen. He couldn't tell if the reaction was surprise or apprehension. "Just hold it a sec." He held up his hand like a traffic cop. "I don't mean for you to get physically involved in any way. No way would I allow you to be put in danger. Your profile on Charlie Christmas was right on target and you know how much that helped us."

Evelyn ran her fingers through her hair. "I don't think I could." She hesitated. "This is entirely different . . ."

"Of course, it's different," he broke in, glancing at Carole, whose eyes were riveted on him. "But she's a killer and she's loose out there somewhere, waiting to kill again. If you could apply your knowledge, improvise and come up with something . . . anything that might help . . . Well, that's textbook stuff, Evelyn, to make a profile on the first woman killer." Sullivan knew that Evelyn's father was a small-town assistant D.A. before his death in a boating accident and she had cut her teeth on his cases, an interest sparked in childhood that grew to fruition in maturity.

Evelyn picked up her drink, avoiding Sullivan's demanding eyes. "I'm not sure there's enough to work with . . . My background might not . . ."

"Your background is all I have to help me on the psychological side." Over Evelyn's shoulder Sullivan saw Castro leaning against the doorframe, drinking a beer. "This is very likely the biggest case I've ever undertaken. I need you. I need everything I can get from a person with your qualifications."

Sullivan remembered the night he spent with Evelyn. In that intimate moment she solved the puzzle as to why a woman as wealthy as she would expose herself to such rigorous academics and dispelled any doubts that Sullivan was merely a surrogate for Andrew Casey, a man whose stature, until that revelation, cast a giant shadow. Evelyn disclosed that she'd married a man whose real kick in life came from making money, business accomplishments, showing off an elegant house. People called her Cinderella because she came from a small town to Dallas and married her boss. She acquired the social graces her husband's pyramiding activities required but became bored in the process. As Andrew Casey accumulated more business and social conquests, Evelyn's real interest turned toward the academic corridors, her hours filled with studies of aberrant behavior, criminology, a thesis on sociopathic and psychopathic personalities, and ended with a master's degree in psychology.

Sullivan lit a cigarette. "Well . . . will you at least give it a whirl?"

Evelyn lifted her chin slightly, her mouth firming at the corners. "I'll give it a try."

Castro sauntered in as if on cue. Sullivan got up, tied an apron around himself and handed Castro a bottle of wine. "Open this while I get dinner on. It's a Jordan, eighty-three, a good year. Just like this one's going to end up. I asked Mary to set the table in the breakfast room. We'd have to yell at each other in the dining room and it's too hot to eat on the terrace."

Evelyn watched Sullivan move around the kitchen, hustling food on plates. When he took charge, there was no doubt as to who was in command. He held a wooden spoon like a weapon and turned to the group.

"After dinner I'm taking everybody somewhere for a nightcap."

"Let's stay here," Evelyn protested. "The bar has everything you'd need."

Sullivan shook his head. "Nope. We're going out to start on the case."

"Where are we going?" Carole asked, helping with the salad plates.

"You'll see when we get there," Sullivan answered. "Let's eat and get it over with so we can go."

Evelyn knew how much Sullivan liked to dine in a leisurely manner, so he had something important to explore. Suddenly, she found herself interested, thoughts circling around the killer.

With dinner barely digested, they piled into the car and Sullivan drove just over the speed limit to the brightly lit caverns of downtown Dallas. Tempted, he passed up the No Parking spot he'd occupied earlier and left the car in the Meridan Hotel's underground lot.

They walked through the quiet lobby peopled by only two old couples and a lone man reading a paper in a chair next to a potted palm. A casually but expensively dressed woman stood by the newsstand, as if waiting for someone.

Seated in a leather banquette in the bar, they ordered and Sullivan's eyes scanned the room. Almost empty, the elegant bar had a seedy feel. Three middle-aged women who looked like secretaries finished with overtime sat at the bar telling jokes in turn. Two businessmen sat several seats away, their suits rumpled from the day's wear, ties loosened, talking quietly. Hovering over a drink, a man who looked to be in his thirties sat alone at the end of the bar. The man from the lobby came in, glanced around and settled at the bar. A young couple in evening clothes occupied the banquette next to Sullivan's group.

When their drinks were served, Sullivan took a sip, his eyes playing back and forth over the group. "I want you to play a game. 'Memory,' I call it. Everyone close their eyes." He watched while they complied. "Now, I want each one in turn to tell me how many people are at the bar." He saw Carole's lids flutter, trying for a peek.

"Seven," she said.

"You're disqualified," Sullivan answered. "The rest of you keep your eyes closed now. The point of the game is this. Your eyes receive every image before them and your brain records and stores the information, just like words printed on a computer. And just like words on a computer, those images can be called up if the proper key or response is touched. Now, Evelyn, thanks to Carole, you know there are seven people at the bar. Describe one."

A frown appeared on Evelyn's forehead as she concentrated. "There are three women together. One has on a knit-type pants suit."

"Why did you notice that?" Sullivan asked.

"Because it looked hot, out of season."

"Good. Association," Sullivan said.

"There's a man by himself," Castro added. "I remember because I always think people by themselves at a bar are lonely. Just want to be around someone."

"Well, don't everybody sit here with your eyes closed or people will think we're weird," Sullivan said, picking up his glass.

Evelyn sipped her drink. "You know, driving over here I was thinking . . ." She tapped a swizzle stick on the table. "The killer hates doctors for some reason. Feels threatened by them, maybe. Could be her father was a doctor, mistreated her. Maybe a doctor did something to her that changed her life."

Carole's orange eyebrows lifted. "Maybe a plastic surgeon. Maybe he disfigured her."

"She can't be too disfigured or she couldn't pick up men," Evelyn answered. "Maybe a gynecologist did something to her that prevented her from having children. Or an obstetrician did something to her at birth, her own or her child's. A pediatrician." Her face lit up. "Why not have a computer check on malpractice suits?"

"That's an excellent start," Sullivan said. "We could find something. I'll have it done tomorrow. There are a couple of wrinkles we can't ignore. Looks like the killer has medical knowledge. She never missed hitting the heart and she's strong. I'll give you the files to study as I finish with them. You'll see that she doesn't pick on just one specialty, though. All five victims were in different fields."

"Then any doctor will do. That tends to back up my theory that her father was a doctor," Evelyn said.

Sullivan smiled at her as he stood and checked his watch. He'd set the wheels of her recovery in motion. "Now you're in the swing. Be right back."

He walked to the far corner of the bar and motioned to the bartender. Sullivan showed the man his identification. He'd read his statements in the files and those of the bar waiters.

"I've already talked to the police," the man said. "Look at this place. Used to be three-deep around the bar. Couldn't hardly keep up with the orders, everybody shouting for a drink. AIDS slowed down the traffic, but this Sequined Stalker stopped it cold."

Sullivan realized the bartender might have actually seen the blond woman the night of the murder, but too many images to record had overloaded the circuits, unlike his Memory game, which forced concentration on a few. He hoped to punch the right button with the room service waiter who remembered the glimpse he got of the killer. "I called Royce Miles earlier. He's a room service waiter. Gets off at ten and is going to meet me here. I told him to check with the bartender and you'd point me out."

Sullivan arrowed through the room and hooked into the

banquette. "You might see my game work in a few minutes. Keep your fingers crossed. I'm going to question Royce Miles, the room service waiter who actually saw the killer leaving the victim's room. I read over his statements. Said he only got a glimpse of her, but she was blond and had a small cocktail hat."

"They are basically out of style," Evelyn commented. "Don't see them much. Only someone funky would wear one these days." She glanced at Carole and looked quickly away.

Castro's fingers did a quick tap dance on the table. "A funky killer or was there a purpose for the hat? A help to disguise her?"

"And what did the killer do with the weapon, whatever it was?" Sullivan asked more to himself than anyone. "Likely she carried it in her purse." As he toyed with the questions, he saw a young man, early twenties, he guessed, come in and speak to the bartender. He looked toward Sullivan and walked to his banquette.

"I'm Royce Miles," he said, ill at ease before the group. Sullivan gestured. "Sit down, please."

The man perched on the edge of the leather seat as if it were hot. He reminded Sullivan of a younger Lieutenant Ross Day, a farm boy come to town to make good. His hands were large, knuckles red and scratched in places, cuticles ragged. Sullivan introduced his companions, whom Miles eyed suspiciously.

"Mr. Miles," Sullivan began. "As I told you, I'm a special investigator on this serial killer case." He showed him his identification, which Miles barely glanced at.

"I've already told everything I know. I don't want to get involved in this. Don't want my name in the paper. Don't want that Sequin coming after me." He shook his head. "No, sir, I'll leave town first."

"Nobody's going to put your name in the paper, I assure you," Sullivan said. "So far you're the *only* person who's actually seen her. You were looking right at her, nobody else around.''

''It was from the other end of the hall, like I said.'' He ran a finger around his collar and pulled on it as if it were choking him.

''What were you serving that night?'' Sullivan asked.

Miles looked startled. ''What?''

''What was on that cart? How many orders? One or two?''

''Two,'' he answered. ''What does that matter?''

''Two covers. What were they? Club sandwiches, a full meal?''

''You could look up the ticket in accounting or something. Why does it matter? They didn't have any connection with the woman.''

''You see her after you served or before you went in?'' Sullivan pressed.

''After.''

''The people you served give you a big tip?''

Miles blinked. ''Why, yeah, he did. It was steaks, they had. He said they looked good and hot. Unusual.''

''What did he look like?''

''Who, the man what give me the tip?''

Sullivan nodded. ''He dressed or what?''

Miles frowned, his eyes narrowed. ''Had on a robe. She did too. Had just got in from Chicago, he said. Was tired, too tired to go out. He was tall, darkish. She was kinda plump, you know. Robe was low-cut. I could see down her front when she sat down.'' He shifted his eyes to the bar, cheeks blushing.

''Fine,'' Sullivan said, hoping to reassure him. ''So you go out, happy about the tip, and you see the blond woman. She had on a hat. What else do you remember?''

Miles shook his head. ''Nothing. She walked fast to the elevator.''

''Nothing?'' Sullivan questioned. ''She's walking down the hall. Think about her.''

''Nothing. I was thinking about getting off duty, seeing

my girl . . ." He hesitated. "The blond woman had a purse." He snapped his fingers. "Yeah, a purse like one I saw when I was shopping for my girlfriend's birthday. Gold, shaped like a shell. Thing was so little you couldn't even carry a pack of cigarettes or a glasses case. Cost eight hundred bucks!"

"A Judith Leiber bag," Evelyn identified it.

"Out goes the possibility that she carried the weapon in her purse," Sullivan commented. "Maybe since it's a sharp object she threaded it into her clothes, like a needle in a sewing basket."

Evelyn quickly seized upon the idea of the hat you didn't see much anymore and the killer's reason for wearing it. "A big, strong hat pin. How about that for a weapon?"

Sullivan nodded, deep in thought. There couldn't be too many stores that carried the expensive purse. That was a positive lead.

"Can I go now? Nothing I said helped much, I don't guess," Miles stated.

"On the contrary." Sullivan touched his shoulder. "You've gotten us off dead center and pointed in a direction. Appreciate it."

The boy looked puzzled as he loped off, glancing back once at Sullivan before he went out the door. Carole said she had work to finish at the paper. She hugged them goodbye.

Sullivan addressed Evelyn. "See how much you've already helped?" He slapped some bills on the check. "I've got a full night ahead with the files." He moved his hand so that it touched Evelyn's. Her eyes lifted and met his. He knew it was only a matter of time before one of them, one night, crossed that great distance between guest quarters and main house. Right now, they all had work ahead, everyone pulling together to stop the monster, as Carole had called her. Sullivan wondered what kind of freak he might come face-to-face with and couldn't picture her.

6

I feel good tonight. Very good, indeed. I think I might finally be rid of Doctor. The look on his face was soooooooo satisfying this time. The best yet. He hurt more. Surprise on his dumb face. Doctor's face with that mouth set in disgust, the shadow of a beard even after he'd just shaved. Dark skin that looked like thousands of dots punched on it. He lathered that face with an old brush like he was from the last century. Never could change once he got set. Old-fashioned leather strop his grandfather left him, hanging in his bathroom. Sharpened his razor on that strop. He sharpened me on that strop. I don't want to think about him anymore. Put him out of my head, once and for all. He is the monster, not me.

I told that reporter I didn't "stalk." Didn't like the name. Suggested a better one. That was a laugh. Now she calls me a *monster*. Little does she know. It's all in the eye of the beholder. I must speak to her again. Set her straight. Scare her a little.

I had to go out after I read the paper. Everything took

,place as I predicted. I am *attuned*. *Attuned* to what people might do. That's what made it so easy. That's why no one will ever catch me. I laugh.

I think about changing clothes. After work, I like to wear slacks or a robe when I'm home. I'm not in the least sleepy. I'm going to have a drink, relax. Not think about Doctor. He's gone. Forever, this time. I can really forget he ever existed. I got him.

I fix a drink, pour in extra scotch and look at the clock. I always stay up late. Get home from work after twelve. Tonight is my regular night off. I can take a night off whenever I have other plans, like in the last few months . . . when I had to get rid of Doctor. I stop myself. I'm not going to think about it anymore.

I walk around the house where I grew up, sipping my drink. It's all mine now. Was Granny's to start with. Her clothes and belongings are still in the attic with the cobwebs. The house is old, full of creaks and strange noises, maybe inhabited by shadowy phantoms. I sometimes feel that long ago some dark magician cast a spell over it.

The cellar with an oubliette is below. On the first floor is the living room, stuffed with beautiful things Momma bought, dining room, kitchen, breakfast room. And Doctor's study. I don't like to go in there as I did as a child to look at his medical books when he wasn't home. Upstairs is my bedroom, Momma's, a guest room where no one stayed. *And* Doctor's bedroom.

I glance at the stairway where I used to sit on the oriental runner and listen to them at night when their voices woke me. Doctor and Momma arguing and fighting in Doctor's study. Doctor talking about me sometimes. Momma defending. I sucked my thumb and hooked my toes around the banister poles while they yelled and called each other names I didn't understand.

Doctor sometimes came home after I'd gone to bed and went to the hospital early, before I got up. I can remember wanting to see him. I was stupid back then. Old black

Claree who didn't like me was all I had to talk to, except
when my cousin came around. Momma stayed locked in
her bedroom most of the day. Drinking, Doctor accused
her. I could smell it, too, when she allowed me in. Whis-
key so strong it stung my nose. Stench of puke from the
bathroom turning my stomach. Shimmering acres of
stained satin in there, Momma all curled up under the
four-poster canopy. Mirrors that shot back reflections so
it looked like an army of me in there. Perfume in diamond-
faceted glass bottles. Little lacy pillows. Clothes and shoes
heaped on the floor.

I look out the window. Sometimes I hear an owl screech.
The yard is more than four acres. Dark with trees and
shrubs where I used to play. I had a secret place out there.
Secret until Doctor found it. I had a dog I thought was
mine. Name was Blackie. Doctor said it was his, called
him Sheffield and told me not to touch it. That was after
the cat. Doctor never understood the cat was sick. I had
to do it. Doctor thought Sheffield ran off. Never did find
him.

My heart jumps when I hear the doorbell. So late. I
think They have come for me. Doctor would be happy if
I got caught, laugh. I get control of myself. Nobody is
coming for *me*. I am too *attuned*.

I walk to the door and ask who's there.

"It's me."

I grew up calling my relative Cuz. My uncle, Cuz's
father, was a doctor, but not like *mine*.

"I knew you'd be up," Cuz says, coming in. Cuz was
always useful to me as a child when I wanted blame laid
elsewhere. I always keep Cuz in mind as a reserve.

"Want a drink?" I have almost finished mine. I want
another before I make my call. I hope Cuz won't stay
long.

"Yeah. Got any wine?"

"Sure." I'd have to open a bottle that will go to waste
later.

We sit in the living room. When I'm home I keep the lights turned low. Sometimes I even sit in the dark. Dark is always more seductive than light. You can hide in it, pretend there is everything you want in the shadows. I can't imagine why anyone would be afraid of the dark. I never was, even as a child. Cuz looks around before taking a swig.

"Read the paper tonight? God, I get the creeps thinking about it."

Even in the dimness I can see goose pimples on Cuz. I like to watch people scared. I know to what the statement refers, but don't let on.

"It's getting so I'm afraid to go out alone." Cuz takes another swallow. I see the Adam's apple move up and down.

"Oh, you mean about the killer? Why would you be afraid? She only kills Doctor . . ." I correct myself. "Doctors. You aren't one."

"You never know. Maybe she'd kill anybody. It's creepy knowing some monster is on the loose right here around us."

Not a monster, I want to say. "I'm not in the least afraid."

Cuz glances around. "I'd be. Way out here."

Way out here! Cuz doesn't live that far away. What my dear kin means is my house is bizarre. "I don't think about it." Not about Doctor, anyway. Not anymore.

"I want you to do me a favor—a big one. I am hoping I can count on you."

"What is it?" I dread what is coming, but can't imagine what it is. Cuz is the type to impose. Do this. Can you help me out?

"I'm going on a vacation for a couple of weeks. To Mexico. I don't want to put Poo in a kennel. Poor baby would have a broken heart. She's no trouble. Will you keep her while I go? Please say you will."

The thought unsettles me. I hate animals, especially the

rat-thing called Poo, floppy-eared, a satin bow in the ball of a head. I think about Sheffield and how Doctor worried about him, actually cried when he decided he wasn't coming back. I sense an excitement. If I think about Doctor, which I don't intend to do because that's over, it might be nice to worry him some more. Poo might do. "Okay, I'll take care of Poo. No problem."

Cuz gets up and the clumsy fool upsets the wineglass, then grabs a napkin and starts to dab my oriental rug Momma bought. I say not to worry and get a towel.

We clean up the mess, and my scheming relative leaves, having accomplished the intended mission. Never comes to see me without a purpose. I'm relieved. What a pig! Phony all the way. Now for my phone call. I don't even have to plan what to say. I know what will scare the reporter. I laugh and dial.

"*Morning News,*" the switchboard operator answers.

"Carole Wheeler's desk," I say, hoping she's gone back to work.

"Hello," she says.

I check my watch and clear my throat. "I read your article. You shouldn't have called me a monster." This started off to be fun, now I feel a rage after speaking the word.

"What would you call yourself?"

"Everything is in the eye of the beholder," I manage to say, my hand tight around the thin crystal glass.

"Wait a minute. Let me get a cigarette."

She's buying time. "You don't smoke."

That stops her. I try to picture her face.

"I don't like the way you dress," I say for another blow. "That black affair you had on tonight is not becoming."

I hear her breathing. She is speechless.

"That *was* you with Evelyn Casey and Hawk Sullivan tonight, wasn't it? I'm *attuned*. I've seen Evelyn's picture in the paper before. Your article said Sullivan was in town.

I knew where he'd want to go first off. Who was the Mexican dude? A cop? He your boyfriend?"

"You were there?" Carole Wheeler squeaks out.

"I'm everywhere. I'm *attuned*." She knows that now. I check my watch. "No more calling me a monster." Doctor did once. I never forgot it. Now I'm boiling, just remembering. I want to say more, but I have to think about the time. Those wheels turning. "Goodbye."

"Wait, I want to talk to you," she pleads.

Good. I like for people to plead. "Don't you think I know your phone is tapped?" I hang up. I used to plead. *Don't hit me.*

I call out like I used to and hear my own voice echo. It is a strange dramatic whisper, like a rapier swishing through air. Again. *"Pleeeeeease don't, Doctor."*

Monster Doctor wouldn't stop. Maybe I won't, either.

7

Sipping a mug of coffee he brewed in the guesthouse kitchenette, Hawk Sullivan strolled over to Evelyn's terrace and sat in the shade of a giant oak. Sprinklered earlier, the sweeping green lawn looked as if it had cried, teardrops hanging from blades of grass. It was still cool, but the sun was already making its presence known. Soon it would strike with full force and set Dallas aflame.

He lit his first cigarette of the day and leaned back to enjoy it, not in the least tired from the late hours spent poring over the files. He felt an infusion of excitement, the old hound ready to chase a new fox. Apparently the attitude was contagious. When his eyes and brain could take no more, he'd gone to the window and raised it so that he could sleep with fresh air, not air-conditioning. A light was on in Evelyn's bedroom. Faint sounds of a Rachmaninoff piano concerto drifted through the night. As he closed his eyes, he wanted to believe that while she worked on the files he'd finished earlier, she was also thinking of him.

"Mr. Sullivan. That was a real good dinner you fixed last night."

He swung around to see Mary standing by the open French doors. The accusatory scowl gone, she was actually smiling. "Miz Casey seemed so different when she went upstairs last night. Almost like her old self." She turned to leave, then edged around. "You gonna fix breakfast this morning?"

He grinned back. "I don't do breakfast." He meant it. To him, dinners were creative, other meals just sustenance.

"Want me to fix you a little something? Pancakes? Anything?"

At least he'd reached a truce with her. "Maybe some juice, a piece of toast. Mrs. Casey not down yet?" He stubbed out his cigarette.

"She's long been gone. Dressed and said she had an errand. Your friend still in bed?"

"He'll be out in a few minutes." Castro had stayed up almost as long as he had, fighting sleep as he hunched over the files.

Sullivan followed Mary into the kitchen and sat at the table. He checked his watch, planning to call Captain Chandler in thirty minutes to inform him of the previous evening's events. For the files, he'd written a careful report of the room service waiter's new recollections and the speculations that followed. Evelyn's suggestion to run a computer search on malpractice suits filed by some individual with a medical background was a good one. The killer was knowledgeable in the medical field and might have some vendetta against doctors. However, Sullivan suspected that the idea had probably already occurred to the homicide detectives, with appropriate action taken. Delving into the files confirmed it. The computer check had revealed nothing of value. The purse Evelyn identified from the description and the concept that the murder weapon might be a sharp hatpin were both big pluses. He was pleased at the new avenues that had opened. The methodical step-by-step investigation would be a slow and grinding job, but a satisfying one if some clue popped up to expose the killer. Or if the Sequin made a mistake.

The doorbell and the telephone rang simultaneously.

"I'll get the door. You answer the phone," Mary said.

Captain Chandler was on the line. He told Sullivan that the Sequin had called Carole Wheeler again. Day and Gilbert, along with Carole, would be in his office in an hour to listen to the recording. The captain wanted to give Carole some instructions. He expected Sullivan and Castro there. Security for the upcoming convention needed to be discussed and planned. The unmarked car he'd ordered for Sullivan was ready for pickup. Sullivan decided to hold his news until he saw Chandler in person.

As Sullivan hung up, he saw Quinn Stewart walk into the kitchen. Stewart was dressed for golf, but obviously not prepared for Sullivan's presence, his expression a mixture of surprise and irritation.

"You're out early," he greeted Sullivan.

Castro came sailing through the French doors, dark hair damp from a shower and plastered to his skull. In that instant Sullivan knew the situation became clear in Stewart's mind. Sullivan lit a cigarette and didn't know why he felt the need to explain.

"Evelyn asked us to stay in the guesthouse. She's going to try and work up a profile on the killer for us. I think it'll do her good to have something constructive to occupy her mind. Put what she knows to use."

Castro blew on a mug of coffee Mary handed him. "She already came up with some good ideas last night at the Meridan Hotel bar after we questioned a witness."

Stewart's cheeks flushed. Sullivan saw the tightness around his eyes, lips firmed into a pencil line. "I don't like it one bit that you're trying to get Evelyn involved in your . . . your type of activities. I'm not at all satisfied about your motives, either . . ." He broke off as if he already had the words but was searching for better ones. "It's been your life to deal with criminals, not Evelyn's. You're accustomed to violence. A person like Evelyn shouldn't even try to cope with such a situation. Look at the last time. If anything in the slightest happens to put her in jeopardy, you're going to have to reckon with me." Stewart's eyebrows lifted, gauging a reaction. "Even under the best of circumstances you lead a vagabond kind of life. Evelyn doesn't fit. You need to give that some real thought."

Sullivan battled to master his emotions. He tried to concentrate on an amusing comment from Carole Wheeler that Quinn Stewart was so uptight he squeaked when he walked. Nothing about him was comical now. He was trying to stake claim to Evelyn, and Sullivan wasn't going to let him. Evelyn had the capability of making her own decisions. He'd seen her in action and knew her strengths.

"Stewart . . ." Sullivan had never called him by name and it seemed strange to say. "Regardless of what you think, I have Evelyn's best interests at heart. I wouldn't in any way put her in danger. You haven't been successful at pulling her out of the funk she was in. If working on this profile stimulates her interests and brings her back to her old self, I'm all for it and you should be, too. After all, she was interested in this field long before either you or I knew her. I've got no beef with you, but I'm going to have if you don't . . ." Sullivan broke off when he saw Evelyn.

"Morning," Evelyn said, coming into the kitchen. She looked from Sullivan to Quinn, then glanced at Castro. With a smile on her face she opened her tote bag, pulled out a large hatpin and laid it before Sullivan. "Your murder weapon. I had to comb through a few thrift shops before I found just the right kind." Hair pulled back into a ponytail, wearing cotton slacks and a shirt, she looked proud of herself. It was obvious to everyone in the room that an emotional overhaul was in process. Even her walk had a special spring, to say nothing of the new sparkle in her eyes.

Sullivan picked up the hatpin by the ball on the end and tested the sharp end for strength. "Could be."

Castro sauntered over to look. "Forensics can tell by comparison if this could make similar puncture marks."

Evelyn poured a mug of coffee. "Mary, I'm starving. How about some bacon and eggs?"

Eyeing Stewart's surprised reaction, Sullivan remembered the hearty appetite Evelyn once had, although she denied that she ate much. "Captain Chandler said Carole got another call last night from the Sequin. Castro and I are going down to listen to the recording. I've got a report for him so he can get some wheels turning about the purse theory." He looked again at the hatpin. "I've got a feeling this is the type of murder weapon the killer used . . . purpose for the hat. We don't know what kind of hat to look for, so the purse is the line to follow."

Evelyn hooked into a chair by the table. "It shouldn't be all that hard to check records. Neiman-Marcus and two boutiques are the only places where the Judith Leiber bags are sold in Dallas. I know. I've bought a few myself."

"So have plenty of other women. It's going to require some manpower after we have the list of people who have bought those bags," Sullivan added.

"It was the small gold shell purse, though," Evelyn said. "That should narrow the field quite a lot."

Castro bit his lip. "If the purses were not charged but paid for with cash, it'll be hard to trace. Clerks might have to be questioned. Still, it's a good lead. Better than anything Homicide had."

Sullivan sighed. "The purse could have been purchased out of town. Dead end, then. Maybe it was bought years ago, even."

"No," Evelyn said. "The shell one is a relatively new item."

Quinn Stewart watched the three volley back and forth

as if he were at a tennis match. When a break came, he said: "Evelyn, I'm on the way to the club. The girls called from Atlanta this morning. They're going to visit me on their Thanksgiving break. I thought we'd have a big dinner at my house this year. Maybe you could help them shop for some school clothes."

Stewart looked so expectant, so hopeful, that Sullivan felt a sting of pity for him. Worse than a "weekend dad," he was a holiday parent. At least he had something Sullivan didn't have and always wanted: children. He remembered painfully when Karin's morning sickness, which they hoped was a prelude to a happy event, was diagnosed as leukemia.

"Sure, Quinn. We'll plan some things for them. I'll be glad to help out." Evelyn glanced at Sullivan, who looked away.

"I'll check with you later," Quinn said, heading for the door.

Sullivan watched him walk away, then turned to Evelyn. "Castro and I better get a move on. I'll get the rest of the files for you to study. Don't know when we'll be back. I'll also check with you later. I've bought some stuff for dinner." He leaned around and winked at Mary.

Evelyn touched his arm as he rose. He glanced down at her hand. "Hawk, last night I was thinking about the profile. I don't know if it would apply to a woman serial killer since there's never been one, but remember, I told you once that all known male serial killers have had tattoos. It's like they need some identification. You might try that as a lead."

Already deep in thought, Sullivan nodded and picked up the hatpin. Castro followed him from the kitchen.

In less than fifteen minutes Sullivan and Castro walked into Chandler's office. The captain was seated behind his desk, Day and Gilbert in side chairs, Carole Wheeler on the couch. Sullivan and Castro settled next to Carole. She looked nervous, pleating her skirt with her fingers. Her eyes darted around the room, holding a moment on Gilbert, who avoided contact.

Chandler touched the tape recorder on his desk, and the throaty rasp of the killer filled the room. Sullivan thought he felt the hairs on his neck stand. To actually hear her speak as if she were in the room chilled him. Then, like an unexpected blow from a fist, he heard that eerie voice speak Evelyn's name, then his.

Chandler switched off the recorder. "This bitch has already proved she means business. I don't think we've seen the last of her. If we had any suspects . . . any leads . . . we could have a voice pattern comparison." He focused on Carole. "Now, when she calls again, and I'm sure she will, I want you to try a few things to distract her mind. She's clever, but maybe if you hit a sore spot, you'll get her off track. Ask her what bugs her in her background. It all started back there, you know."

Carole nodded. "I'll ask Evelyn Casey for some questions that will sting the Sequin. Sullivan's asked her to work up a profile on the killer."

"Mrs. Andrew Casey, the oil heiress?" Chandler asked.

"Yes," Carole confirmed.

"I heard the Sequin mention the name Evelyn Casey on the tape, but it just struck me who she might be," Chandler said, his expression surprised.

Before Sullivan could say anything, Carole explained Evelyn's background, gesticulating wildly with her hands, rows of bangle bracelets clanging as she talked. Sullivan's mind was trapped on the previous evening. Without doubt, the killer had been close. He ruled out any of the three middle-aged women at the bar. Had to be the casually dressed woman waiting by the newsstand. He couldn't get a clear picture of her face. Damn it! Only the clothes, the posture. His mind was spinning, ears ringing with the voice mouthing Evelyn's name, Quinn Stewart's words turning in his head.

"She's going to do a profile?" Gilbert asked, lips curled into a smile. "Something like the psychic we had?"

"Evelyn's qualified," Carole protested. "She hit the profile on the nose last time."

"We'll take anything we can get," Chandler answered, his tone ending that subject.

Sullivan pushed up from the couch and laid the hatpin and his report of the previous night before Chandler. "I think this might be a facsimile of the murder weapon."

Day and Gilbert leaned forward, eyeing the object. Chandler picked it up, head cocked to one side. Day glanced up at Sullivan, astounded at the find. Gilbert shot a glance at Carole, jaw pulsing. Carole had an uncharacteristic hurt look about her, a dog kicked by the master. Sullivan had the vibe that those two had held a conversation long before the meeting. He had a strong feeling Gilbert was pissed by her article, took it to mean Homicide, without Sullivan, was ineffectual. He had a vision of Carole the night before, frightened by the call, trying to contact Gilbert. Maybe went to wherever he lived after calling the station. Found out he wasn't working at all, but with the lady sergeant from the task force.

"Day, when we finish here I want you to get this to Forensics." Chandler checked his watch. "They should be able to give us a report right away."

Sullivan summed up his report. "The purse is a good lead. I think we should get on it right away." He explained that the shell-shaped purse was a fairly new item and sold at only three stores in Dallas.

Gilbert's cold eyes swept over Sullivan. "How'd you get that information out of the room service waiter. I questioned him myself and couldn't get anything except he saw a blonde with a hat."

"I read your report," Sullivan answered. "I just got lucky with him." Sullivan started to light a cigarette, then remembered the sign on Chandler's desk. "Mrs. Casey tells me that there has never been a serial killer without a tattoo. Maybe that's a line to pursue. Check with some tattoo parlors for women who've gotten one. Can't be too many women with tattoos or too many tattoo parlors here.''

Castro added, ''In a port like San Diego there are dozens, but I would think . . .''

''Find a tattooed woman,'' Gilbert cut him off, ''and maybe we've got the killer?'' He chuckled inwardly, shoulders moving. ''You know what's the most common criminal name in the south and southwest U.S.?'' Gilbert opened his hands as if holding a book. ''Wayne . . . my name. I've heard guys say let's arrest all the Waynes around and surely the perp will be in the group. It's about the same thing.''

''I never heard it, but if that's true about the tattoo, what have we got to lose?'' Chandler said. ''We don't have many other places to look. Getting this purse search going will probably take until Monday, this being a Saturday and the store closed tomorrow. The threat of AIDS has practically ruined the tattoo business. I know for a fact there's only one tattoo parlor in the city. Voodoo Tattoo in the west end. Sullivan, you, Castro and Gilbert give it a try. We can have Distinguishing Marks in ID Section run a scan on any names you might get. If one of the names pops up, we'll run a search on known offenders, pick up on the record. The Sequin might not even have a record. Might not even be from Dallas, a drifter.'' Chandler sighed and leaned around the men to catch Carole Wheeler's attention. ''Carole, your last article was good, well meant, but now that we've heard the Sequin's call it's done a couple of things that might spell damage. The killer knows Hawk Sullivan's name, is aware that he is here to help us. From publicity about the other serial killer case, she's linked him to Evelyn Casey. I don't want anyone put in jeopardy by revealing too much about them. You see, when I'm quoted in the paper, I'm referred to as only Captain Chandler or if Day or Gilbert is interviewed, it's Lieutenant Day or Gilbert. No first names given. A killer couldn't track us in our personal lives, if he had a mind to. Could only reach us at the office. There are a lot of nuts out there that might want revenge. So keep things on a last-name basis from now on.'' Chandler cleared his throat. ''I've appreciated your cooperation all the way on the case and I want to ask for more.'' He picked up the hatpin. ''I don't want anything about the suspected weapon to get out of this room. I'll let you know when you can use the information. If I see one thing in print about this, you won't have any more information from this end.'' Chandler nodded, confirming his statement. ''We're gonna talk security for the convention now. I imagine you've got work to do. You do your best to keep the Sequin talking.''

Carole leaped up, looked at the back of Gilbert's head, then left. Chandler studied some diagrams on his desk before he spoke. Sullivan presumed he was giving Carole time to clear out of the outer office. Chandler's words had so stunned him that he wasn't thinking clearly. In the excitement over seeing Evelyn and the stupid reasoning of publicity for his agency, he'd made a grave mistake of allowing Carole to write the article. He'd never dreamed the Sequin might predict their moves after reading the article or link him to Evelyn.

Chandler stood, hands gripping the edge of his desk. ''I want a man in every elevator twenty-four hours a day. I've got the shifts worked out. I've already talked with the man at the Hyatt who runs the convention business. We'll have people at the cocktail party before the banquet and at the dinner. He says uninvited guests do wander in sometimes. We're working on something with name tags. We'll have men in the lobby and bars watching for prostitutes and pickups. The bell captain has been warned about anyone trying to arrange for any prostitutes. The Chairman of the doctors' group is going to give a discreet warning at the first meeting. We'll have another briefing and assignments the day before the convention.'' He waved his hand. "That's about it for right now. Day, get to Forensics. Tell 'em this is a rush. The rest of you guys check out the tattoo thing and get back to me. Sullivan and Castro, you'll work on the purse line starting Monday. I'll make some arrangements with the store now, so they can be ready for us then. I'll be here waiting for what you come up with today. It's about time we got lucky."

8

Lieutenant Wayne Gilbert drove Sullivan and Castro through the west end of downtown Dallas. The once dilapidated and near-abandoned area had undergone a face-lift. Facades of turn-of-the-century buildings had been sandblasted and rejuvenated, warehouses turned into chic restaurants, dry-goods stores of old transformed into tony boutiques. Elegant women in expensive casual clothes strolled the sidewalks, the section now an obvious rival for Neiman-Marcus on the opposite end of town.

Gilbert explained that the unique area afforded quarters to law offices and housed many corporate headquarters. "There's where the FBI has relocated."

Sullivan wondered if Gilbert had purposely driven him by the agency of which he was once in charge to make him feel outdated. Sullivan glanced back at the quaint four-story building, wrought iron edging the entry, windows shuttered and underlined with planter boxes. He would enjoy jawing with the few old-timers, if any were still around, and meeting new faces he knew would look like boys to him now.

He lit a cigarette and thought about his dilemma concerning Evelyn. The call from the Sequin had unsettled him. With the profile, he had handed Evelyn a new lease on life. What damage would it do if he snatched the case back? What damage would it do if he allowed her to continue? Maybe he and Castro should get their own place, leave her completely out of the picture until the case was resolved.

"I know you were with the FBI here. You grow up in Dallas?" Gilbert asked, turning right into a part of town that had not been rejuvenated, storefront windows smashed and buildings shabby.

"Washington," Sullivan answered. "Moved to San Diego when I was twelve." Sullivan's dad had been a fair college baseball player who wanted to make the major leagues but instead opened a sporting-goods store in Washington to keep old memories alive. His wife developed uremic poisoning in the latter stages of her second pregnancy. Being good Catholics, the mother was sacrificed during birth so the newborn, Hawkins Sullivan, could enter the world unharmed.

Memories burned on Sullivan. Unlike most kids who grew up in stages, Sullivan remembered the exact day when he took a single bound into maturity. He was playing in his front yard when his older brother dashed into the street to retrieve a ball just as a fast car turned the corner. After so many years he could still hear the awful crunch. He could picture his father's questioning expression after the funeral when he looked at the six-year-old who was left. Maybe the old man wasn't wondering why his favorite son had been taken, the golden boy who brought home the grades and awards, instead of Hawk, the klutz who looked up to his older brother and tried in vain to emulate him. Sullivan never knew for sure. He only knew that after that

tragedy his father looked at him but never really saw him.
From that day on, Hawkins Sullivan had two loads to carry.

Soon after his son's funeral, Sullivan's dad had told him
that sporting-goods stores fared much better in California,
where more lines of equipment such as surfing and fishing
gear were in demand. Sullivan suspected the old man had
simply had his fill of Washington and all he'd lost there.
The two packed up their green Buick and headed west to
make a new life.

"You were transferred to the FBI San Diego office after
Dallas, right?" Gilbert asked.

"That's correct," Sullivan answered, looking straight
ahead. More than likely Gilbert knew the move was a
demotion before the final boot.

Gilbert turned toward Castro in the back seat. "Capt'n
said you were with Homicide in San Diego. A sergeant."

"Yep. I was going to take the officers' examination.
Now I like being private, though. Stand a chance of making some money."

"A captain's salary's not too bad. Steady. Then, if you
want to go higher . . . it's possible with the right breaks."

Sullivan studied Gilbert's strong profile. So he was
bucking for Chandler's job. Might snag it, too, if he was
the one to catch the Sequin. Ambition was good most of
the time, but not always.

"I guess that call from the Sequin shook you," Gilbert
said. "Now she knows more than she did to start with."
He glanced back at Castro. "Knows Sullivan's name and
Mrs. Casey's, but can't figure who the Mexican dude is."
Gripping the wheel tighter, he moved his thumbs up and
down. "Wonder what she'd think if she knew Mrs. Casey
was trying to work up a profile?"

"That won't happen. I'd get off the case myself, first."
Sullivan was aware he was under Gilbert's close scrutiny.

"Here's the place." Gilbert wheeled into a parking
space.

Sullivan stubbed out his cigarette, unhappy with the

mood into which he'd settled. Getting out, he glanced at the small shop, the sign VOODOO TATTOO in snaking letters. A bell above the door tingled as they entered.

The front room passed for an art gallery, pictures of every imaginable tattoo available displayed on the walls. Green dragons on hind legs, ready to strike. Curvy outlines of women, any name written below. Daggers dripping blood. Fish in an elaborate underwater scene, complete with an octopus lurking behind seaweed. A rising sun peeping over a blue horizon.

"Jesus, look at all these. I almost got one when I was a kid," Castro said. "Thought it was muy macho."

"Then you could have been a serial killer suspect," Gilbert answered.

"Yeah." Castro popped his palm with a fist. "Serial killers always pick on a certain type. I know just the kind I'd go for."

Sullivan watched Castro and the slick detective eye each other until the moment passed. The trio turned when they heard a noise. Two hands, fat as stuffed sausage, rings on every finger, pushed through the beads and parted them. A man came through the maze as if he were swimming. He was short and bald except for a few strands hanging to his shoulders, a miniature sumo wrestler. In a sleeveless T-shirt, his arms were covered with blue and purple tattoos.

"Help you?" the man asked, eyeing the men. "I'm Sam Ching. I own this establishment."

Gilbert pulled out his identification. "Homicide. We'd like to ask you a few questions."

Ching's ferret eyes darted in their sockets. He had no eyebrows, but skin folds gave the appearance that he had. "What about?" His breath caught in his chest.

Sullivan knew that the word "homicide" usually brought the same reaction as "gestapo." "Do you tattoo many women?"

Ching batted lashless lids. "Some. Not as many as men, of course. Why?"

"Let me handle the questions, Mr. Ching," Gilbert answered. "You remember any of the women that struck you as . . . maybe weird?"

"Weird? They're all weird mostly. I mean, the art of tattoo is for men, in my opinion. Years ago when it began . . ." He threw up his hands. "Well, now, it's a different world . . . everywhere."

Sullivan hoped to find a lead here, a suspect of some type to get them rolling, but knew any suspect could have been tattooed years ago. And, of course, in another city. As Chandler pointed out, serial killers sometimes drifted, like Ted Bundy from Utah to Colorado. "The Green River Killer," not as yet apprehended, had moved from the Seattle area to southern California. Their chances of finding something here were thin. "Mr. Ching, how long have you been in business?"

"Ten years last month." He pointed at the floor. "Right here in this shop."

"About how many women a year do you tattoo?" Castro asked.

Ching shrugged, turning down his lips. "None when I first started out. In the last six years . . . maybe five to ten a year."

"Your customers pay mostly in cash or check?" Gilbert glanced around, assessing the place Ching called an establishment.

Ching's smile showed a gold front tooth. "Either one. I take checks if they have good identification. I keep good records, too. Take names and addresses before I do the work. Have them sign a release. No lawsuits later. Send out fliers when I have some new designs I think customers might like. Good advertisement. Many come back when they see some new artwork they like." Ching looked pleased with himself, a real businessman.

"We'd like to go through your records and get a list of

all the women customers and addresses.'' Sullivan wondered if Ching's customers were the type to give their correct locations. Out of the corner of his eye he saw Gilbert check his watch in an irritated manner. It was the weekend and obviously he had things on tap. "I guess this might take some time." Sullivan figured the better part of the afternoon.

"Not really," Ching answered. "You see I keep a separate file for women customers. Send out fliers to them with designs they might like where men wouldn't. You know . . . butterflies. Flowers. In this business women don't go for the same type tattoos men do. It's a specialized business. You have to know tastes. Most women like small tattoos. You know Cher has one."

"Maybe we should pull her in for questioning." Gilbert's tongue played inside his cheek.

"Homicide, you said. You think I might have worked on some killer? The one I read about, the Sequined Stalker?" Ching grinned, small eyes alive with excitement. "What advertisement."

"You got a desk or a place where we can work?" Gilbert asked, ignoring the question.

"Come right on back to my office." Ching turned and waddled away.

They passed several open rooms that reminded Sullivan of doctors' examination cubicles. Sullivan supposed Ching did his work in those areas. He got a quick glimpse of a cabinet that held different-colored dyes in small bottles and a row of needles. He wondered how Forensics was progressing with the hatpin. Thanks to Evelyn, if he singled out the murder weapon in less than twenty-four hours on the case, Gilbert would resent him even more. The investigation should be a team effort, but something in him wanted to beat Gilbert to the Sequin.

Ching pulled out his records and laid them on a table. He provided them yellow pads and pens, then left to attend to his skin artistry. They divided the files and started copying names and addresses.

In less than thirty minutes, they compiled a list of forty-two names, types of tattoos and addresses. Sullivan stared at the list, hoping against hope the Sequin might be among those listed. When things looked easy, they only got harder.

Gilbert picked up the list. "Okay, let's get this list back to the station so the ID section can run a computer scan. If any names come up, we'll personally check 'em out. If not, I'll get a couple of sergeants on the task force to foot it out all weekend with the list, see if they find anybody suspicious . . . strong woman with a medical background. No law against having a tattoo, but they can ask a few questions . . . where were they the night of the last killing. Day might have something from Forensics by now."

Asking questions about the Sequined Stalker, Ching followed them down the hall to the front door. Sullivan thanked Ching, who wanted to know if he should call them when the next lady came for a tattoo. Gilbert said he would be in touch. Ching insisted he might be of help.

As they drove away, Ching was still at the front door mouthing. Sullivan lit a cigarette, thinking what spice it was to the ordinary person to be involved in a police case, especially to finger a serial killer or to envision himself personally cornering one. If they knew as much as he, they wouldn't be so anxious. Those officers assigned serial murder investigations were, from experience, terrified of them and approached only with great trepidation. That, or they wouldn't last long.

Sullivan heard Castro and Gilbert talking, but didn't listen to the words, his mind centered on Evelyn. He knew that all male serial killers went for a certain type—but only when killing of their own free will. Ted Bundy sought dark-haired girls. John Wayne Gacy, young boys. The Green River Killer, prostitutes. From personal experience Sullivan knew that Charlie Christmas murdered only shy, lonely, vulnerable women, but when cornered he attempted, like a rabid animal, to kill anyone in his way. The Sequin went for doctors, but might she switch? Working on the profile that might uncover the killer could place Evelyn in danger if the Sequin got wind of it.

Gilbert pulled into the wire-fenced parking area next to the station. "Capt'n said your issue car would be in slot ten. That's it, to the right. Key's in it. Give me your rental key and I'll have a patrolman return it."

They walked through the busy station, uniformed officers hurrying past, plainclothes detectives lugging sets of files, some carrying grease-stained bags of food. Realizing how hungry he was, even the short-orders smelled good to Sullivan. In the Homicide Division every desk had an ashtray, and cigarette smoke hung like fog in the air. Gilbert stopped at one of the desks, gave a detective the list from Ching's with instructions to take it to the ID Section for a scan and report back. Gilbert ushered Sullivan and Castro to his small office, cordoned off from the open area by glass. Day's was next to his, he explained. They could see he wasn't at his desk. Both offices were similar, a gray metal desk, swivel chair to match, two straight-back wooden chairs for visitors and walls lined with file cabinets. There were no personal items in either office.

Gilbert leaned back in his chair and unbuttoned his suit jacket. "I can send out to the deli. Anybody for a sandwich?" His offer was rote rather than hospitable.

Sullivan didn't care to have a meal with Gilbert, but his stomach overruled any prejudice. Besides, he and Castro were stuck there until they had some results. Gilbert crooked his finger and beckoned a young rookie to his office. All three ordered hot pastrami on rye.

Sullivan spotted Day walking through the activity in the outer area, moving his legs as if bogging through a muddy field. The overhead neons cast a light so bright his scalp shone.

"Forensics says we got a fit. It definitely could be a

hatpin,'' he said, coming in. He smiled and cracked his knuckles. "It's a step in the right direction.'' His eyes darted from Sullivan to Castro. "Get anything on the tattoo?''

"Waiting,'' Gilbert answered, propping his feet on the desk. "ID's running a scan. Shouldn't be long.'' He checked his watch. "If nothing pops we'll knock off for the day. I'll get some investigators on the list, anyway.''

Identifying a murder weapon in a case was always a top priority and Sullivan should have been pleased for the part he'd played, but instead of triumph, he felt deflated. He had to make a decision concerning Evelyn.

Day faced Sullivan. "The capt'n called the head purse-buyer at the downtown Neiman-Marcus. Margo Martin. They got two other stores here, but everything goes through that channel. She confirmed that they and two other of those small stores . . . whatcha-call-'ems . . .''

"Boutiques,'' Gilbert filled in.

"Yeah . . . boutiques. Neiman's and those two are the only ones who carry those purses. I've got two investigators going to the . . . small stores. Sullivan and Castro, you can start at Neiman's with Margo Martin on Monday morning. She'll be waitin' for you.'' He perched on the edge of the desk. "We'll just wait, then.'' He lifted his elbows and flapped his arms. "Air-conditioning feels good. Hot as hog's breath outside.''

The young officer pushed through the door with a bag of sandwiches and they dug in. Day swung his feet back and forth, still commenting on the weather. Gilbert put his sandwich down and looked toward the squad room.

"Here comes Nelson Collins from ID. Got a smile on.'' Gilbert blotted his lips with a napkin and straightened in his chair.

A stocky redheaded man in a suit shiny from age burst in. Everyone looked expectantly at him.

"Got anything?'' Gilbert asked.

"Bible says, 'Ask and ye shall receive.' My computer

says that, too. One name came up. Joyce Morrow. Two counts of assault. Both on men. One of them who filed a complaint was a doctor. Got her phone and address. A scan at Distinguishing Marks confirms she's got a tattoo of a butterfly on her right shoulder. She's a lady wrestler. Got a mug shot. Not bad-looking for such a profession. She's called Joyce the Choice." He chuckled, then his expression changed. "Get this. She was a medic in the Marine Corps."

Gilbert pushed away from his desk. "Well, let's take a look at this strong woman with a medical background who has a tattoo and once assaulted a doctor. Could be we're gonna come face-to-face with the Sequin."

9

Evelyn looked up from her papers when the doorbell rang. She had worked all day on the profile. Her eyes burned and her neck was stiff, but the exhaustion she felt was what she'd call "a good tired," although she wasn't positive anything valuable had been established. Dodging around the scattered reference books, she hurried to the door, hoping Sullivan was back. She actually felt like a changed person. She had a purpose, a challenge to meet. All due to Hawk Sullivan. The thought of him filled her with anticipation.

Evelyn opened the door and found Carole in the threshold, shaking her head. She wore a green cotton warm-up decorated with different-size checkered bows and matching Keds. A green scarf was fashioned gypsy style around her orange curls. "I may have done it. Talked to Hawkeye?" Her voice was uncharacteristically pitched, urgent.

"Done what?" Evelyn asked, stepping aside to let Carole enter.

Bracelets clanging on freckled arms, Carole gestured as

the Sequin's words spilled from her mouth. "God! Evelyn, I just didn't consider the possibilities."

Evelyn stood still, absorbing the news, trying to sort out the consequences. She fought down old fears, but still felt a shiver run through her. "Well, so she knows my name. That doesn't mean anything." She tried to sound casual. "What did Hawk say?" Evelyn turned and headed for the den.

Carole hurried to keep up, taking small steps in Evelyn's tracks. "He looked pretty upset."

Evelyn knew he'd blame himself for getting her involved and wouldn't want her to continue. "I don't see any problem." She did, but didn't want to look at it. After she and Sullivan had dealt with Charlie Christmas the newspaper accounts were filled with the accurate personality profile she'd constructed. Now Sullivan was in town and the killer had seen Evelyn with him. The Sequined Stalker knew what she looked like, so obviously she'd seen her photo somewhere. Before the incident with Charlie Christmas, her picture had often been in the society columns, especially when Andrew was alive. Maybe the killer had recognized her from those days. That was the way she was going to view it.

"I'd slit my wrists if I caused you any problem," Carole said, flouncing down on the couch and folding her legs yoga style.

Evelyn sank into a roomy lounge chair and rested her head on its back. "The only problem I'm going to have is with Hawk."

"He's not going to want you involved. He'll want you to stop work on the profile. Are you going to stop?"

"No," Evelyn answered with authority.

"I didn't think so." Carole looked at the books, Evelyn's littered desk, wads of discarded paper. "Are you getting anywhere?"

"I don't know. Everything applies to a man. I'm trying to adapt it, but who knows if it's accurate?"

"The captain wants me to try to keep the Sequin talking if she calls again. Hit on something in her background to throw her off guard and make her lose track of time. I remember some stuff from the Charlie Christmas profile. Serial killers are sociopaths . . . feeling nothing for anyone except themselves. Unable to form any real attachments. Sly, conniving, clever. They use knives or strangle victims, never guns, to achieve intimacy with them. In this case, possibly a hatpin." Carole waved her arm. "I know they receive lesser amounts of satisfaction with each killing, which prompts them to continue. Tell me some real background meat I could use on her."

Evelyn sat erect, her mind racing with bits of information. "A serial killer has been constructing power fantasies since early childhood, building a life around them. Appears outwardly normal. Probably tortured animals, maybe had sex with them." Evelyn paused.

Carole snapped her fingers. "Okay, good. How about I ask her . . . real innocently at first . . . what's your favorite animal? Dogs? Cats? When she answers, I zap her with, 'How did you torture them?' "

The thought of Carole sparring with the killer made Evelyn shudder. That the killer had observed them, been so close, was even more frightening. "That's probably as good a question as any."

"What about sex?" Carole leaned forward, deeply intrigued.

Evelyn ran her fingers through her hair and shook her head. "Serial killers, at least males, had adolescent sexual tension, probably held unusual attitudes about pornography and prostitutes. Later in life, normal sex doesn't work for them. Murder is a substitute for sex."

"Okay, say most of that doesn't work for a woman." She rolled her eyes. "I could ask her about her sexual past. The homicide guys listening would get a kick out of that."

They both laughed. Evelyn pushed up and walked to the

bar. "It's getting on toward cocktail time. Want a Perrier while I have a vodka?"

"Sure. Why not? A double. I'm in the mood."

Evelyn glanced at the empty bowl on the counter. "I'll get a lemon from the kitchen. Be right back."

Carole observed her as she walked away, wishing she had Evelyn's flair, her confidence. Evelyn would have never pulled the stunt Carole did the night before. The Sequin's call had given her a good excuse to contact Wayne. She could have called, but decided instead to go to his apartment, faking more apprehension than she actually felt, in hopes he'd ask her in for a drink that might lead to more. Although she hated to admit it, she was desperate for his company, his attention. Would do anything to lasso him.

When she arrived his car wasn't in his slot in the dark parking lot. Feeling alone, her plan soured, she started to leave just as Wayne drove up and parked next to her. She jumped out, babbling the news. He seemed nervous, on edge, glancing toward the street as if something else was on his mind. She touched his sleeve and he edged away, saying the monitors had the conversation on tape. He was tired. The situation would be dealt with in the morning. With a curt good night, he moved toward his apartment.

Turning on her ignition, she watched him climb the wrought-iron stairs to his second-story apartment. As she drove away, a car exactly like his, police issue, pulled into the slot next to his. She slowed in the street long enough to glimpse a woman get out of the car and walk toward Wayne's apartment. She knew a woman was on the task force. Working closely with Wayne, the woman would have the inside track. Carole had accelerated, feeling a wedge in her chest.

Evelyn came in with the lemon, sliced it with her bar knife, dropped it in her drink, then handed Carole hers. "I was just thinking . . . you might shake the Sequin up with something from her childhood. Again, this has applied with males. Cold, abusive father. Problem mother, maybe an alcoholic, possibly seductive. Likely both parents abandoned the child, physically or emotionally. Can't identify with either parent. As you know, Charlie Christmas was an orphan.'' Evelyn settled in her chair.

Carole took a sip of Perrier and wrinkled her nose at the bubbles. '' 'Bet your mom was a drunk.' I could say that, or 'Your dad beat you much? Punch you around when you were little and couldn't fight back. A mean bastard, wasn't he?' That might provoke her. Go on, give some more.''

Evelyn felt the same enjoyment as she had when first studying her field, learning, accomplishing. ''The transformation from sociopath to psychopath eventually happens and a blend of those characteristics turns the person into a psychotic. The psychotic walks a fine line between the psychopathic and sociopathic personalities, performing crimes that are spur-of-the-moment violence, which is typical of the sociopath, and also exhibiting careful victim selection, which indicates premeditation and planning, a psychopathic trait. You can see that the combination makes the killer more formidable.'' Evelyn tried to conjure up some picture of the killer, her personality, but drew blanks. She sipped her drink. ''We've got one thing that's common with serial killers that applies to the Sequined Stalker.''

''What?'' Carole was anxious for an answer, leaning forward at such an angle that Evelyn thought she might pitch right off the couch.

''It's well documented that some psychopaths try to get as close to the police investigation as possible, following the progress in the papers, returning to the crime scene. To them, notoriety is almost as important as the killing itself. Serial killers have an established ritual which means something to them, gives a purpose. Very unlikely they would deviate from the ritual.''

''She'll keep calling, keep poking around, then. She'd better not get wind of your profile.'' Carole finished her drink in one gulp. ''I better get going. My room's a mess

after the move. That Mississippi belle is a real neato.''
Carole rummaged in her tote bag. ''I must have left my
key in the car. I hope nobody steals it.'' She spilled the
contents of her purse on the floor and crouched down,
scraping various items into a pile.

Evelyn wondered who'd steal Carole's yellow VW bug,
plastic rose attached to the aerial, that had barely made
the trip from San Diego to Dallas, especially since it was
parked in front of her house. She leaned forward and
picked up a photograph that had landed in her chair.

On all fours, Carole reached for the picture. ''That's
my roommate, Dorothy Virginia. Cute, huh?''

Evelyn glanced at the photo and handed it back, her
mind on the situation at hand. She wondered why Hawk
hadn't come back or called. Already she was planning her
spiel. With him she'd have to use reverse psychology, come
up with something he didn't expect. She saw Carole to the
door.

''Hawk going to cook again tonight?'' Carole asked.

''He said so.'' If he didn't hurry she'd have to start
some initial preparations. The dinner he planned required
time. What was keeping him? Had they run across some
lead? She was dying to know if a hatpin could be the
murder weapon. If so, she had proven she had some worth
to the case. Her information on the purse could also prove
valuable.

''Maybe Wayne will call me to go to dinner,'' Carole
said, but her expression denied expectation. ''I'll wait
around for a while, but not too long.'' She lifted her chin
slightly. ''If he doesn't call . . . la-de-da . . . My roommate and I will go out and get to know each other.''

Evelyn thought how body language was such a telling
sign. Carole would wait all night for Wayne's call if necessary. ''Does he go out with anyone besides you?''

''Why not?'' Carole shrugged. ''I would. See you.''
She hurried down the sidewalk, half skipping, half hop-
ping.

Evelyn walked to the empty kitchen, hoping Hawk would be there soon. In the course of only one day the house seemed empty without him.

For fear of alerting Joyce Morrow with a call, Gilbert had driven Sullivan, Castro and Day to her address, a large home surrounded by several wooded acres in the suburb of Addison, Texas. A quick check into her background had revealed that Joyce Morrow, unmarried, earned over a hundred thousand dollars a year. Garbed in fancy clothes, ''Joyce the Choice'' was a popular wrestling personality on local television.

The quartet rang the doorbell, waited, rang again. Gilbert checked his watch. When no one answered, they walked around the house, peeped in windows, then inspected the empty garage. Sullivan suggested that someone in her position would probably have an answering machine. They hauled back to the car and drove to a nearby service station. Gilbert got out to use the pay phone.

The phone rang four times, then the line clicked and he heard a froggy voice: ''Hi. This is Choice Joyce. I'm at Crank's Gym. Leave a message or call me there.'' She gave the number and Gilbert called it for an address. He made one more call, then strode back to the car, once more checking his watch.

He slammed the door, looked at the expectant men, then told them about the answering machine message. ''I called Nelson Collins in ID Section. He's going to call Joyce Morrow's number and tape her recording. Then he can work on a voice pattern comparison with the tape we've got of the Sequin. Might have to get some help from the FBI. Collins says since we're comparing two tapes, one that is likely disguised, the other a planned message, there could be enough distortion with unnatural patterns to throw the analysis off.''

''So now we drop in at Crank's Gym,'' Sullivan said.

Gilbert chuckled, though he seemed edgy. ''Ought to

be interesting. What a name. It's Crank Case's Gym. Wonder if Crank is a man or a woman.'' He drove away, shaking his head. ''This is getting freakier by the minute.''

''I got a miniature recorder in my pocket.'' Day smiled. ''Good thing, isn't it? When we talk to Joyce the Choice I can record her live. Maybe that'll help some.''

In the back seat with Castro, Sullivan lit a cigarette and watched the Dallas skyline, buildings illuminated in the growing twilight. Evelyn would wonder where he was. He could have found time to call, but he wanted to tell her in person his decision that as a precautionary measure she should stop work on the profile and distance herself from him and the case. It had been a tough conclusion to reach, but imperative. When the case was over they could resume the interrupted relationship. What about time and distance? he asked himself. He'd be San Diego–bound at the case's termination, with no reason to hang around. He was aware of Castro's stare and realized he'd made a slight groan.

''What's with you, man?'' Castro asked quietly.

''Not a thing,'' Sullivan said, looking straight ahead. ''I was just thinking about Joyce the Choice. Be great if we got lucky, but I'm not holding my breath. Still, so far everything fits. I want to see her face. Look at her eyes.''

Gilbert looked toward the rear. ''Can you tell by that?''

Sullivan didn't answer.

Gilbert slowed on Harry Hines Boulevard, a street lined with strip joints, lights flashing around signs that promised nude dancers, dark warehouses, liquor stores and small brick and tile businesses closed for the night. Passing the brightly lit Parkland Hospital Medical Complex, Gilbert turned down a small street checkered with empty lots and slowed in front of the only building on the block, a square concrete construction with no visible windows.

They opened the glass front door to a cavernous room full of activity, noise bouncing off walls. Shouts, curses, threats, sounds of flesh slapping against canvas echoed through the steel rafters. Dressed in tights, women in small rope-ringed arenas writhed on mats like snakes in mortal combat. A few punched leather bags with the skill of trained fighters. The stretching and lifting equipment was engaged by biceps-bulging, sweating females in workout suits. Forms on stationary bikes pedaled as if in a triathlon division. Several muscled, well-proportioned women skipped rope, as light on their feet as ballet dancers.

The foursome stood, mesmerized by the sight. The smell of perspiration and old socks mixed with liniment reminded Sullivan of his high school gym.

"I wouldn't mind tangling with a few of these pieces," Gilbert said, eyes on a woman pumping iron.

"Pieces," Day exclaimed. "Wayne, these ain't pieces, they're hunks, mountains."

Sullivan looked at Day, amused. He'd noticed that Day reverted to the vernacular of his past when absorbed, the gaping farm boy at the county fair. Sullivan could have pegged Day as a police detective in any crowd. They were the same in every city. Brown jacket, loud tie over polyester. And always brown shoes, clumsy cordovans that exaggerated shoe sizes. Gilbert could pass for an executive. Sullivan supposed at the moment he and Castro could be taken as beachcombers, in their casual dress. Especially himself.

"Might not want to tangle if one of them's the Sequin," Castro said.

"That must be Crank Case over there at the desk," Sullivan said, almost laughing at the name. Tough name to match a tough clientele.

They walked over to the desk where the balding man in a T-shirt worked on ledgers. His teeth clamped an unlit cigar like a dog that had no intention of letting go of a piece of meat.

"Crank Case?" Gilbert asked, keeping a straight face as he showed identification the man didn't look at.

"Yeah, what of it?" The teeth that weren't missing resembled kernels of corn and were just as yellow. He squinted and his face turned into a design of wrinkles running at odd angles, crossing and intersecting into diamond and triangle patterns on skin weathered and ravaged by alcohol.

"I understand Joyce Morrow is here. We'd like to talk to her," Gilbert answered, glancing at his watch.

"What for?" Crank shot back, bloodshot eyes narrowed.

"That's none of your concern. I asked you a fucking question and I'm waiting on the answer," Gilbert returned, jaw clenched in irritation.

"You didn't ask me no question. You just made a statement." Crank licked his lips. "You guys leaning on Joyce just 'cause she beat the shit outta couple of wise-asses trying to hit on her in bars, thinking they could take her on? The Choice showed 'em." He turned around and spit on the floor.

Gilbert reached across the desk and with both hands grabbed the little man by the shirt. "Listen, you motherfucker, for two bits I'll haul you in." He glared at the man, holding him tight. "I'm not going to take any shit off you." He shook him like a rag doll.

Sullivan didn't think Gilbert's attitude was commensurate with the provocation. This wasn't Russia and a badge didn't empower the holder to mistreat people. "Hey, we're not here to lean on her," he said. "Just want to talk. Doesn't have anything to do with those assault charges."

Crank lifted his arm. "Okay. Cool out. I'll take you back to where she is." He squirmed in Gilbert's grip.

Gilbert released Crank Case, then pushed his own arms forward to free his shirt cuffs that had hiked up above his wrists. "That's better. Let's go."

Crank Case shuffled off in a huff, the group following. Several women broke from clinches and hammerlocks to watch. "She's finished and in the shower rooms. You can't go back there. Wait by the door.'' He leaned toward the opening, mouth open, ready to call.

Gilbert laid a hand on Crank's shoulder. ''Is there a back door out of that shower room?''

Crank shook his head. ''Just windows.''

''Don't say the word 'police' or I'll squeeze your head off your shoulders,'' Gilbert warned.

''Joyce,'' he yelled. ''Some people here to see you.''

''Be right out,'' she answered, contralto voice echoing on the tiles.

Sullivan took a deep breath and looked at Castro. Day cracked his knuckles. Gilbert lifted his head and rotated his shoulders. It seemed to Sullivan that the background noises had dimmed somewhat.

''Help you?''

They all turned to the figure in the doorway. As well proportioned as a beauty contestant, Joyce Morrow wore a sleeveless warm-up that fit like wallpaper. Outlined through the shiny material, her legs were muscular, but trim like a fit racehorse. The small butterfly tattoo on her shoulder was visible. Arms strong-looking but not wrestleresque. Her blond hair was a skullcap of tight curls. Glowing complexion. A sensual mouth. Wise eyes that probably missed nothing.

Gilbert whipped out his identification, which she took and studied as if memorizing. She lifted her eyes and stared at Gilbert.

''So?'' she asked, completely composed, unlike most people, who became rattled when Homicide showed an interest in them.

''We'd like to talk to you. Is there some private place we can go?'' Gilbert answered, eyes roaming over the female before him.

''There's a lounge over there.'' She motioned with her head. ''What's this about?'' She surveyed the others present, taking her time.

"Just a few questions. That's all," Gilbert said, obviously wanting to take the lead.

Joyce Morrow pivoted and moved across the room with all the assurance and hauteur of a model in a fashion show. Four sets of eyes followed, Gilbert's the most intense. No wonder she was a local wrestling television star, Sullivan thought. He had seen lady wrestlers on the tube before, some wearing capes, even tiaras, into the ring, gaudy behavior, exaggerated moves, wild gesticulation. He intended to watch her. He also intended not to lose sight of the fact that she had a two-count assault record and a background that so far fit the mold of a killer. It would be interesting to see if Gilbert kept the same considerations in mind when questioning her, which should be a delicate, even artful effort. Sullivan hoped Gilbert wouldn't think with something other than his brain. Gilbert hadn't read her the Miranda warnings or asked if she'd like a lawyer present. It was rightfully Gilbert's or Day's show, but Sullivan might find it difficult to keep a lid on if things went in the wrong direction.

In a room lined with vending machines Joyce and Gilbert sat on a couch designed for two. The rest pulled plastic chairs close to the lieutenant and the wrestler. Joyce's eyes sought out Castro and held on him, obviously evaluating. Day stuck his hand in his pocket casually, as if searching for something.

"Anyone have a cigarette?" Her question was directed toward Castro. "I still smoke one or two a day. I shouldn't."

Her attention made Castro flush. He motioned toward Sullivan. "He's got some."

Sullivan was quick with the pack and a match. He kept his eyes on her. She was smooth, maybe too much so. Gilbert leaned forward to gain her full attention, giving the woman a bright smile.

Joyce blew out a cloud of smoke, not inhaling. "You're from Homicide, so obviously this doesn't have anything to

do with the charges in my past. Once your name gets on
that computer, it keeps cropping up, but I just want to set
the record straight to start with. In my profession we get
a lot of ribbing. Sometimes it even gets mean, out of hand
when some drunk recognizes you, thinks it's macho to
take you on. I think you get the picture." She waved her
hand. "So has anyone I know killed somebody?"

Interesting, Sullivan thought, that she would connect
the visit to someone other than herself. The normal reaction would be fear of oneself as a suspect, terror of being
railroaded if innocent.

"I don't know who you know," Gilbert said, plucking
at invisible lint on his trousers. "I understand you were a
medic in the Marines."

Joyce nodded, eyes blinking, obviously thinking into the
past. "Correct."

Gilbert allowed an awkward silence to follow, then
asked: "Do you own any Judith Leiber purses?"

Joyce looked puzzled. "Yes, I do, as a matter of fact.
Several. Some people might think that's a crime." She
took another drag off her cigarette. "I want to know what
this is about." Joyce lifted her arched eyebrows in anticipation.

Sullivan wondered how Gilbert would get around the
question and if he was clever enough to establish whether
she actually owned a shell-shaped purse without arousing
suspicion. He knew a way. It was hard not to jump in and
take charge.

Gilbert pursed his lips. "Sure you're entitled to know.
A Judith Leiber bag was left at a homicide scene. We're
checking out everybody in the city who owns one."

Joyce smiled and nodded slightly, knowingly. "So you
got my name from Neiman-Marcus."

Sullivan had to give Gilbert credit. Left to fill in the
blanks, a suspect would sometimes give more information
than a clever interrogator ever requested. Now Gilbert
knew she had a charge at Neiman-Marcus and bought her

purses there. The type of purse in question could be easily
checked. Also, if guilty, she now felt safe: she hadn't left
a purse anywhere.

Gilbert uncrossed his legs and leaned forward, resting
forearms on knees. "Just one last question." His tone was
easy, patient. "For the record, can you tell me where you
were last Tuesday night?"

Joyce grinned. "You're not a fan or you'd know. I was
on television."

Sullivan saw the flash of disappointment in Gilbert's
eyes. He felt it also. Their only suspect had the metroplex
viewing audience as witnesses to her whereabouts.

Gilbert checked his watch, then stared at Joyce Morrow.
"What time is your program? I'll try not to miss it next
week."

"Seven-thirty to eight-thirty. Channel eleven."

Gilbert straightened. "That's pretty early to finish. What
did you do afterward? Go somewhere? Anyone with you?"

Joyce shook her head. "I went straight home to watch
it again on tape. I was alone. It was a tough match and I
wanted to analyze it in private."

Gilbert stood. "That's about it. Appreciate your cooperation."

They followed his quick steps through the gym and piled
into the car. Gilbert started the engine and edged away
slowly, his eyes on the well-lit parking lot. When Joyce
Morrow came out a side door, he gunned away to Harry
Hines Boulevard, then pulled off the road and wheeled
into a driveway by a shuttered store. As she drove past he
edged into the stream of traffic heading downtown.

Gilbert glanced at Day. "I'm going to follow her until
she lights someplace, then put a team on her. One from
my group and one from yours. I want her under twenty-
four-hour surveillance. We'll work out the shifts. I've got
a feel about her. She's slick. An actress."

Day took the recorder from his pocket. "I'll turn this
over to ID so they can get cracking. Probably have to

rouse the FBI tonight for some help.'' Day scratched his head. "If we're gonna put a team on, we're gonna have to use my sergeant on her tonight. We need a woman on each shift, in case she goes to the ladies' room or somethin'.''

Gilbert scowled. "Yeah, I know," he answered, his irritation clear.

Gilbert followed Joyce Morrow's Mercedes at a discreet distance down the expressway leading toward the bright lights of downtown Dallas. When they reached the city's concrete caverns, Morrow pulled up in front of the Hyatt Hotel, left her car with the valet and walked into the hotel bar's sidewalk entrance.

"Son of a bitch," Gilbert said, slowing next to the curb. "Wonder if she's casing the place." He drummed on the steering wheel. "I'm going to get a court order to tap her home phone. She makes one call to Carole Wheeler, we've got her.''

10

Driving the ummarked car, Sullivan braked before Evelyn's entry gates. He and Castro, along with the two homicide lieutenants, had waited until the surveillance team was in place at the Hyatt, then left. Gilbert had seemed irritated, short-tempered to those around him. Sullivan suspected he'd planned the evening around the female sergeant and due to the situation was powerless to salvage the date.

Castro turned to Sullivan. "Olga said if I saw J.R. while I was in Dallas to get his autograph. She's a kick."

Sullivan chuckled as he cruised down the driveway. He knew Castro already missed Olga, but would never complain when there was a job to do. Sullivan agonized over his confrontation with Evelyn. Tenacious as she was, Evelyn had probably worked diligently all day. Now, Sullivan was about to snatch away her assignment and renewed enthusiasm before she even hit her stride.

"Look, I know you're upset about the Sequin's call and want to talk to Evelyn about it. You do what you have to do and I'll take the car and grab some of that Tex-Mex food I've heard so much about. We passed a restaurant that looked good. I'll eat, have a beer or two, then pack it in for the night after I call Olga. Okay?"

Sullivan opened the car door. "Okay. See you in the morning. We'll move to a motel."

Sullivan watched Castro drive away, then walked up the front steps and rang the bell. The carriage lights had been turned on. He took a deep breath and glanced up at the sky. It looked like rain, a welcome relief, an emotion he'd feel when this was behind him.

Barefoot, wearing a simple aquamarine cotton caftan that matched her eyes, Evelyn opened the door. "Back?" She leaned forward and pecked him on the cheek. She had arranged her blond hair into a sleek bun at the nape of her neck. Her perfume was subtle and mixed with the aroma of soap and shampoo.

He drank in the sight of her and wanted to pull her close, but hesitated. "Sorry we got tied up so long. Let's go to the den and have a drink. Do some talking."

"Any news about the hatpin?" she asked, leading the way.

"Looks like it's a fit." He knew the fact would only egg her on to try and make more discoveries.

"The purse?"

Sullivan glanced around the neat den, Evelyn's desk uncluttered, her row of books in order. He walked to the bar. "We'll start on that Monday at Neiman-Marcus."

"Well, at least I was some help." Her tone was almost blasé as she sank into her chair and propped her feet on the matching ottoman.

A touch surprised and puzzled by her attitude, Sullivan handed her a drink and the napkin he'd remembered to add, then perched on the arm of the couch. He disliked sitting on couches, especially one lined with throw pillows and cushions filled with down where you fought to keep from sinking and drowning, constantly feeling the urge to escape.

He lit a cigarette, looked at the flame, then blew out the match. "So what did you do all day?" He was positive she had talked to Carole.

"I tried to work on the profile. I got tired. Bogged down. About the only trait I could pick up that would fit a male or a female is that a serial killer shows some signs of exhibitionism. What kept you so long today?" Evelyn asked, sipping her drink.

Putting off the inevitable a little longer, he explained the follow-up on the tattoo angle Evelyn had suggested, which had brought the lady wrestler into focus. While he was becoming more impressed with what he thought of as "computer cops," the human factor, the grinding step-by-step detective work, still had its merits. A computer could slot someone innocent where they didn't belong. "So here's someone who fits all the points we have so far. The exhibitionism makes her even more suspect." Strike another one up in Evelyn's column, Sullivan thought, dreading what he had to express next in light of her contributions. "I want to talk to you about something . . ."

"I have a few things I want to say first," Evelyn broke in, avoiding eye contact. "Carole told me the Sequin mentioned my name. If there's any damage done, it's already happened and nothing can change it." Evelyn waved her hand as if to put said fact behind her. "I wanted you to stay in the guesthouse because it was convenient and suited you . . . me, too. Now that's all changed. I know you. You wouldn't feel free to leave me alone in light of what she said and I'd be nervous about you moving, too. You'll feel trapped here now. I'm sorry about it, but, of course, you are stuck with me. You'll stay here now out of a sense of duty, not preference. I'd like it that you stayed of your own accord, but that's something we'll both have to deal with, like it or not . . ."

"Whoa!" Thrown off balance, Sullivan held up his hand.

"Just let me finish." Evelyn pushed up from the chair. "About the profile. I don't like to make excuses or try to weasel out of something. I know you expected me to come through. I did try." She paced back and forth, working herself into a frenzy. "I really did. I'm aware the reward is greater than the risk here. This could be a big chance for me to gain a national reputation, a real chance to do something interesting with my life, have a career. I'm not the social, country-club type. I do like to accomplish."

Her words bounced off him like rubber bullets. What was she saying? That she couldn't manage the profile? "You've already contributed . . ."

"Oh, it could be so much more if only I were capable of making any headway. Think how awful it must be to question your choices when it's too late. Have to drink stronger martinis every night to forget taking the wrong path." She continued to pace. "I know there's growth and then status quo." She stopped in front of Sullivan and dropped her arms to her sides as if they were dead weight. "Hawk, not everybody can accomplish on some grand scale. They just have to slip by the rough spots and move on with the tide."

He stubbed out his cigarette, astounded by her attitude. He had pictured the scene so differently, visualizing himself demanding she quit work on the profile, having no further involvement in the case. He expected her to be persistent, challenging his decision, steadfast in her determination to continue.

He freed himself from the pillows and stood. "I guess this means you're finished with the profile." He felt strangely deflated now that she had reached a decision he had intended to promote himself.

Evelyn's eyes locked on him and held. "No, it means I'm just getting started. I don't want to face all those consequences later. I didn't get far today, but who knows about tomorrow?''

He stood there, shocked, then his crooked grin appeared and turned into a laugh. ''Talk about psychology. Lady, you are too much.'' He lifted his shoulders and opened his palms. ''What can I say?'' For her to go to such lengths, he had to let her continue. Chalk another up to her. He reached out and drew her close.

They swayed and hugged there in the middle of the room, each wanting the moment to last, both afraid for it to end. Sullivan took her chin in his hand and turned her face to him.

''I'm late as it is. If this keeps up I'll never make that dinner.''

Evelyn brushed her cheek to his. ''I think I just lost my appetite for food.''

She took his hand, led him out of the den, down the hall and up the stairs to her bedroom. She pulled the caftan over her head and tossed it aside, standing naked before him.

''You planned this.'' He smiled, crinkles around his eyes bunching, and looked at her with such longing, such anticipation, he thought he might burst from a desire not felt since the last time he was in that room.

Evelyn freed his shirt from his trousers, unbuttoned it and shoved it back. Touching the scar on his shoulder, she looked up at him, then covered the mended flesh with kisses she felt she'd stored a lifetime.

He swayed toward the bed, pulling her along, leaving his clothes as they went. They covered each other with kisses, greedy for the fulfillment long gone unsatisfied. The cool of the sheets and the warmth of her body sent him almost beyond control, but he held back, wanting to draw out the time as long as possible. He heard her gasp, sensed a tremor, then felt the pressure of her fingers on his back and was swept into an explosion of pure joy.

Relishing the pleasant aftershocks, he lay still until the

sparks dimmed and were finally extinguished in his mind's eye. He brushed Evelyn's hair from her face and kissed her long and gently.

"That was the best ever for me," she said quietly, stroking his shoulder, fingers running through the hair on his chest.

"And for me," he answered, letting his mind ripple along. He reached out and grasped her hand, his thumb making circular motions on her palm, their legs entwined.

They quietly discussed the past, the gap in their lives without the other's presence. With one giant step, Evelyn had recovered from the trauma she suffered. As a result of Sullivan's earlier words, she now saw the episode for what it was, a life-threatening roadblock around which there was but the one detour. By pulling the trigger, she had saved other lives, her own included. Once aired and examined, pent-up emotions with nothing to feed on lost their force and dissipated as quickly as a hurricane that takes to ground. She felt the aftermath of quiet and peace. They were wordless for a time, each lost in tranquil evaluation of new emotions, arranging in their minds future scenes and plans that fell short without the other included.

"You'll go back to the guesthouse tonight, won't you?" Evelyn propped up on an elbow, finally breaking the silence.

A hard choice, but the answer was affirmative. Sullivan didn't care for himself, but his sense of propriety for Evelyn's sake dictated otherwise. He nodded.

"I suppose it's best, with Castro there."

"And Mary downstairs. And Quinn, who pops in on a regular basis." He managed to grab his shirt from the floor without leaving the bed, retrieved a pack of cigarettes and lit one. "Has your appetite come back? I whip up a mean omelet."

"I'm ravishing." Evelyn laughed. "I knew a woman who said that once when she meant 'ravenous.' "

Sullivan grinned. "I think you're ravishing, too. You'd better get dressed before I think about it too much."

It rained Sunday morning, and with the humidity setting record highs, Dallas turned into a steambath. Sullivan's clothes clung like cellophane. He had slept as soundly as he ever remembered and without dreams. Castro was asleep when Sullivan came to the guesthouse the night before, and was snoring and mumbling in the next room, sometimes calling out a command Sullivan couldn't decipher. Brewing coffee in the kitchenette, Sullivan tried not to make any unnecessary noise.

He lit a cigarette, waiting for the machine to perform. Like normal people, he and Evelyn had the whole day free. He made plans. He would like to take her someplace for a leisurely brunch, have a Bloody Mary, talk about things not related to the case. Wander through art galleries. Later, he and Castro could watch the Dallas Cowboy's exhibition game on television. Listen to a symphony while he fixed the dinner he had intended to prepare the night before.

The shrill telephone ring cut his thoughts. He couldn't decide if he should answer or wait for Evelyn to pick up the line in the main house. After the third blast, he grabbed the receiver.

"Help you?"

"Gilbert, here. I just talked to Margo Martin from Neiman-Marcus. She thought you and Castro should get a head start on those charge accounts while the store is quiet. Be at the front entrance, sixteen-eighteen Main Street, in an hour. She'll open up the store for you."

Plans shot, Sullivan felt a zap of irritation. "Right. Have a report from the team on Joyce Morrow?"

"Two men and a woman joined her at the hotel bar. Gave her a present. Rectangular box about six by nine inches. Wrapped up with paper stamped with 'Happy Birthday' all over it and tied with a big bow. She never opened it. They shared a bottle of champagne, Joyce one glass only. They left together, got their cars from the valet. Sergeant Gray got the other car's license number. Called it in to DMV for a check. Joyce drove to her address. Hasn't been out since. A new shift's on her this morning. Pretty strange.''

"What's that?'' Sullivan asked.

"Date of birth . . . I just happened to notice on Joyce Morrow's sheet. Yesterday wasn't her birthday. It's February tenth.''

"Huh.'' Sullivan expelled the expression, puzzled. One thing for sure, Gilbert was bright. That small but important fact would probably have slipped by less observant investigators. "I don't guess you make anything of it yet.''

"Not yet. Gimme a buzz if you find anything today. Check out Morrow's account first.''

Sullivan hung up and called to Castro. In moments, Castro stood in the doorway yawning, shorts wrinkled and twisted. "What's up, man?'' Castro ran his hand over his chin.

"You, finally,'' Sullivan answered, pouring a mug of coffee.

"We going to move to a motel this morning?''

"No.'' Sullivan took a careful sip. "Changed my mind about that. I've decided it's best not to leave Evelyn here alone.''

"Just being cautious,'' Castro said, mouth pursed, eyebrows lifted.

"Just being cautious,'' Sullivan parroted, and filled Castro in on Gilbert's call.

"Don't they take a day off around here?'' Castro asked, heading back to dress.

"Look at it this way,'' Sullivan yelled toward the bedroom. "The sooner we finish the case, the sooner you can get back to San Diego.'' The same applied to him, too. After last night, he wasn't anxious to leave. Evelyn was completely ensconced in Dallas, background and business roots firmly planted. His place was in San Diego, a home he loved, a business to run. He took another swig of coffee, deciding not to worry the problem to a frazzle now that he'd ironed out a few old ones the previous night.

Castro sailed through the door, natty in a powder-blue silk long-sleeve shirt, matching slacks and polished loafers with tassels. "Clothes to go to Neiman-Marcus in."

"I could spot you anywhere. The picture of a detective," Sullivan teased. He wore reasonably new khakis with fewer cigarette burns than usual. His Izod, though, still held the store box folds. His worn Gucci loafers were a Christmas present from Karin's last holiday.

They hurried across the lawn, dodging puddles. Evelyn's French kitchen doors were open and Sullivan told Castro he wanted to pop in and give her their schedule.

She sat at the kitchen table, hovering over the Sunday paper, her finger hooked through a coffee mug handle. Her hair was pulled high atop her head, held by a rubber band, curls corking down. Sullivan wanted to touch her neck. She turned when she heard them.

"Morning. What's up?" she asked, cheeks flushing slightly. She adjusted the neck of her robe to show less chest.

Sullivan remembered that blush of modesty from the morning after they'd first made love. It was something he might call endearing, if he thought in such terms. "Gilbert called us to get started at Neiman-Marcus on the purse thing. Time to hop to."

Her disappointment showed. "My clue ruined Sunday. I shouldn't have brought it up until the weekend was over. I just called Carole. I was a little worried about her yesterday. She was in great spirits, though. Said Wayne Gilbert called her after you finished last night and took her out. I think she's stuck on him. I hope he's a good guy. What do you think?"

Castro glanced around while Sullivan floundered for an answer he wanted. Sullivan knew of two women in Gilbert's life. Undoubtedly there were more. How many women did a man need? he wondered. All he wanted was one. "I'll say this. If I were in a jam I'd rather have Gilbert than Day working on the solution. If I were looking for a pal, I'd rather have good ole Ross baby, as Gilbert calls him." Sullivan wondered if Carole had any inkling she was second choice. Maybe she'd rather be that than no choice at all.

"I believe I get the picture," Evelyn answered. "Have an idea when you'll be finished?"

"Not a clue," Sullivan answered. "I'll be in touch as soon as I know something."

Sullivan gave her a salute, turned and walked down the hall, Castro on his heels. He looked back once. Her eyes were still on him. Opening the front door, they galloped down the steps to the car and headed toward the world-famous store, all theirs for the day.

The streets were almost deserted, but slippery from rainfall. Sullivan took his time and when he reached the downtown area, finding most parking lots closed, decided to leave the car in front of Neiman-Marcus. He placed his identification on the dash so it could be seen through the windshield, then locked the car.

"So this is Neiman-Marcus," Castro said, standing next to Sullivan, peering into the thick double glass doors. "I sort of thought it would be different, more special. Looks just like any fancy department store on the West Coast."

"That's what hype will do," Sullivan answered, about to rap on the glass. He saw a woman come out of the elevator and walk toward them as if stepping on eggs and trying not to crush the shells.

In a chic black suit, the woman pulled a key from her pocket, crouched, turning her knees from them, and opened the locks at the base of the doors. She lifted to full height and jerked open the door.

"I'm Margo Martin," she announced in a clipped voice, the geography anything but Texas. "Head purse-buyer."

Sullivan had the feeling he should salute. Her black hair was pulled back so severely into a knot Sullivan was sure her scalp ached. Certainly the coif was responsible for the slightly slanted eyes. He introduced himself and Castro.

"Lieutenant Gilbert called early this morning and insisted we get started. Marvelous way to spend a Sunday." A slight frown appeared on the taut forehead. "We'll go up to the business offices on the sixth floor." She pivoted and slinked toward the elevator bank.

"Hardly touches the ground, does she?" Castro said out of the corner of his mouth, eyes full of mischief. "Could that be called stalking?"

So Gilbert, not Margo Martin, was the one who rearranged the day, Sullivan thought. He had the distinct impression Gilbert considered the tattoo and purse angle to be phantom clues he intended them to chase while the lieutenant, in his haste to best them, pursued more positive lines. No matter what his motive, there was no denying the probe had served up Joyce Morrow. And, for safety's sake, Gilbert had her covered, but probably expected little to come of the exercise. However, the birthday present *had* hooked Gilbert's interest.

Sullivan glanced around at the empty store. Expensive glass display cases filled with costly merchandise lined the aisles. Mannequins so lifelike they looked ready to speak, torsos twisted into impossible positions, sported the latest fashions. A small enclosure, labeled "The Bazaar," presented hats held high on Lucite stands. As they stepped into the elevator, the treasure trove resting on dove-gray velvet in the jewelry department further down caught Sullivan's eye. The gems sparkled even in the dim light. One item probably cost more than his entire worth. Evelyn Casey could purchase anything she desired and never feel a strain.

The elevator doors closed without a sound and Sullivan felt only a slight movement as they ascended. Margo Martin looked impatient, her eyes on the flashing numbers.

"Ever have sales?" Castro asked.

"Of course." The purse-buyer batted lashes so thick with mascara Sullivan could see beads of black on the hairs.

Castro grimaced as if he'd been reprimanded.

The doors opened and they stepped out on the floor where millions of dollars changed hands. Appropriately there was a restaurant, the Zodiac Room, where gourmet food was devoured as quickly as the cash in the back offices.

Margo Martin led them to an office filled with desks and computers. She showed them a typical charge receipt, explaining the codes. Every salesperson had a number that identified who sold a certain item. Every item had a number, denoting the type of merchandise. Every transaction had a number quickly traceable. Each store branch had a number.

She sat down before a computer. "Even though I'm the head purse-buyer it's necessary that I know the computer system to keep my department running correctly." She flipped on the switch and the screen lit up with commands. "What you want narrows the field considerably. First, we get to purses in general." The screen changed, displaying information. "Then we scope to manufacturers." A new list flashed in green letters. "In this case we want Judith Leiber." She keyed in another command. "Now we want a certain item, the shell-shaped purse, number six-four-seven-two-zero." She turned to the two men looking over her shoulder. "Now I can print out every sale of this number, the date bought and the purchaser."

"First, I'd like to check a specific account," Sullivan said. "A Joyce Morrow."

Margo Martin's fingers tap-danced on the keys. She leaned forward, squinting, as the screens scrolled. "Good customer. She's bought quite a few Leiber bags. But no, no shell, not this year. This item has been on the market three years. I'll go back." She punched in another command and waited until the information jumped up. "No shell. They're awfully small. Decorative, but not really functional. You're lucky it's not a big seller. Of course, she could have paid cash. We have some cash sales on the item, not many. Ten, it says. The purse costs eight hundred dollars retail. Not many people carry around that much cash. Likely men buying for a mistress, don't want the item on their account."

"If Joyce Morrow has a shell bag, it could have been a gift. She has a fondness for Judith Leiber bags that anyone close to her would know," Sullivan mumbled, not ready to cross her off the list. "Along with checking those listed who own the shell purses, we'll have to check out the cash sales with the clerks, see if they remember anything about the customers." Sullivan lit a cigarette, eyes searching for something to use as an ashtray. "I saw some hats on the first floor." He laid his palm diagonally on his forehead, fingers splayed, in an attempt to describe what he meant. "Fancy ones, with little nets . . . veils."

For the first time Margo Martin smiled. She opened a drawer and presented an ashtray. "Cocktail hats. They're making a slight comeback. A touch too frou-frou for most women."

"Could we run a check on those sales?" he asked. The Sequined Stalker had been active just over five months. If they could find a buyer who had also purchased a shell purse, it might spell *bingo*. It was a wild shot, he knew. The hat could have been purchased anywhere, at any time in the past. Still, he always tried to cover as many bases as possible, though many proved dead ends.

"What manufacturer?" Margo Martin asked. "Those on display are all different labels."

Sullivan shrugged. "I don't know. I guess we'll have to check them all. Do those little hats come with hatpins to keep them on?"

"Those went out in the Dark Ages. You'd find those at costume shops now . . . secondhand thrift stores. Little stretch cords that fit under the hair are used now to hold hats in place. Want me to get the printout on the purses rolling?'' Margo Martin asked, batting her eyes like a set of whips.

Sullivan nodded. ''Might as well.'' Checking the names was going to be tedious and time-consuming. To say nothing of the hats. Gilbert hadn't offered any manpower from the task force. Obviously his attitude fell somewhere within ''You brought it up. You check it out.''

Turning a switch, Margo Martin punched a key. The printer shuddered slightly, then started clacking at a rapid pace. Sullivan watched the names and addresses appear on paper. He wondered if he might be looking at the true identity of the Sequined Stalker as the list grew.

Margo Martin swung around and locked eyes with him. ''You've got your hands full.''

Thinking about the upcoming convention and the time frame he was under, Sullivan twisted his lips. ''In more ways than one.''

They know.

Doctor always did.

Came for me like they will, too.

Everybody that looks at me knows what I've done, can see right into my mind no matter how hard I try to keep them from it. Their eyes see through the epidermis, past capillaries and cells, deep into the dermis where a network of nerves twines like electrical cord, pierces through boné and marrow into the cranium, hones in and spotlights the cerebellum and medulla oblongata, the vortex of my being.

I release the curtain from my hand and walk away from the window. I want to feel better. I am silly. No one is out there. No one knows anything. How could they? I am too *attuned.*

The stupid dog runs in yapping. He reminds me of the past. I kick at him. "Get away, Poo." He stops in his tracks and cocks that nobby head to one side as if he can't understand. Beady-eyed spoiled rat-thing looks hurt. I could show him what hurt is.

I walk to the door of Doctor's den and peep around, not really wanting to go in there. The smell of Doctor is still there. It couldn't be, but it is. Trapped in the curtains, buried in the walls. Moving like a mist over the bookcase and his *Gray's Anatomy*, where I learned everything. His cracked leather bag and all its contents still sits on the window ledge, waiting to be grabbed for a house call. Nobody but Doctor made house calls. Momma accused him of other things when he came home.

Knives and doctor tools are in that leather bag. When I picked it up things clinked. The blades are sharp shiny metal, handles smooth like pebbles. I liked to take them out. Found out how sharp the blades were when I cut my finger. I twisted a Kleenex around the cut and watched the blood ooze onto the tissue.

I found Doctor's catalog and paged through the drawings of the instruments, learned what they were for. Ones with short blades are called scalpels. The pointed-blade ones are lancets. Long blades are bistouries. Round skinny things are surgical needles. The hollow tube, a cannula, which a trocar fits into. The ones that squeeze are harelip clamps. I stole one of the surgical needles and hid it in my room. Might have a use for it. Doctor found it and beat me for taking things that didn't belong to me. Momma screamed at him for it. The argument lasted for hours.

I was caught by surprise the first time the constant battle between them ended differently. Usually they'd argue themselves into exhaustion, hateful words finally trickling off into a final jab. I knew to run from the stairway then, before Momma started up, and hide under the covers in my room. Doctor always stayed in his den, reading or whatever he did. After a while I'd hear his heavy footsteps on the stairs.

This time was different. Their voices woke me. I went to my place on the stairs to listen. Doctor was talking.

"Something has to be done."

"What do you mean by that crack?"

"The cat. The cat. Your child cut the cat open. It's more than abnormal. Something has to be done before it gets out of hand."

My real father died when I was a baby. After Momma married Doctor, *he* adopted me, but referred to me as *your* kid when he was mad.

"*My* child, as you say, was only playing doctor, wants to be like you, though God knows I don't know why. Big heart-doctor. Mr. Cardiologist with the big heart himself. Ha!"

"Don't you understand?"

"It was only a stray."

I smile out there on the stairs and rub the banister.

"Jesus! I don't care if it was a stray. It's wrong and I'm going to beat it into the kid. Sheffield might be next."

"No, wait. Calm down. Come over here."

Doctor liked his dog better than me. He's right, Sheffield is next. I'm going to cut off his head. Stab him in the heart. Put him where Doctor can't find him. Down in that hole in the cellar. Punish Doctor.

Everything is quiet for a while and it scares me. I get up and tiptoe to the door. Peep through the crack. Momma is rubbing the front of Doctor's trousers. She unzips them and his Thing comes out like a stiff snake. She rubs it and it gets bigger. I wonder if she knows a magic trick. She takes off her robe and parts her legs.

Oh, no, look at her!

Doctor put his Thing in her. Is he going to the bathroom inside her? I want to throw up.

Up and down.

Oh, no.

Doctor's stabbing her with his Thing. I don't know what to do. She moans. He is hurting her. Killing Momma. I have to help. My feet are glued to the floor. I watch. Do something. What? Run in and kill Doctor? He would kill me.

I run upstairs to my room, shaking. Jump under the covers. I'm next. Doctor is coming to stab me. I throw up under my pillow. Momma is dead.

My teeth chatter. I am hot and cold at the same time. I bite my nails until they bleed.

I hear Momma walking up the stairs, laughing, talking to Doctor, words so slurred now I can't understand her. After Momma's asleep, Doctor comes into my room and tells me if I yell and wake Momma he'll whip hard. Makes me turn over while he draws the razor strop back and flails away. I bite into the pillow to keep quiet. He hits hard, but whispers, "Bad. You're bad. Do bad things."

I don't want to think about those days. I walk away from Doctor's den and go up to my room. I look at my clothes in the closet. I have to decide what to wear next.

When I was twelve I started trying on Momma's clothes. I'd gotten smarter then, but my grades were bad. The teachers were against me. I could understand some of the things that mixed me up as a little kid. Like Doctor stabbing Momma. But I couldn't understand why he didn't like me in her clothes. Came into my room when I was dressed up, then ran for the strop.

He finally quit caring about anything. Didn't give a shit. Stopped pretending. Sometimes I ran into him when he was coming out of the house and I was waiting on the curb for the school bus. He'd say, "Good morning." Look at the ground, embarrassed or something. Had stopped asking how school was or if I made any friends. Had stopped watching me fake doing homework at my desk. I didn't exist anymore as far as Doctor was concerned.

I turn around to look in the full-length mirror and see Poo in the door. "Well, what are you looking at? Spying on me like Doctor did before I stopped existing? I could put those beady eyes out so you couldn't snoop around." One quick stick. Another. Blind. "I could give you a shot

of Lidocaine from one of Doctor's rubber-tipped bottles.
Maybe you ought to hurt a little.'' *Yeah! Doctor! Hurt a
little.*

Ummmmmmmmm. The buzz is starting. First came
when I was a teenager. Ummmm. Just a little at first. Got
louder. *Ummmmmmmmmm.* A steady hum like a swarm
of insects. Hear it? *Ummmmmmmmmmm.* The chorus gets
louder. *Ummmmmmmmmmmmmm.* The voices from hell
start. Low guttural chanting, not human, words slurred
like a record played at a speed too slow. Restless souls
growling from hell. Some I put there myself. *Um yea um
yea um yea,* low deep, rattling. *Um yea um yea.*

Oh, no. It's coming. I can't stop it. Hot breath from the
devil on my face. *Um yea um yea um yea.* Can't stop it.
Don't want to. *Um yea um yea um yea. DoctorDoctor-
Doctor. Killkillkill.*

12

On Monday morning Sullivan and Castro waited in Captain Roger Chandler's office for the task force to assemble. Sunday had vanished in an exhaustive and unproductive exercise except for confirmation that Joyce Morrow hadn't charged a shell-shaped bag. She had bought other Judith Leiber purses at Neiman-Marcus, so it seemed likely that if she owned one, it would have been on her account. Still, her ownership of such a bag couldn't be ruled out.

After compiling the Neiman-Marcus list, Sullivan had flagged Day, who was overtiming it in his office with reports, and asked him to run the names through the computer. None had records except a few with minor traffic violations.

Sullivan and Castro then set out to pare down the list, going from address to address with standard questions. Finding a majority of occupants away from home and time-consuming return visits necessary, Sullivan and Castro trudged along as best they could. As Sullivan suspected, all of the women contacted were wealthy and substantial citizens with airtight alibis for the night in question. Most were fascinated by a visit from Homicide, a few insulted.

When he and Castro decided to knock off, it was well into evening. "Time flies when you're having fun," he remarked sarcastically to Castro as they stopped in front of Evelyn's. Quinn Stewart's Jag and Carole Wheeler's yellow Volkswagen sat in the driveway. The television's blue cast reflected in the den window. If three was a crowd, five was a gang bang. Wolfing a hamburger around five, neither was hungry and retired to the guesthouse, anticipating a good night's sleep. Sullivan read a detective paperback, smoked and tossed until midnight, then drifted into an uneasy sleep filled with a series of dreams that woke him at each conclusion.

Now Sullivan focused on the captain, clearing his mind of yesterday's thoughts.

"I'm adding four more women to the task force," Chandler was saying. "We need them for the shifts on Joyce Morrow." He fingered Gilbert's reports. "A check into this Crank Case turns up the fact that he's Joyce Morrow's uncle. Early this morning he went out to her house with a gift-wrapped package about the same size she was given at the Hyatt. If there's some event going on in her life, we don't know about it. The team had a pair of binoculars, of course, and saw the package also had Happy Birthday paper on it." Chandler shook his head.

"Could be some dope scam," Sullivan suggested. "A clever way for merchandise or money to change hands."

"That came to me, too," Chandler answered. "I think I'm going to have to notify Narcotics with what we've got. I don't like to have two operations going on an individual at once. I have no control over their division and I sure don't want this blown someway if she's the Sequin."

Gilbert sauntered in, looking fresh and rested, an invisible cape of after-shave trailing behind him. He nodded to Sullivan and Castro. "Anything new on the voice patterns?" he asked the captain.

"They're working. So far, the results are inconclusive and looks like they may stay that way. Have anything new?" Chandler lifted his eyebrows, a man ready for any crumb that would help.

Gilbert nodded, lips twisted as if locking in some secret as long as possible. "About an hour after Crank Case delivered that package to Joyce Morrow, she made a call." He hesitated, eyes shifting from man to man, drawing out his drama.

Captain Chandler moved forward, almost lifting off his chair. "Well, for Christ sakes, what did she say? Did she call Carole Wheeler?"

For an instant, Gilbert's tongue puffed a knot on his cheek. "She dialed a number we're checking out. A man answered with 'Hello' and Joyce the Choice said, 'The cock crows Wednesday night,' then hung up."

Chandler screwed up his features. "What the fuck kind of talk is that?"

Sullivan wondered the same thing.

Day and the rest of the task force filed in, stationing themselves around the room. Sullivan figured the attractive woman who sidled up to Gilbert was the sergeant on Day's team. The four women hanging back were the new additions. From the looks of them, Gilbert was going to have a field day.

Chandler introduced Sullivan and Castro, then stood and walked to a blackboard. "Two of you from each team have been assigned to start checking out the two boutiques for the shell purse purchases. Sullivan and Castro, here, have started on Neiman-Marcus, which is a much more extensive list. I'm going to assign two more from each team to share the list they have. You'll work today and tomorrow, then, of course, tomorrow night we'll be in place at the Hyatt." He picked up a piece of chalk. "I want to give you the layout and your stations."

"The plan looks foolproof to me," Day ventured, eyes riveted to the blackboard.

"When you're dealing with a warped and clever mind, no plan is foolproof," Chandler said matter-of-factly and without a reprimand.

He was right, Sullivan thought. The minute a person forgot that fact, he'd already started to fail.

Gilbert cleared his throat and lifted his hand, drawing attention to himself. He fastened his eyes on Sullivan, a humorous pleat playing at the corner of his mouth. "Anything new with the personality profile Evelyn Casey's working on?"

Sullivan returned Gilbert's stare. "Nothing tangible, but one thing she said struck me. A serial killer often shows signs of exhibitionism. Whether that applies to a woman, she wasn't sure."

Some of the group turned to each other, mumbling speculations about Joyce Morrow. The captain called for order.

After Chandler finished his instructions and dismissed the group, Sullivan and Castro settled into the routine developed on Sunday. A fruitless morning rolled into lunchtime and they broke for a sandwich. Sullivan telephoned Evelyn from the fast-food restaurant and asked her to suggest a place where they could meet for dinner. No matter what, he intended to recess long enough to touch base with her.

Late in the afternoon, weary from the oppressive heat and worthless visits, Sullivan and Castro stopped in front of a residence much less pretentious than the ones they had previously encountered. The neighborhood was middle-class, small versions of rambling Texas ranch-style homes, economy cars and RVs in driveways, bicycles and toys on sidewalks.

"A monthly mortgage payment on one of these is probably equal to the price of a Judith Leiber purse," Sullivan commented, getting out of the car.

Castro agreed. "Man, I could just see Olga paying such a price for a purse even if she was rich. She'd as soon cut off her hand first. I guess that saying that the rich are different is true.''

''All in how you look at it. They've got to spend it on something.'' Sullivan rang the doorbell. ''Hard to see how someone who lives around here could part with such dough. What kind of wingding would they go to with a purse that cost eight hundred dollars? Not your basic country-club set here.''

The door was opened by a slightly chubby woman with very short hair, and a cigarette between her fingers. Without makeup, her cheeks were scrubbed rosy and reminded Sullivan of two apples. She wore jeans, loafers and a faded oxford button-down shirt, the tail out. A silver watch burrowed into her wrist. With some fixing, she could be attractive, Sullivan mused.

Straining forward, eyes squinted, she blinked and gave them a myopic stare. ''Hep you?'' she asked, country style, lifting thick unplucked eyebrows.

''Alice Merritt?'' Sullivan studied her, wondering if he might be looking at the Sequined Stalker. Other than Joyce Morrow, she was the best candidate so far.

She nodded, taking a long drag on her cigarette.

Sullivan showed his identification. ''Could we ask you a few questions?'' He tried to stifle any excitement he felt, erase the illusions of her making some slip, then confessing. Things didn't often happen that way. But maybe . . .

Eyes rounded, Alice Merritt glanced from Sullivan to Castro. ''What in the world about?'' She set her jaw and seemed to grind out her words through clamped teeth, rather than speaking them, a not uncommon regional trait. ''Homicide? Why would you want to talk to me?'' She flicked her cigarette in the yard.

''It's about a purchase you made. Charged at Neiman-Marcus,'' Sullivan answered. He tried to imagine this woman dressed in sequins and feathers, wearing makeup and a blond wig, picture her carrying the delicate purse, perky cocktail hat atop her head, and had trouble with the vision. Yet her tastes had obviously run toward the expensive purse or she wouldn't have purchased it.

Alice Merritt looked from side to side, casting down the street. "Better come in 'fore the neighbors see you. Gossip enough around here without two *po*-licemen on my front step," she said, then stood back, holding the door.

Sullivan was a little chagrined, having defined in his mind the universal appearance of detectives, positive no one would take him as one. Certainly Castro wouldn't be suspected. Maybe they *did* have that aura.

He glanced around at the room full of furniture so new it looked straight out of a warehouse sale, protective plastic slipcovers over the upholstery. Paintings of ocean crashing against rocks, crumbling Greek temples and feather-headdressed Indian portraits on velvet lined the walls. The television set with its giant curved screen dominated the room. The place spoke of cash, but money ill spent. Sullivan smelled something with onions cooking.

"Please sit down," Alice Merritt said, and camped uneasily on the couch, fidgeting with a loose string on the plastic's seam.

Sullivan and Castro sat in chairs padded and stuffed to bursting point. Spying an ashtray with the logo "Put it out at Jake's," Sullivan lit a cigarette.

"You bought a Judith Leiber shell-shaped purse at Neiman-Marcus," Sullivan stated.

Alice Merritt blinked. "Yes, I did. Does something like that bring out Homicide to a person's doorstep?" She tried to laugh, but was obviously uncomfortable with snappy retorts. "I charge there sometimes when I want to splurge. You don't have to pay the full amount of your bill each month if you don't want to, like at some stores." She pulled a pack of cigarettes from her breast pocket and lit one with a disposable lighter.

Sullivan eyed Alice Merritt, making her feel more uncomfortable. She rustled around on the squeaky plastic, avoiding eye contact. There was a certain naïveté about her. Could be an act, he thought.

Castro caught her attention and smiled. "Do you have a medical background of any sort? Ever been connected in any way with that profession?"

Sullivan saw her make some association, saw the sign of recognition in her eyes. "No," she answered quickly. "I was a high school gym teacher in Waxahachie before I came to Dallas. What's this purse got to do with Homicide?" She dropped her palm to rest flat on the plastic. Her nails were bitten to the quick. She lifted the hand holding the cigarette and took several quick puffs.

Sullivan blew a smoke ring. "It concerns a case we're working and we're checking everyone who owns one."

Her face clouded for an instant, then relaxed. "I don't have the purse anymore. I lost it." She massaged the plastic, making circular motions, then reversed directions.

As sure as a lie detector would prove, Alice Merritt wasn't telling the truth. "With a search warrant, we could take a look around." Sullivan didn't say he had one, didn't say he didn't. Castro glanced at him.

"Go ahead and look," Alice Merritt said, grinding out the butt in the ashtray. "I lost it. I left it in a rest room. In the Anatole." She had selected her path and was gaining momentum with the story. "I went back when I realized what I'd done and it was gone."

It was gone, all right, Sullivan thought. But where? He locked eyes with her. "You wear glasses?"

She looked puzzled. "Yes. Most of the time. To drive with . . . read . . . watch TV."

"And you smoke," Sullivan added. "Take glasses and cigarettes with you every time you go out, right?"

A frown rippled on her forehead. "Right."

"You'd never buy a purse for yourself that those items wouldn't fit in. They will not fit in that shell bag," Sullivan said evenly, his eyes steady on her.

All color drained from her face. She was struck speechless.

Sullivan leaned forward. "Alice, may I call you that? I think you'd better level with me or we'll have to go downtown to the police station to do some talking. Some of those guys aren't too nice." Sullivan paused, letting his words sink in. "Where were you last Tuesday night?"

Alice's jaw pulsed. Torn by some decision, she looked like it was the first time she realized she was in trouble. "Look, the purse was a gift I bought for someone. I . . . I just don't want to get my friend in trouble. I thought I could get by without having to tell." She balled the tail of her shirt in her hand and squeezed it. "I owe her so much. I came up here from Waxahachie hoping to make it big. She tried to help me. I just didn't have it, not like her. She got me a good job anyway. We were just browsing around in Neiman's one day and she admired the purse. I went back and bought it for her. Least I could do. She gave me my name, 'Alice from Dallas.' I know it don't ring any bells. I don't have her showmanship . . . her ability. She got me a job as a trainer. She's a good person. She couldn't have done anything wrong. I wouldn't hurt her for the world . . ."

"Alice," Sullivan broke into her spiel, "who did you give the purse to?"

She looked up. "Joyce Morrow. Joyce the Choice. Please don't get her in trouble. She hasn't done anything."

Sullivan and Castro exchanged glances. The fact that Joyce Morrow owned the type of purse in question had now been established, but Sullivan was presented with another problem. He didn't want Alice to talk to Joyce about the visit, alert her. He smiled at Alice and tried to look relaxed. "Well, Alice, that's fine. We don't have any problems. We've already checked out Joyce Morrow and she's clear. See, she was on that list of people who charged a shell purse at Neiman-Marcus, too. Must have gone back after you and she saw it and bought it. She must be a nice person. Didn't want to mention it to you when you gave her one.''

''Just like her. Didn't want to hurt my feelings,'' Alice added, looking relieved.

''Course now you wouldn't hurt hers by letting on you know.'' Sullivan planted his seed.

''Course not,'' Alice agreed.

Sullivan and Castro stood. At the door, Sullivan looked back. ''Alice, you wouldn't happen to have a tattoo, would you?''

''Sure. Like Joyce.''

Back in the car, Sullivan turned to Castro as he started the engine. ''Looks like Joyce Morrow has all the ingredients that go in the cake.''

''If she'll just make a phone call to Carole,'' Castro said.

''Or if she makes some attempt tomorrow night at the convention, they'll nail her on the spot.'' Sullivan accelerated.

''She'll be on television. Remember, it's Tuesday, her night. Hope the bar at the Hyatt has a set. I want to watch her.'' Castro grinned.

''She's finished with the show around eight-thirty, then we'll see what Joyce the Choice is up to.'' Sullivan lit a cigarette and checked his watch. He wanted to be alone with Evelyn like normal people meeting for dinner, but hated to leave Castro to his own devices in a strange city with nothing to do for the evening again. He had to toss out something that would snag Castro and let him off the hook. He cut his eyes at Castro. ''How was that Tex-Mex the other night?''

''Great. Could eat it every night. I'd better never mention it, but Olga's isn't half as good.'' Castro leaned toward the windshield, checking out the sky. ''Clearing up. Be nice to see some rain in San Diego sometime. Hope my yard's not burning up. Olga said she'd water, but she forgets chores she doesn't like to do.''

"Tonight's Monday night, too. Probably a good exhibition game on."

"Yeah," Castro agreed, nodding.

"Be good to grab some hot stuff and watch the tube. When I called Evelyn earlier she said she felt like getting out. Wanted us to meet her at this little French restaurant close to the Highland Park Shopping Center. Guess we'd better go."

"Nah. You go ahead. I'll drop you off and she can bring you home. I'll just get some Tex-Mex takeout and watch the game," Castro answered, looking straight ahead.

Sullivan drove to the canopied entrance of the small restaurant and Castro slid to the driver's seat. Sullivan leaned down as Castro took the wheel.

"Call Homicide and tell them what we found out about the purse. We'll still have to keep checking until we finish the list. Well"—he tapped on the door—"wish my dinner was going to be as good as yours."

Castro revved the engine. "That's why you wore a coat this morning." He chuckled, gunned the car and drove away, leaving Sullivan standing there.

Sullivan looked after Castro, then turned and went into the restaurant. He pulled a tie out of his pocket and put it on in the men's room after washing up, scrubbing his face with a damp paper towel.

He asked the maître d' for Mrs. Casey's table, feeling a touch uncomfortable the reservation belonged to the lady. The intimate room had a curved brick ceiling, giving the effect of a wine cellar. Small vases of fresh flowers sat on tables covered with white cloths. A few early diners chatted quietly as soft gypsy violin music drifted through speakers. This was his kind of place. He felt relaxed, content in the atmosphere, the case temporarily out of mind. He ordered a Jack Daniel's on the rocks and lit a cigarette.

When Evelyn came in, he saw the maître d' bow slightly

and take her hand. One of her old haunts, Sullivan thought, wondering what memories the restaurant evoked. Heads turned as she glided toward the table. She was dressed in black, a chunky gold chain around her neck, her hair pulled back into a bun topped by a large bow. Light played on her cheekbones when she smiled.

Sullivan stood and seated her. "What took you so long?" He touched her shoulder before returning to his chair.

"You've been here for hours, I take it, with all the empty glasses lined up in front of you." Mockingly she glanced at the blank table before him.

The waiter arrived with Sullivan's drink and took Evelyn's order. She rested her forearms on the table edge and leaned forward, clasping her hands. "So bring me up to date."

Sullivan related what he knew. "If this Joyce Morrow would just make a move, we'd have her dead to rights. So simple. Only things don't usually happen that way."

The waiter served Evelyn's drink and she took a sip, her eyes alive and sparkling with interest. "Do you think Joyce Morrow is the Sequin?"

He laid his hand on hers. "I don't know. I want to think so, so much that it almost clouds my judgment. I want to get the Sequin." He stabbed out his cigarette.

Evelyn sighed. "I know you do. I wish I could help. I'm having trouble with the profile. I can't fit her into any exact slot. So many of these traits with serial killers aren't natural to female behavior." She touched her forehead. "She's a different animal. Special, if you could call it that. I think I might go to one of my old professors at SMU for some ideas. He's worked on some important cases."

She might not find anything constructive, Sullivan thought, but at least she had a renewed interest in her field and was in much better spirits than when he arrived in

Dallas. It was some accomplishment. "Sounds like a good plan."

Evelyn leaned down and picked up her purse. Opening it, she pulled out a newspaper clipping. Her expression turned serious. "This was in the evening paper, Carole's rival. I didn't want you to see it, but knew you'd hear about it sooner or later."

Sullivan looked at her, a sudden uneasiness taking him, and accepted the clipping. He squinted in the dim light, eyes moving over the column that heralded the coming convention and the tight security Homicide was expected to provide. The reporter recapped the crimes committed by the Sequined Stalker and concluded with the statement that socialite Evelyn Casey, who had experience and background on the subject, was piecing together a profile of the first woman serial killer.

"Jesus!" he groaned, dropping the paper as if it were hot. "This tears it." He lit a cigarette. "Now the Sequin knows for sure about your involvement."

Evelyn locked eyes with him. "Well, I'm not going to stop. The Sequin wouldn't know if I did."

"We could have Carole write an article saying that you couldn't get anywhere on the profile and stopped."

Evelyn's lips firmed. "No. The Sequin probably wouldn't believe it now. Besides, I don't want that kind of publicity if I'm going to make a name for myself."

"You won't make any kind of name for yourself if the Sequin takes a notion to stop you," Sullivan snapped. He picked up the article. His words to Gilbert that he'd quit the case before he'd place Evelyn in danger came shouting back. This was Gilbert's doing. Gilbert had brought up the profile in front of the entire task force so that he couldn't be pinpointed as the leak. Clever bastard, Sullivan thought. Gilbert was on his list and that wasn't a good list to be on.

"Maybe you'll catch her tomorrow night," Evelyn said.

Then it would be over before any more damage could be done, Sullivan thought. But he knew enough not to count on anything except that his evening was now shot and the fact that with reckless disregard for Evelyn's safety Gilbert had put her under a microscope for the killer to examine.

13

The day dawned bright and clear. After a quick cup of coffee, Sullivan and Castro left the guesthouse to get an early start on their list. Both were marking time until the convention that evening. Sullivan saw Evelyn seated on the terrace in a chair facing the guesthouse. She had no intention of missing them. Sullivan waved and walked in her direction, Castro heading for the car in front.

Their previous evening had ended with a meal consumed in silence. He was sorry about his gruffness and imagined Evelyn had felt as he had as a boy at the table with his father. During those stony silences Sullivan couldn't swallow or think of anything to say to a person who was irritated with life in general and him in particular. Now he had behaved in exactly the same manner.

"You're starting out early," Evelyn said, hair held back by a plastic bandeau. She wore a cotton warm-up and sandals. Books lay in her lap.

"Look," Sullivan said, standing on the terrace steps,

one foot resting on the landing. "I'm sorry about last night. The article unnerved me."

Evelyn studied him. "Why is it that you always blame yourself when something happens that you have no control over? Think the burden rests with you?"

He thought about what she said. "I don't know. My nature, I guess. Are you going to start analyzing *me* now?"

Evelyn's lips twisted in a crooked smile. "That might be a hard job. I think I'll stick to serial killers."

Sullivan grinned. "I don't know what time I'll be back tonight. Probably late. Castro and I are going to try and watch Joyce Morrow on the set in the Hyatt bar. Maybe you'd like to see her, too."

"I'll be watching," Evelyn answered. "Hawk," she called as he started to leave. He turned back. "Good luck today."

"You, too. I'm not worried about any repercussions from the article."

She read the answer in his face, but listened to the lie. "Neither am I."

He nodded and walked around the house to the car. He and Castro drove through the gates, ready to begin the exercise that would consume the day. Sullivan had to admit that the anticipation of the evening brought a certain thrill. There was the possibility the entire operation might be wrapped up within forty-eight hours.

At six o'clock, after an unproductive day, Sullivan and Castro gathered with the task force in a meeting room off the Hyatt lobby. Sullivan was so irritated with Gilbert he could barely stand to look at him for fear he might lose his temper. The room buzzed with conversation, a sense of contagious excitement charged the air. The men wore dark suits or sports coats and ties, the women were well attired in dinner dresses. The younger officers, particularly the females, seemed especially intrigued by the operation.

Equipped with a walkie-talkie, every person was also wired, not only mechanically but emotionally as well.

Captain Roger Chandler, who could be mistaken for a banker in his three-piece suit, called for order. "You know your stations, your shifts, you know what to look for, you've seen photos of Joyce Morrow. There's one thing I want to say before you take your places. There was an unfortunate leak to the press concerning Mrs. Evelyn Casey."

Sullivan whipped his attention toward Gilbert, willing him to look his way. He was positive Gilbert felt his stare burning into him, but the lieutenant kept his eyes on Chandler, his features impassive.

"Now, I will not tolerate any of my team talking to the press unless I authorize it," Chandler continued in a commanding tone. "I appreciate any help I can get, but I did not request Mrs. Casey to work on a profile. She embarked on it of her own volition and although I don't want any citizen placed in jeopardy, I don't feel it's my responsibility to take any security steps in her behalf. Mr. Sullivan and Mr. Castro are staying on her premises and I take some consolation in that. I'm not accusing any of you of talking to the reporter who wrote the article. Mrs. Casey could have talked to friends and the information could have sifted through to the reporter. She could have even told her herself."

Gilbert slowly turned his head in Sullivan's direction and locked eyes with him. Sullivan felt his face flush with anger. He'd like to bash the smirk off Gilbert's lips and had to actually fight to control himself. Castro nudged him.

Chandler continued. "All I'm saying is do not speak to any member of the press without my okay. Absolutely no interviews. The article stating how heavy security will be tonight and tomorrow night might have scared off the Sequin. However, these serial killers are very daring, I understand, think they can outwit anyone, so there's a chance we might still get lucky.'' Chandler waved his hand. "Okay, that's it. Get moving and good luck.''

Sullivan and Castro moved with the crowd, then broke off and entered the large convention room where a cocktail-buffet for the name-tagged ophthalmologists was in progress. Chatter and laughter against the tinkle of glasses abounded in the festive atmosphere. They paused on the edge of clusters of people, listening to their small talk, eyeing the women present, most of whom looked as if they belonged to the men they accompanied. Middle-aged women dressed in their best, a majority slightly dowdy, a few fashionable, but no prizewinners.

With difficulty, Sullivan shifted his eyes away from the bar, rows of bottles open and ready to be served by the white-jacketed bartenders. A Jack Daniel's would go nicely now, he thought, and turned his attention to the well-laden buffet table where Captain Chandler stood talking to a man whose stick-on tag bore the words "John Kevin Hunter, M.D., Chairman." Roasts and hams were accompanied by a variety of salads and cold vegetables. Sullivan sampled the smoked salmon and Castro pushed a stuffed egg in his mouth.

After an hour of slinking and snaking through the crowd, sampling more food as they went, Sullivan and Castro went to the elevators and rode up and down, listening to swatches of conversation from the few passengers that made the trips with them. To fight the boredom, Sullivan tried to play mental games, attaching professions and imaginary lives to the individuals. A white-haired man and woman he pegged for a retired couple turned out to be in the cast of *Dallas*, now shooting the fall series. Castro perked up and listened intently to the couple's conversation, dying to ask about J.R. Ewing.

Sullivan checked his watch. They would be relieved before long and spend their break in the bar, where they'd just manage to catch the tail end of Joyce Morrow's televised match. He would like to have just one quick drink, but he was on duty and needed a clear head. Fingering the breath mints in his pocket, Sullivan was tempted.

Unbeknownst to Sullivan and Castro as they rode the elevator, Evelyn and Carole were seated in a low-backed booth in the bar off the lobby, watching television. Joyce Morrow entered the arena wearing a green satin cape over her matching leotards.

"Look at that!" Carole exclaimed, almost jumping up. "What an outfit! She looks like a green female Superman. Neat."

Evelyn watched Joyce the Choice gesticulate wildly at her roaring fans when she stepped into the spotlight. Arms lifted high above her head, Joyce jumped and turned in the ring, facing each segment of the audience. Her opponent came through the ropes to wild boos.

Carole sipped her Perrier. "Think Sullivan will be pissed that we're here?"

"Probably," Evelyn answered, still watching the set. The activity on the screen was semi-outrageous, in her opinion, but nevertheless entertaining.

"That doesn't bother you?" Carole asked, adjusting her turban, the jeweled pin on it slightly askew. She noticed a man in the next booth eyeing her.

"Not a bit." Evelyn picked up her vodka and turned to Carole.

Carole looked just over Evelyn's shoulder at the man who watched them. "My excuse for being down here is that I have to be on the spot if something breaks with the Sequin. What's yours?"

"I don't need one." Evelyn laughed.

"If I didn't know Hawkeye so well, I'd be kind of afraid of him. I used to be. He can be so . . . gruff sometimes. Like an old mean bear." Carole took on a wistful quality. "He's good-looking, though . . . in a special kind of craggy way. I like it when he smiles."

"He doesn't really mean to be so gruff," Evelyn said, toying with a swizzle stick. Her eyes wandered around the jam-packed smoky room. "See those two women at the end of the bar? I'll bet they're detectives on the task force."

Carole eyeballed them. "Yeah. Bet so. The place is crawling with them. See that couple in the corner booth? They haven't said a word to each other. Bet they're on the team, too. Look, there's a nice-looking woman alone at the bar. Maybe she's a pickup. Maybe she's the Sequin." Carole rattled the ice in her glass. "I'm still irritated about that article Judy Thomas wrote. Bet Quinn was upset." Carole screwed up her face. "He reminds me of everybody's first husband. Probably likes elevator music."

Evelyn chuckled, shaking her head. She continued perusing the room, an excitement widening in her. She could be in the same room with the Sequin. Her eyes flashed back to the screen where Joyce the Choice and her opponent were locked in combat on the mat. She blinked and squinted for a better look. The Sequin could be performing right before her very own eyes. "I'm not making much progress on the profile. I think I'll talk to an old professor at SMU."

"My roommate, Dorothy Virginia, says that she doesn't think the police will ever catch the Sequin . . . she'll just move on to some other place." Carole hesitated. "Oh, no . . . the man in the next booth . . . He's getting up . . . Looking straight at us."

Evelyn and Carole turned as the short man stood in the dimness, facing their table. "Buy you girls a drink?"

"No, thank you," Carole answered. "We're waiting on some policemen to join us."

The man chuckled as if he didn't believe the reply. "Can't blame me for trying," he said, and hooked back into his booth, his eyes still on them.

"What a creep," Carole whispered, glancing over Evelyn's shoulder. "Doesn't he know the Sequin might get him, asking strangers for a drink and God knows what else he has in mind. He's been trying to eavesdrop, too."

Carole stuck her thumbs at the corners of her mouth, stretched it wide, inverted her hands, fingers pulling down the skin under her eyes, and stuck out her tongue, grade school style. The man quickly looked toward the bar as if he hadn't seen her.

"Jesus, Carole," Evelyn said, astounded.

"I wouldn't have done that if he hadn't been such a wimp," Carole said, as if that explained her behavior.

Sullivan and Castro appeared in the bar. The lone woman got up and left. Evelyn decided she was perhaps a replacement for them instead of a pickup. Sullivan looked shocked when he spotted them. Evelyn waved and smiled brightly, innocently as she could.

"Well, join us and watch Joyce the Choice," she said when they walked over to the booth.

Lifting his eyebrows, Sullivan slid in next to her, Castro on the opposite side next to Carole. "Just out for a little evening of fun?" Sullivan asked. "Kind of like fire truck chasing."

"Yeah," Carole answered. "We almost got picked up by the jerk behind us."

Sullivan glanced at the man, then focused on the television set, lips forming a smile. "Look at that. Showmanship at its finest."

Castro craned his neck to watch. "Get a load of those broads. Gonna tear each other's heads off."

Sullivan turned his attention to Evelyn. "So far, nothing. Pretty humdrum. The captain has this place covered. I, for one, am going to have a drink." He hesitated. "A double Pepsi. Castro?" Sullivan motioned to the waiter.

"A Coke," Castro answered, still watching the set.

Carole hooked pretzels on her fingers as they discussed the case. Each speculated on the outcome of the evening, coming to the unanimous conclusion that it would end with no action. In the dim room, Sullivan's eyes roamed from one person to the next.

"The chairman of the convention has advised all participants to be in their rooms no later than eleven," Sullivan explained. "Said they could do everything they intended by then. Besides, there's a breakfast meeting tomorrow morning at seven-thirty. After this curfew takes place, the captain has urged the guests not to leave their rooms. The task force will patrol the halls for an hour, then we'll knock off for the evening."

"We'll wait here for you and you can follow us home," Evelyn said.

Sullivan checked his watch. "You'll be falling-down drunk by then."

"I'll pace myself," Evelyn countered.

Sullivan sighed. "Okay. Suit yourself." He squeezed her arm and left, Castro following.

They took up their next assignment on the tenth floor, standing at the end of the hall. To make it simple, the hotel had reserved the eighth, ninth and tenth floors for the overnight conventioneers. At least Sullivan could smoke in peace. He slanted against the wall near the ashtray stand filled with sand. Castro sat on the window ledge, feet swinging back and forth.

When the elevator doors opened, Sullivan and Castro drew to attention, peering down the hall. A couple stepped off and weaved toward their room. Sullivan remembered them from the cocktail party. A second elevator door opened and a lone man got off and walked quickly to his room. He glanced up and down the hall, then entered his room. Sooner or later everyone was coming home to roost, Sullivan thought, bored with the lengthy process.

Four floors beneath Sullivan and Castro, Dr. Howard Richards walked down the carpeted foyer. The lights were dim and he had the sensation of moving in slow motion through a narrow tunnel. His head spun from more than his normal amount of drinks. The occasion called for some celebration, he reasoned.

He stuck his key into the lock, opened the door and

stepped into the dark room, his hand searching the wall for the electrical switch. He flicked on the lights, closed the door, then hooked his suit coat over the back of the desk chair. He glanced at the phone, reflecting on the call he had made earlier, sighed with relief at his decision, then went into the bathroom to wash his face and hands.

Over the running water he thought he heard a faint knock on the bedroom door. He turned off the faucet and cocked his head. The knock came again.

"Who is it?" he called out, shaking droplets of water from his hair.

"Message," a slightly Hispanic-accented feminine voice warbled.

He was tempted to tell her to shove it under the door, but decided the messenger expected a tip. Padding to the door, he opened it just as he remembered too late that the message light on his phone had not been blinking red. Startled, his eyes went immediately to the blond wig.

Before he could speak, she lunged at him with all the fury of a wounded jungle cat. Kicking the door behind her shut, she brought one arm from around her body and raised it high in the air. Metal glinted in the light. He tried to dodge, but the sharp point hit him first, driving him down.

He felt pain, searing and white-hot in his chest. Saw sequins falling like rain around him. Then darkness and warmth engulfed him.

The elevator doors parted on the tenth floor and Captain Chandler himself got off and galloped down the hall toward Sullivan and Castro, a frown on his forehead. Alerted, Sullivan and Castro stood erect.

"God damn it," Captain Chandler spat out.

Sullivan felt a catch in his chest. "What's happened?"

"The surveillance team on Joyce Morrow lost her after she left the Sports Arena. Got caught in all that traffic. Now we can't pinpoint her whereabouts. Traffic put out an APB on her over an hour ago. Maybe some cruiser will pick her up. Got a team watching her house. She hasn't showed up yet.''

Downstairs in the bar, Evelyn carefully sipped a second drink, trying to make it last. Carole was on her fourth Perrier. When the commotion started, they looked up, startled to see Joyce Morrow and an entourage of four come into the bar. The bartender lifted his hands in a triumphal salute to her. Waiters waved. Obviously the bar was Joyce Morrow's haunt. Several in the room cheered for the lady wrestler, who wore a fancy black warm-up decorated with rhinestones.

Joyce Morrow's group circled into a large banquette and one of the men presented her with a birthday-wrapped box. ''Would you look at that!'' Carole croaked. ''A gift again.''

''And it's not her birthday,'' Evelyn added, staring at Joyce Morrow, her mind spinning with the puzzle.

Carole tapped her fingers on the table. ''I'll be right back.'' She leaped up and waltzed across the crowded room to Joyce Morrow's table. Evelyn watched in amazement, wondering what antic Carole was about to pull. Out of the corner of her eye, Evelyn saw a woman in a booth across the room turn sideways and whisper in a walkie-talkie she was doing her utmost to conceal. The man with her leaned forward to further shield her from view.

Carole stood before Joyce Morrow's table. ''Hi,'' she said to the lady wrestler. ''I'm a reporter with the *News*. Carole Wheeler. I just wanted to say I'm a fan of yours.''

''Why, thank you,'' Joyce Morrow said, and smiled.

Carole's eyes were on the box. ''Is this your birthday?'' She looked up, waiting for an answer.

''No,'' Joyce Morrow answered. ''It's a friend of mine's this week and I'm having a surprise party for her.''

''Oh, I see,'' Carole said. ''Well, nice to meet you.'' She flounced off and threaded her way back to Evelyn's table.

''Find out anything, Sherlock?'' Evelyn asked.

"Yeah," Carole answered, and leaned forward. She told Evelyn what the wrestler had said.

The news lifted Evelyn's eyebrows. "Well, I guess that explains the mysterious packages."

"Not exactly. The box had holes punched in it. All around. Wonder why? Who'd buy somebody a present, then stick holes in it after taking the trouble to wrap it?"

Evelyn glanced at Joyce Morrow, who sipped a frosted orange drink. "Strange. I don't understand it."

More people pushed in, crowding the room. Evelyn tried to look through gaps in the crush, keeping Joyce Morrow in sight. When the lady wrestler finished her tall drink, she rose, took the package and left. The woman with the walkie-talkie and her escort jumped up to follow, but their exit was blocked. They dodged around several people in a hopeless jam, then finally broke free and hurried toward the lobby.

After several minutes passed, Sullivan and Castro pushed through the crowd to Evelyn's table. Ducking around a group, Gilbert seemed to materialize as if by magic at the same time.

"Carole, what are you doing here?" Gilbert flashed a bright smile.

Carole beamed. "I wanted to be where the action was." She looked at Sullivan, then turned to Evelyn. "This is Wayne Gilbert. Lieutenant with Homicide." She glanced up at Gilbert. "Wayne, this is Evelyn Casey."

Gilbert's smile widened. "How do you do?" He nodded. "Not much action around here tonight, after all, except the team lost Joyce Morrow in the crowd after her match."

"She was just here," Evelyn said, feeling Gilbert's eyes all over her.

"I've got part of the birthday thing figured," Carole said, looking to Gilbert for approval. "It's not her birthday, but a surprise for her friend."

Gilbert broke into a laugh aimed at Sullivan.

"But wait a minute," Carole said. "The package had holes stuck in it."

"Holes?" Sullivan repeated, and frowned.

Gilbert waved his hand as if batting the subject aside. "Aw, those people." He moved as if about to slip into the booth uninvited. "Why don't we have a drink?" He kept his eyes on Evelyn. "The capt'n is about to batten down the hatches. We're off duty now."

Evelyn looked straight at Sullivan. "A couple who were in here made a beeline after Joyce Morrow. They had to be on the task force. The woman had a walkie-talkie."

Sullivan glanced at Gilbert, irritated. "I'm sure they picked up on her, but she was still out of circulation for an hour or so."

"I'm sure they called a cruiser to tail her if she happened to be able to get her car," Gilbert said. "Nobody can get a car from valet parking out there in that crunch, even with the extra help they laid on. Maybe Morrow's still stuck there, too. Anyway, they're on her now, even if it is a wasted effort." He edged next to Carole.

Sullivan remained standing, Castro behind him. "I think we'll be heading out now that it's over. Ready, Evelyn?"

Evelyn slid around the booth and stood. Just as they started to leave, Captain Chandler pushed through the crowd, his face gray and troubled.

"Got another one," Chandler said, running his fingers through his hair as if ready to jerk it from the roots. "I don't see how the Sequin could have pulled it off, but she has. Another doctor murdered in his room. Let's get humping.

14

Captain Chandler, Lieutenant Gilbert, Sullivan and Castro sprinted across the lobby like racehorses released from the starting gate. Crowds of people drew back wide-eyed, ogling the charging quartet. Holding the elevator door with his shoulder, Lieutenant Day waited expectantly. Beside him stood the hotel manager, his face a mirror of disbelief and shock. Uniformed officers sliced through the swarm, forming a human chain around the elevator banks.

The men crowded into the elevator and Day let go of the door. "Six," the manager shouted, and Day's stubby finger hit the button.

Captain Chandler tapped anxiously on the railing circling the elevator, his eyes on the floor numbers flashing above the door. "The victim has been identified as Dr. Howard Richards. The night maid found him when she went in to turn down the bed. Room six-two-one."

"He has a Dallas address," the manager added. "We blocked out the eighth, ninth and tenth floors when we got the list of out-of-towners attending the convention. I looked on the master list and he was one of the locals who was a part of the convention.''

His mind a jumble of questions, Sullivan flicked his eyes from man to man. Each one's expression was more confused than the next. Why did this Dr. Howard Richards take a room if he lived in town? Did he meet someone and on the spur of the moment get a room? After all the security lectures? But, of course, the words of caution were only directed to the out-of-towners with reservations, were never pointed to the local group who would presumably return to the safety of their homes after the conclusion of each event. Still, Sullivan imagined that the murders, headlines in Dallas, were well known to the entire group of doctors.

The elevator doors opened on the sixth floor and the men spilled out in the hall where a group of uniformed officers stood guard. The door to the hotel room was wide open. Members of the task force pushed forward. A black maid, her back hunched and spasmed, wept into her hands.

''Have someone take her statement,'' Chandler said to Gilbert as he walked into the room. ''I want all the guests on this floor checked to see if they saw anything. First thing in the morning at the doctors' breakfast start questioning them and their wives. I want to know if Richards was with anybody at the cocktail party, who he talked to, what he said, if he left with anyone. I wonder why his wife, if he has one, didn't come to the party like the other local wives.''

Sullivan's eyes went to the well-dressed man who lay sprawled on the floor, a badge of red widening on his white shirt. Then he saw the sequins, a small crooked trail like snail tracks. The officers crowded in, circled the deceased, but kept their distance. The investigation would have to wait until the medical examiner, the Crime Scene Unit and Forensics finished their jobs.

''Poor dumb sumbitch,'' Day said, staring down at the corpse.

"How did the bitch do it?" Gilbert asked no one in particular. "How did she pull this off right under our noses?"

The manager twisted his tie as if he intended to choke himself. "Jesus Christ! We're ruined once this hits the papers." He turned to Captain Chandler. "Some security."

Chandler's face remained impassive. He glanced over his shoulder toward the door, obviously anxious for the team to arrive, then turned his attention back to the dead man. Day and Gilbert spoke with their teams.

Sullivan squatted close to the victim, cocking his head for a better look. His thoughts immediately went to the man's wife, if he had one, and the shock she was about to receive. He felt more sorry for the living than the dead. He wanted a cigarette, but wouldn't dare light one. He straightened and glanced at Castro, whose eyes scanned the room like a bank's revolving camera.

The medical examiner arrived with two assistants, hunkered down by the victim, pulled on paper-thin rubber gloves and took charge of the corpse. The Photo Unit crowded in and started taking stills and videos. The Crime Scene Unit and men from Forensics bolted through the door and began their routine. The sequins were bagged, rugs and furniture vacuumed for fibers and hair. They hit like a horde of locusts, passing through the bathroom, taking samples from the toilet, bagging glasses, ashtrays, examining the empty closet, Fingerprint Unit spreading grayish powder everywhere.

After the victim's position was outlined in chalk, his hands were bagged in plastic, rubber bands placed at the wrists. The medical examiner had his assistants place the corpse in a body bag for removal to the morgue, where the autopsy would take place after identification by next of kin. As each team finished they hurried away to test and study their findings. Then they would relay the conclusions to Homicide, who would apply the human element to the equation.

After giving the lieutenants more instructions, Captain Chandler left to speak with the press in the lobby. Alone finally, the officers from Homicide speculated back and forth with Sullivan and Castro. "The doctor had no clothes here, no bag, no toiletries, not even a toothbrush, so it looks like he didn't intend to spend the night," Sullivan stated. "His wife, if he has one, can shed some light on it." Already he dreaded knocking on the door at the doctor's address, four men from Homicide in the middle of the night with news that a loved one had been murdered. Rather than telephone the doctor's residence, Chandler thought this was best, his standard approach under such circumstances. Sullivan agreed with the captain. Still, the task was a difficult and painful one.

Gilbert clucked his tongue. "Looks to me like the ole boy intended to have a quickie, then go home. I can't see how he hooked up with the Sequin so fast."

"Listen." Day cracked his knuckles. "Joyce Morrow was unaccounted for for over an hour and turns up in the bar here. Maybe she came straight here after they lost her leaving the Sports Arena, went upstairs with the doc and killed him, then pretty as you please goes in the bar and has a drink like nothing happened. That's mighty brazen, but the capt'n says those kind are daring, you know. Male serial killers, anyhow. We don't know squat about women." Day lifted his eyebrows. "But don't you see, that would be sorta like reverse psychology. Who would kill somebody, then go sit in the bar at the same hotel? Anybody would think a murderer would leave the scene of the crime as fast as they could. So somebody clever would do just the opposite so they wouldn't be suspected. See?"

Day's exhaustive powers of deduction and the gaps in his reasoning made Sullivan want to tap himself on the head. Day hadn't offered an opinion on how Joyce Morrow and the doctor might have hooked up, if in fact they had. There was a strong possibility Joyce Morrow and the Sequin were two entirely different people. "Can't the tickets at valet be checked for time in and time out on cars? We know what time she came in the bar. If we could put her at the hotel almost an hour earlier . . ."

"Can't do it," Gilbert cut him off. "Time's not kept. Valet just gives out a claim check with your number on it. It's five dollars to park no matter how long you stay."

Castro cleared his throat to get the floor. "Well, serial killers like to gloat about what they've done. Now that the Sequin's started calling, she'll do it again. If it's Joyce Morrow, we got her nailed. She doesn't have a clue her phone is tapped."

Lips slightly down-turned, Gilbert made a little grunt. "As Day said, we don't know squat about any woman serial killers." His eyes darted to Sullivan. "Under the circumstances we can't even question Joyce Morrow about her whereabouts during that missing hour. If she's alerted that she's a Sequin suspect and under surveillance, she'll no doubt figure her phone is bugged and never make that call we hope for."

Sullivan lit a cigarette. "We'll check with the desk clerks and see when this room was reserved . . . when the doctor registered. That'll tell us something." Sullivan could actually feel Gilbert bristle at the suggestion he was probably about to make himself.

Gilbert gave Sullivan a superior look. "Let's go." He paused, then looked from Sullivan to Castro. "You guys are here to help us solve the killings, but looks like you can't help us stop them."

Gilbert turned on his heels and headed for the door before Sullivan could say anything. Sullivan didn't have a quick retaliation, anyway. Best let the situation ride when someone was intentionally baiting you, Sullivan thought.

After they walked out of the room, the guards closed the door to the crime scene and yellow-taped it. They rode in silence to the lobby floor, which had now cleared. Sullivan was sorry to have left Evelyn and Carole to go home alone. He supposed Carole was typing away by now for the morning edition. Evelyn was likely digging into her books for some scrap that might help.

Gilbert strode to the reservations desk like some general, his parade following. He flashed his badge at the clerk. "The man who was murdered here tonight, Dr. Howard Richards, room six-two-one. I want to know when the reservation was made, when the doctor checked in."

The clerk shuffled through a deck of reservation cards as if ready to deal a hand. "No previous reservation." He snapped his fingers. "I remember now. A slow time at the desk. He checked in during the cocktail party tonight, about six-thirty. Came in and asked if we had a room available. No luggage. Signed in, gave me a credit card for an imprint and took the room key." He picked up the bill. "One local phone call is all the charges."

"Wonder who to," Gilbert said, looking at the reservation card to confirm the home address.

Sullivan hurried to keep up with Gilbert as he advanced through the revolving glass door and onto the sidewalk. They piled into Gilbert's car and he pulled away, tires screeching. Day tossed out more speculations as they sped through the city, downtown streets now almost deserted.

"This is going to take up the whole night," Gilbert said, wheeling onto the Central Expressway. "Break it to Dr. Richards' wife, if he has one, question her if she can handle it, then take her to the morgue to identify the body. Geez." He drummed on the steering wheel. "The capt'n gives his orders, then goes home."

Sullivan wanted to ask him what else was priority over his job, but smoked instead. Castro sat so far down on the seat it looked as if he were resting on shoulder blades. Day droned on with ideas.

"Something's different here," Sullivan thought out loud, staring at the tiny glow of the cigarette tip.

Gilbert jerked his head around toward the back seat. His face under the passing streetlights was without expression, but not his eyes. They were at once alert and angry, holding on Sullivan for an instant. "What are you saying?" he asked, turning back.

"Not anything," Sullivan muttered. "Not just yet," he added.

Gilbert glanced in the rearview mirror. "Carole Wheeler got lucky tonight, even if the doctor didn't. Right on the scene, like she was expecting something to happen. She'll beat all the other reporters with a story. Couldn't believe that Mrs. Casey was down there in the flat middle of everything. You'd think with the Sequin knowing about her she'd be nervous. Women! They're fearless or don't know to be afraid."

Sullivan felt himself tighten. It was not so much the chauvinistic remark that irritated him, but the lumping of Evelyn into the category of women in general. He had almost reached the end of his patience with Gilbert. If their lack of affinity for each other came to a head, it would mean trouble, which they already had more than their share of.

Gilbert turned to Day. "This was a spur-of-the-moment thing for the doctor to do. I still say he had no intentions of spending the night. He planned that quickie with someone he knew. We'll check out every woman he was associated with. I'd bet my life he's acquainted with somebody who turned out to be the Sequin. Be interesting to see if he has any connection with Joyce Morrow."

When Gilbert stopped in front of a columned Colonial-style house in Evelyn's affluent Highland Park neighborhood, Sullivan stubbed out his cigarette. On top of receiving shocking news, Dr. Howard Richards' wife was about to be subjected to some embarrassing questions and shattering revelations about her husband's activities. Sullivan hoped there wasn't a wife. Maybe the doctor wasn't married.

The four men walked to the dark house and rang the bell. Gilbert stomped invisible dust off his feet, then rang again. Day cracked his knuckles, the pop breaking the stillness on the circular porch. A shaft of light from the house next door caught Sullivan's eye. From the window he saw a shadowed head peeping around a wall of drapery held back by a hand. The hand let go and the window turned into a dark square.

Gilbert jabbed the bell again and waited for the response that didn't come. "Maybe nobody's here." He exhaled loudly.

"I'll walk around back and look in the garage," Sullivan said, hurrying down the steps. He moved quickly down the driveway between Richards' residence and the one next door. Again, the neighbor pulled back the drapery for a peek. The garage at the rear was open. Sullivan spotted the Jaguar and an empty slot. He rounded the car, placing his palm on the hood as he turned, then patted the door and walked back to the porch.

"There's a car in the garage," he said as Gilbert pressed the doorbell.

At the sound of a bolt being released, the men faced forward, flooded by the porch light. The door opened and a woman in a robe was silhouetted in the threshold.

"Yes?" she asked, flicking the wall switch that illuminated the entire downstairs area. Her jet-black hair was brushed back so stiffly that it looked shellacked into place.

Gilbert showed his ID. "Mrs. Howard Richards?"

"Yes, of course I am."

Sullivan thought she seemed quite proud of the fact, as if the title lent a certain exalted status. He judged her to be somewhere north of forty.

"Could we come in?" Gilbert asked.

"What's this about?" Light played on her face, exaggerating her strained expression. Suddenly her features looked sharp enough to cut wood. "Homicide?"

"I'm afraid we have some bad news," Gilbert said,

more gently than Sullivan thought him capable. "Your husband, Dr. Howard Richards, was found murdered in a hotel room at the Hyatt tonight."

Mrs. Richards looked as shocked as if a pan of ice water had been thrown in her face. "Howard murdered? How?" She stepped back to allow them to enter, tugging the belt of her robe tighter. "I was asleep. Maybe I still am. I hope I am." She touched her temple.

Gilbert gestured toward the room to the right. "Let's sit down in the living room."

Sullivan knew that the newly bereaved said the strangest things. The first words were usually of denial. Then came questions before shock took hold. Everyone was different. He watched Mrs. Richards lead the men into the living room. Her waist had started to thicken slightly, but her figure could still turn heads. She had a certain imperious bearing. She settled on the couch, protectively arranging her robe around her. Gilbert and Day sat on either side of Mrs. Richards, Sullivan and Castro in armchairs pulled close. She slipped a wad of Kleenex from her pocket and dabbed at dry eyes.

"Mrs. Richards," Gilbert said, "I don't know your first name."

"Loraine," she answered, hands clasped together, obviously bristling at the idea he might address her so familiarly. "What happened?" she asked, posture erect.

Sullivan noted the sense of economy that seemed a part of Mrs. Richards' very nature, her movements, her emotions, her words; an attractive woman, in a severe, cold way. The furniture in the room ran to the expensive but not comfortable. It occurred to Sullivan that Mrs. Richards matched the place. Some people could suck the warmth out of anything.

Turned toward Mrs. Richards, forearms resting on his knees, Day explained that her husband had been found stabbed. "I know this is a bad time, but we're going to have to ask you to go downtown with us to identify the body. First, though, we'd like to ask you some questions, if you feel up to it. Otherwise, we'll get that trip downtown over with and come back to talk tomorrow. Is there anyone we can call for you? Children? Some relative? A friend?''

Mrs. Richards shook her head. ''No. Our son was killed five years ago in a car accident.'' Her emerald eyes held on the door as if she were looking for someone to come walking in. ''There's no one in particular to call. Ask me what you want and then I'll dress.'' She looked down and dug at her eyes with the Kleenex. ''Poor Howard.''

Sullivan supposed that with the son's accident, Mrs. Richards was no stranger to unknown men ringing her bell with bad news. He spotted the smallest ashtray he'd ever seen on the minute French end table by his spindly chair. He lit a cigarette and studied Mrs. Richards.

Gilbert fixed his eyes on a point just over Mrs. Richards' shoulder. ''Why didn't you go to the convention party with your husband tonight?''

''I wasn't feeling well. I stayed in bed and watched television, then fell asleep.'' She blew her nose. ''Anyway, I don't like that type of thing . . . all those visiting 'firemen' you'll never see again.'' The corners of her mouth were set. Sullivan imagined she always had the last word on any subject. He wondered what kind of passions, emotions, lay beyond that chilly exterior. As she'd said, ''Poor Howard.''

Gilbert kept his gaze steady. ''Mrs. Richards, do you know why your husband took a room at the hotel?''

She lifted her arched eyebrows, inverted Vs. Suddenly she became aware of Sullivan's stare and returned it. ''Howard called and said he'd had too much to drink and didn't want to drive home.'' Mrs. Richards shifted her eyes to Gilbert. ''Didn't want to get picked up by the police. It happens often.'' Her words took her quickly aback. ''His having too much to drink happens often, I meant. He said he'd buy a toothbrush at the hotel drugstore. His clothes were fresh . . . not like he'd worked in them all day.''

It looked to Sullivan that Gilbert's theory about Dr. Richards' quickie was on target. The party had been in progress only thirty minutes when the doctor requested a room. In that length of time he couldn't have had much to drink. Unless he'd hit the bottle earlier.

Glancing self-consciously at Sullivan, Mrs. Richards said, ''Could we just go downtown and get this over with?'' She stood, clutching her robe. Sullivan's attention remained trained on her. ''I'll throw on something.'' She tried to remain attentive to Gilbert, but her attention kept wandering back to Sullivan. Again, she dug at her eyes that had now turned red from the probing.

Sullivan smoked one more cigarette as they waited quietly for Mrs. Richards' return. Wearing a black skirt, matching blouse and mid-heel pumps, she stood in the doorway, then made a tentative step toward the front door. The men rose and escorted her to the car.

The ride back downtown was awkward, no one talking. Between Sullivan and Castro in the back seat, Mrs. Richards twisted a Kleenex, tearing off small pieces and rubbing them into balls. Sullivan felt her vibes: something he couldn't identify was rolling off her in waves. Maybe she had an inkling the doctor's excuse sounded phony. Could be the reason for her controlled behavior. Out of the corner of his eye he shoplifted a glimpse of her. She caught him and edged closer to Castro.

In the parking lot, she glanced up at the half-lit building and shivered. They entered and went immediately to the basement floor where the county morgue was housed. The area was exceptionally cool and lit like a stage, harsh blue rays turning faces a ghastly purplish and Mrs. Richards' hair into raven's feathers.

Captain Chandler stood in the empty hall, talking with the medical examiner and another man. With the echoing footsteps approaching, he looked up. ''Mrs. Richards?''

He touched her shoulder. "I'm Captain Roger Chandler. Homicide. I'm so sorry about your husband. I know this is a difficult time."

"Thank you, Captain," she answered in a quiet, controlled voice, then bit her lip.

Chandler introduced the ME and an assistant coroner, then pushed open the double swinging doors and held them for her. Centered in the room, a steel examination table glistened under the overhead light. Walls were lined with pull-out vaults, case numbers under plastic displayed in brass rectangular brackets. The assistant coroner pulled out a vault. Everyone stared at the figure beneath the cotton covering. The ME pulled back the sheet as if unveiling a statue, leaving the material draped at the waist of the nude body. The fatal wound puckered on his chest.

Mrs. Richards gasped, then made a small croaking noise deep within her throat. Visibly shaken, she inched toward the body and stared down. She reached out, thought better of it and dropped her hand to her side. "It's Howard. I was hoping for some mistake."

Captain Chandler cleared his throat. "Mrs. Richards, the autopsy will be done tonight. I'll stay here for it, then go over to Forensics and work with them. I like to get these things behind us as quickly as possible. If all goes according to schedule, the body can be released day after tomorrow for burial."

Sullivan stared at the tile floor. No matter what Gilbert thought, the captain was as conscientious as any man he'd ever known. The lieutenant would do well to emulate, not criticize.

Gilbert draped his arm around the widow. "We'll take you home now."

Walking through the cavernous area, Sullivan edged up to Gilbert. "I guess this is about it for the night. My car's at the Hyatt. It's walking distance."

Gilbert nodded and guided Mrs. Richards out of the building.

Sullivan and Castro broke away and trudged down the deserted sidewalk. Sullivan stuffed his hands in his pockets and took a deep breath, grateful that the night air had turned cooler.

They retrieved the car from valet parking and Sullivan took one last look at the hotel as they drove away. Heading to Evelyn's, both were pensive, the depressing aftermath settling over them.

"That Mrs. Richards is some cold cookie. Gilbert's a smart-ass, but he's right about us not being able to stop the killings," Castro said as Sullivan braked in front of Evelyn's house. The entire place was lit like a public building.

"We'll just have to solve them, then," Sullivan huffed, getting out.

Evelyn opened the door and stood framed in the entry. "I heard the car door. Anybody hungry? I made some sandwiches."

Sullivan bounded up the steps, followed by Castro. He knew their welfare was at that moment secondary to Evelyn. Her curiosity took first place. She wore a lounge robe that hugged her form. He took appreciable notice. "I'm thirsty," he said, a crooked smile on his lips.

Evelyn brought a silver tray piled with sandwiches into the den while Sullivan mixed drinks. Open books lay scattered on the floor, pages marked by pieces of string. Evelyn positioned herself on the ottoman, arms wrapped around her knees as Sullivan recounted what had transpired. "Something's different here." He tossed down half his drink.

Sullivan pushed up, went to the window and looked out. Stars dotted the black night, scattered across the darkness like gems on velvet. Somewhere out there a killer lived under the same sky. He whirled around, facing Evelyn and Castro. "What do you think is the most normal question a woman would ask if she was told her husband had been murdered?"

Evelyn frowned slightly, concentrating. Suddenly her eyes glittered with triumph. "Who could have done it?"

Sullivan nodded. "Exactly. First thing she'd wonder. I kept waiting, but Mrs. Richards never asked anything like that."

"Yeah," Castro said, eyes narrowed. "Never asked if we'd arrested anybody. Had any suspects."

Sullivan's eyes swept over Evelyn. "Remember your emotions when your sister was murdered? There is a natural urge to know who did it, then the desire for revenge is so strong it temporarily overshadows the sense of loss and grief. Mrs. Richards put on what she thought was a good act, not overdoing the weeping widow bit, but she left out that one human emotion."

The attention was all Sullivan's, his words sinking in.

"You don't miss much," Evelyn finally said, admiration in her eyes.

Sullivan made a face. "I get by. People generally see what they expect to see. We all went to Mrs. Richards', dreading it, expecting to have a shocked widow on our hands. Sometimes you have to look a little harder." Sullivan picked up his drink and took a swallow. "Everybody in Dallas who can read knows about the Sequined Stalker and how she operates. Why wouldn't Mrs. Richards immediately connect her husband's murder to it? She has to know that's what we're thinking. Maybe she wouldn't dare mention it."

"What are you saying?" Evelyn reached out to the tray without looking at it, picked up a sandwich and bit into the triangle.

"I'm not saying anything," Sullivan answered. "Just speculating. When something's out of kilter you have to look at all angles." He looked from Evelyn to Castro. "What if Loraine Richards is the Sequin?"

"Good Lord!" Castro set his beer bottle down on the table hard enough to crack it. His onyx eyes lit up like a pair of lamps just plugged into a socket. "Since Mrs.

Richards wasn't curious enough to even ask if we had an idea who murdered her husband, it points to the theory that maybe she already knew who did.''

Sullivan watched Evelyn's stunned reaction and dragged on his cigarette. He could almost hear the wheels of their minds turning. ''Could be she murdered her own husband to further hide herself from the police. It wouldn't be the first time such a ploy has been used. 'The Purloined Letter' story. Hide something in plain sight. Serial killers are extremely clever.''

Castro leaned forward in his chair as if ready to spring. ''Sullivan, you might have something here. Anybody would have mentioned the Sequin. It had to be in her mind, so why didn't she bring it up? She's playing it cool, wanted us to connect it first.''

''But she's married,'' Evelyn said, eyes blinking rapidly. ''Few serial killers have been married. They are unable to form any lasting attachments . . .'' She hesitated and bit her lip. ''That's male serial killers, though. Maybe female ones are different.'' Evelyn focused on Sullivan. ''You said she seemed cold, controlled. That's one of their traits. She's certainly daring, another strong trait. Those types think they are omnipotent.''

Lifting his finger, Sullivan continued. ''Or maybe she had been planning to kill her husband and saw the perfect opportunity to have it blamed on the Sequin.''

''Another reason for not mentioning the connection,'' Castro said, pushing up. ''I'm going to run out to the guesthouse and look at that printout from Neiman-Marcus. If she has one of those shell purses . . .'' He bolted out before finishing the sentence.

Evelyn went to the bar to freshen her drink. Sullivan moved in close and took over the job. She looked up at him. ''There's a textbook case I know about . . . maybe this would fit. What if the only real victim was just murdered tonight, Dr. Richards.''

Sullivan frowned. ''You mean Mrs. Richards killed all

those others just to set a pattern to hide murdering her own husband.''

"That type of murder does have a precedent in criminology," Evelyn answered, taking her drink. Their eyes held for a moment.

Sullivan lit a cigarette and let it dangle at the corner of his mouth. He squinted, bunching lines on his temples. "That's pretty far out. Maybe too far."

"Okay, but you said to consider every angle. That was one," Evelyn said. "Going on the theory that Mrs. Richards killed her husband . . . him only . . . wanting it blamed on the Sequin, how could she have gotten him to take a hotel room, then gone there and killed him?"

"I'm working on it," Sullivan answered.

Castro came in holding the printout. "Mrs. Richards didn't buy a shell purse at Neiman-Marcus, but, as we know, that doesn't mean she doesn't own one."

Sullivan blew a smoke ring and watched it float, then dissipate. He turned his attention to Evelyn and Castro. "I touched Mrs. Richards' car hood when I was in the garage. The weather's hot, so I felt the door for comparison of the metal. The car has been driven tonight. My old theory is when you see something peculiar in a homicide, look to home first. Mrs. Richards could be completely innocent, but I've got a strong feeling something's wrong here. Tomorrow I'm going to find out just what it is. I know exactly where to start.''

15

By eight o'clock Sullivan and Castro were up and jogging beside the banks of Turtle Creek. Rows of ducks, followed by two majestic white swans, glided along in the murky water.

"Why couldn't we have taken the car?" Castro asked, not even winded.

Sullivan fought to keep his huffing and puffing to a minimum. When he returned to San Diego he vowed to jog regularly on the beach. The thought of going home made him sad. Without Evelyn, the future seemed bleak and empty. He wondered how he could make their diverse worlds blend. Pushing the feelings aside, he struggled to bring his mind back to the case. "I don't want the unmarked police car just like the one Loraine Richards rode in last night parked next door while we question her neighbor. Right now she feels safe. I want her to stay that way until I'm ready to pop her. Besides, this is good for you, Castro. You should do it more often. Aren't you enjoying it?"

Castro gave him a look. "Not particularly. Plus, I keep expecting Immigration to stop me and ask for papers." He grinned, showing the slight chip in his front tooth.

They clopped by the brick walls of the Dallas Country Club and crossed the street. "There's the Highland Park Shopping Center," Sullivan said. "The first shopping center built in the United States. It's been brought up to date with awnings and fancy storefronts. I want to stop by the newsstand at the drugstore over there."

Sullivan dug in his pocket for the change he'd brought while Castro continued to jog in place. Sullivan opened the newspaper and the headlines screamed at him. "The Sequined Stalker Strikes Again," he mumbled to Castro. The article was by-lined by Carole, details sketchy, mainly a recap of the other murders, but information as soon as available was promised.

"Look." Sullivan punched at an article. "From San Diego. A mass murderer on the loose. A whole family slain. Little kids." He strained to see the article, refusing to admit he needed reading glasses.

"Plenty of nuts in this world," Castro commented, still moving. "Let's get on with it. We need to get back to checking that purse list. By now Day and Gilbert are questioning all those people who were at the party last night. Maybe they'll come up with something. Ought to hear from Forensics later today."

Sullivan tucked the paper under his arm and set off, Castro on his heels. "I'll check in with Chandler when we finish this and one other stop I want to make."

"Where's the second one?"

"Dr. Richards' office. I looked it up in the phone book. Right here in this shopping village, office on the second level. He's got two partners, so it'll be business as usual today. They couldn't cancel all those appointments. I'd like to talk to Dr. Richards' secretary."

They sprinted down two blocks, then slowed, turning

right on Arcady, Loraine Richards' street. Other joggers nodded to the pair as they passed, a common bond there.

Castro took a deep breath. ''Be something if Joyce Morrow called up Carole today, gloating about the killing. Mrs. Richards would be out of the picture. Zap! Guilty of nothing but being a cold bitch.''

''Be something,'' Sullivan repeated.

They stopped in front of the house next door to Loraine Richards, then walked up the sidewalk and rang the neighbor's bell. The house was a gray replica of a small French château, mansard roof steeply pitched. Sullivan saw someone pull back the drapery, as he had noticed the night before. The peep space was a mere inch or so. The drapery fell together and Sullivan heard footsteps.

''Who is it?'' an elderly feminine voice called out.

''Dallas Homicide Department,'' Sullivan said as quietly as possible, leaning toward the door. He suddenly realized he'd forgotten his identification. ''We were next door last night,'' he offered, as if that made the difference.

A little birdlike woman opened the door and craned forward. White wisps escaped from the bun at her neck, giving the impression of a mountain sheep's curled horns. Her legs were sticks jabbed into lace-up shoes. She wore a flowered shift southern ladies of old called housedresses.

''I saw you last night,'' she said, her teeth clicking.

Sullivan smiled. ''I know you did. That's why I wanted to talk to you. Thought maybe you could help us.''

With liver-spotted hands, she touched a brooch so passé the style had come back and was now called Art Deco. Old as she was, her eyes sparkled like a child's on Christmas morning. ''I will if I can. Poor Dr. Richards over there,'' she said, nodding toward the house next door. ''Read about it in the morning paper. Knew something was up when I saw you all last night. Knew right off you were the police.'' She glanced at the house again. ''I would take some food over, try to be neighborly in a time like this, but that Mrs. Richards has always given me and everybody else in the neighborhood 'the air.' Don't expect she'll have many callers. It'll be for Dr. Richards' sake if anybody comes at all.'' She stuck out her hand. ''I'm Betty Cain. Come on in. You boys had coffee yet this morning?''

''We'd love some,'' Sullivan answered, and introduced himself and Castro. She reminded him of an old neighbor he'd drop in on after school when his own house was empty. The lonely widow whose grandkids never visited always had a plate of cookies ready.

Furnished with antiques that spoke of old money, Betty Cain's house was well kept and had none of the stale smell of an elderly's lair. Fresh gardenias floated in a crystal bowl on her dining table. Following her to the kitchen, Sullivan watched the veined legs that looked like they might break with each step. The kitchen was homey, not a blaze of stainless steel, a touch outdated but not exactly a Norman Rockwell. A round table of richly polished wood with four padded chairs was set in an alcove. The radio on the counter was tuned to a classical station and purred out a Strauss waltz. Sullivan looked at Betty Cain. Already they were soulmates.

She poured coffee into three blue china cups and served them. ''Want a bun?'' she asked, hesitating before she joined them at the table.

''No, thanks,'' Castro answered. ''I'd have to jog to Oklahoma City to burn that off.''

Sullivan leaned back. ''I'll have one.''

She padded over with the pan just out of the oven, glove on her hand. Sullivan reached for a steaming bun. ''No,'' she said, ''take the other one. It looks better.'' Sullivan smiled and complied.

Back at the table, she edged into her chair. ''Terrible thing. That Sequined Stalker so close to home. I hope you catch her.''

Sullivan bit into the bun and burned his mouth. He chewed carefully, moving the wad from side to side.

"You've got a pretty sharp eye, Mrs. Cain. Did you see Mrs. Richards leave the house last night?"

Her head bobbed. "Sure did. See, when a car backs out of that driveway, the headlights reflect in my windows. Loraine Richards left a little before nine. I know because I was upstairs watching the end of my favorite show, 'Matlock.'" Her eyes twinkled. "I like detectives."

"How do you know Mrs. Richards was driving the car, Mrs. Cain?" Castro asked, little finger extended as he raised the coffee cup to his lips. "You were upstairs, looking down on the driveway?"

Sullivan watched her pale cheeks flush. "Well, to tell the truth, I heard her back door slam and I looked out to see who was leaving. Saw her get in the car and drive off." Mrs. Cain opened a porcelain box on the table and took out a cigarette. She struck a stick match on the bottom of her chair like she was ripping something from underneath, then grabbed an ashtray from the counter. "Want one?" She smiled, clearly enjoying the session.

Sullivan took a cigarette and lit it. "What time did Mrs. Richards come back?"

Mrs. Cain hawked out an enviable smoke ring. "News and weather were over, sports just starting. Ten-twenty."

Sullivan and Castro exchanged glances. The timing worked perfectly. "What else can you tell me about Mrs. Richards?" Sullivan asked.

Mrs. Cain tapped her forehead. "Well, let me think. They fought a lot. See, the houses are close together on this street. Being summer and all, I'm out on my patio in back a lot. So're they. The doctor left her several times. Stayed off a week once, but he always came back. She's a hateful thing. Always treated me like I was some old bag lady. I had her know I made my debut here in Dallas back in nineteen and twenty-five. I was a real cutter back in those days." Mrs. Cain lifted her chin. "She was his nurse, Loraine was. No need being so highfalutin with me."

Sullivan caught his breath. Loraine Richards had medical knowledge. Things were tightening into place. He was almost afraid to move, afraid to look at Castro, the excitement gripping him. "What else, Mrs. Cain? Anything more you can tell me?"

"Betty. Please call me Betty." Mrs. Cain flicked her ashes. "She yelled at him a lot, Loraine did. Accused him of having an affair with someone at his office, named Vivian." She rolled her eyes. "I was sitting out there, having my martini. Our yards are fenced in, but I heard it plain as day. She'd scream like she wanted to kill him. Guess the Sequined Stalker beat her to it." She clamped her hand over her mouth. "Shouldn't've said that." Betty Cain straightened in her chair. "Just last week they had a blowup about something. I couldn't catch what it was 'cause they came out on the patio already into the argument. They sat out there having a drink and went on and on. Then the next night she was all honey. It was strange, her trying to make up so. Not like her, but I think she was afraid he was actually about to leave her. Then she'd only have half the money she had, them splitting up. Money is real important to that woman. She'd be just another divorcée, not *the* wife of a doctor. I told you she was always putting on airs about money and all. She told me one time about this huge place out on the edge of town that she'd inherited from her family. I drove out there just to look. Old run-down house on a wooded lot."

"What did she say when she was trying to make up with the doctor?" Sullivan asked, suddenly feeling as if he were at a gossipy coffee klatch.

Betty Cain took a sip of her coffee. "Loraine said she was sorry, thought they needed to get away alone, get out of the same old atmosphere and try to work things out. She suggested that they go overnight up to some resort cabins on Lake Dallas. He said he'd be operating late. He's an eye surgeon, you know."

Sullivan had a feeling Dr. Howard Richards would have

been dead sooner if he'd gone to the lake. Only he couldn't prove it. Why had the doctor taken the room at the Hyatt on the spur of the moment? He didn't think a quickie or intoxication had anything to do with it. Loraine Richards did. But how?

Betty Cain tapped on the table to retrieve Sullivan's attention. "Dr. Richards said he didn't want to go that far off 'cause some patient might need him. I think he just didn't want to go. I wouldn't blame him if he had a girlfriend. I think he wanted to leave Loraine, but was torn. You know, their boy got killed. I think he felt sorry for Loraine."

Sullivan pushed up from the table. "We better get moving. You've been a big help."

Betty Cain brushed crumbs off her lips and followed them to the door. "Now, don't tell anybody what I said about Loraine so it could get back to her. It's already bad enough. I've got to live next door to her for the rest of my life."

Not if I can help it, Sullivan thought.

Betty Cain opened the door a crack, looking as if she hated for them to go. Her eyes brightened as if she had another delaying morsel to throw them. "Loraine acts in a little-theater group. Thinks she's a Kate Hepburn or something. She looks like Morticia to me. Remember them, the Munsters on TV? Maybe you're too young."

Sullivan pecked the lady on the cheek. "Betty, you're still a cutter."

He and Castro sprinted back to the shopping village and climbed the stairs to the second level where several doctors' offices were located. They found Dr. Howard Richards' at the end of the building. Sullivan told the receptionist they were from Homicide and got a look of disbelief.

"I figured we'd be hearing from you," she answered, eyeing them, but obviously not expecting what she saw. "We're closing the office at noon. Everyone had to come in this morning and take care of the appointments we had. We're calling now to cancel the rest. Dr. Richards was such a nice man." The middle-aged receptionist lowered her eyes.

"We'd like to talk to Vivian," Sullivan said. "Her last name suddenly escapes me."

She looked up, a knowing expression on her face. "Vivian Anthony. She doesn't work here anymore. Quit last month. She lives in a duplex not far from here. Forty-two-sixty Druid. Close to the high school. I know she's at home. I just talked to her."

"Do me a favor," Sullivan said, heading for the door. "Give her a jingle and say we're on the way. Just want to ask her a few questions."

"We could take a cab," Castro suggested, loping down the sidewalk.

"We don't have any money," Sullivan answered, feeling winded. He slowed to a walk.

Though they were still in the exclusive Highland Park area, the houses and yards grew smaller. Young children rode bikes on the sidewalks, training wheels keeping them balanced. High schoolers in fancy cars flashed by, heading for summer school classes.

They turned on Druid, watching the house numbers. Vivian Anthony lived in a sand-colored duplex in the middle of the block. Her door was open and she stood behind a screen door. Sullivan introduced himself and Castro. She asked them to come in.

Vivian Anthony was a slender woman, attractive in a plain sort of way. She looked like everybody's idea of the perfect schoolteacher, no femme fatale, this lady. Her eyes were red and puffed, brown hair uncombed. "I was so stunned when I picked up the paper this morning. I just can't believe Howard's gone." She sank down on a couch that could be converted into a sleeper.

The airy room was filled with plants, sunlight filtering through leaded arched windows. Framed posters lined the walls. Sullivan hoped she smoked. His questions were delicate. There were no ashtrays on the tables.

"Bonnie called me from the office and said you were coming. I suppose when I read the paper I knew someone would want to talk to me." She made circular motions on the fabric with her thumb. "I guess it was fairly common knowledge around the office that Howard and I were . . ." She paused and looked out the window.

Sullivan was thankful she was making it easy for him. "Yes, well, I understand you quit at the office a month ago."

"I had to break it off with Howard. I couldn't see him every day under the circumstances." Vivian exhaled as if she were tired. "His wife was never going to let him go. And Howard had such guilt feelings about her . . . with the son and all. Actually felt sorry for her. It was almost like she had some unnatural control over him. He wasn't weak, but was trying to let her down gently. He kept telling me to hang on. He'd work something out."

"When was the last time you talked to him?" Sullivan asked.

Vivian blinked. "Just yesterday afternoon, late. He said he was in the lobby at the Hyatt. Had decided he'd had it. Wasn't going home. He was going to take a room there for the night until he could make some other arrangements." She broke into sobs, shoulders bent forward and shaking. "Just as things were going to work out . . . the Sequined Stalker got Howard. I can't believe it. Just one night. How could she have gotten to him?" Tears rivered down her cheeks.

Bingo, Sullivan thought. The one call Richards made from his room was to his wife, letting her know he wouldn't be coming home. Seizing the opportunity to have his murder blamed on the Sequin, an idea likely already germinating in her mind, she wrangled his room number out of him and went there. Loraine Richards was very clever to have made up the story that her husband called with the excuse he'd had too much to drink, leaving the detectives with the only conclusion they could draw: the doctor had taken the room for a liaison with someone who turned out to be the Sequin.

Sullivan touched the shoulder of the truly bereaved woman. "I'm sorry about your loss. Thanks for your time. We'll see ourselves out."

"Please catch Howard's murderer," she called after them.

Sullivan turned around. "I intend to."

Castro looked at Sullivan as they retraced their path to Evelyn's. "Loraine Richards is a killer, but I've got a feeling she's not the Sequin."

"I think you're right." Sullivan panted, picking up his pace.

"How are we going to prove it?" Castro wiped his forehead on his sleeve.

"I don't know. I'm thinking. Nobody but Homicide, Carole, Evelyn, us and the Sequin herself knows the murder weapon is probably a hatpin. The papers have intimated it's an ice pick. If the doctor was murdered with a hatpin, his wife is either the Sequin or innocent. If he was murdered with an ice pick, it'll make me think Loraine Richards killed her husband and tried to make it look like the Sequin's work." Sullivan was itching to rubber-hose Loraine Richards with words. He knew something that would scare her.

Moving down Evelyn's driveway, Sullivan saw that her car was gone. They chugged to the guesthouse and found a note from Evelyn telling them that Captain Chandler had called. She had gone to her office, then on to SMU.

Sullivan dialed the captain and, cradling the receiver on his shoulder, lit a cigarette. "Sullivan here," he said when Chandler answered.

"I have a few things in," Chandler said, his tone matter-of-fact. "I'll give you the first, which is bad news. Dr. Richards' heart was punctured by what the ME concludes is an ice pick. The wound is much larger than on the previous victims. So this is the worst headache we could have. A copycat murder. It'll distract from our main case. Could be the Sequin has changed her style, but I doubt it. We're going to have to check into Richards' personal life. See if he had any enemies.''

Sullivan knew of one and told Chandler about it. ''With what I've gathered this morning, I'd like to go talk with Mrs. Richards.''

''Okay, but play it right. No false accusations. Day and Gilbert are still questioning the guests. Nothing so far. Forensics said the sequins found in the room hadn't been sewn on a dress as the others had. Likely just thrown in for a connection. They've got several hairs from a blond wig. Give me a call after you've talked to the wife again. Then you and Castro get on the Neiman-Marcus list. Maybe the Sequin will call Carole Wheeler today, saying it's not her work. I hope so.''

Sullivan and Castro showered and dressed, Sullivan putting on his only dark suit. ''It looks more official,'' he told Castro.

Without calling, they drove to Mrs. Richards' residence. Getting out of the car, Sullivan saw Betty Cain peeping through the drapery. He purposely looked the other way, although he had the urge to wink. A few cars were parked in front of Mrs. Richards' house.

Loraine Richards opened the door, a surprised look in her eyes. She glanced around at her few guests, then turned her attention to the pair from Homicide. ''I thought we were finished with everything. This is not a good time for me. Can't you see I have friends here?'' She started to close the door.

Sullivan grabbed the edge. ''I'm afraid we're going to have to talk now.'' He emphasized the last word. ''Somewhere in private.''

''All right,'' she huffed. ''In the study.'' She looked in at her guests in the living room. ''Excuse me for a moment." She lifted her shoulders. "I have to talk to these policemen."

Sullivan watched her walk down the hall. She had good legs, trim ankles. She did look a little like Morticia, all in black, the mourning widow. The den must have been the doctor's contribution, a room more comfortable than the stiff and formal living room. The couch was upholstered in a plaid. Two leather chairs flanked the fireplace. Rich oriental rug over wooden peg floors. Yards of leather editions in bookcases. An English antique desk only the deep-pocketed discerning would select.

Loraine Richards sat in a chair and crossed her legs at the ankles. Castro dropped on the couch, sinking down. Sullivan stood before the fireplace, arms behind him.

"What more could you have to ask me?" Loraine Richards snapped, directing her words to Sullivan. "I mean, my husband's just been murdered. I wouldn't expect any decent policeman to trouble me any more at such a time."

Sullivan glared at her until she finally moved uncomfortably. "I never said I was decent."

She straightened and blinked. "I beg your pardon."

What Sullivan had noticed most about Loraine Richards the night before was the expression in gemstone eyes. Sharp, very sharp. "Mrs. Richards, you might like to call a lawyer to be present. We'll wait."

She stiffened as if struck by a whip. "What is the meaning of this? Why on earth would I need a lawyer?"

Sullivan thought he might as well mention the words that Mrs. Richards couldn't seem to utter. "The Sequined Stalker."

She looked puzzled, frowned, then glanced at Castro as if looking for support. "The papers said she murdered my husband."

"Yes, we think she did," Sullivan said evenly. "Where did you go last night?"

"You were with me. We went downtown."

"Before that."

"Oh." She hesitated. "I told you I wasn't feeling well. My nose was stopped up. I drove to the drugstore in the village to get some decongestant spray."

"Where did you go after that?" Castro asked, showing her he was no ally. "Tell it exactly like it was."

Sullivan added more fuel. "We have witnesses."

Loraine Richards clenched her jaw. "Listen, if anyone said they saw me anywhere, they were mistaken. I was at home. Right here." She pointed to the floor.

All they had was a nosy old woman's word. Wasn't much, Sullivan thought. He needed to zap a little fear into that ice wall, see if he could melt it. "You were your husband's nurse, so you have medical training. The Sequined Stalker never misses." He knew she had to be familiar with what the papers had revealed about the Sequin. "You own a blond wig, Mrs. Richards?"

"Do I look like a person who'd wear a blond wig?" Her teeth were bared like a dog's. It wasn't a pretty sight.

"Where were you Tuesday night a week ago?" Sullivan pulled a slip of paper out of his pocket. "And on the fourteenth? The sixth of July? The tenth of June? May twentieth? May first?" He glared at her. "Dates the Sequined Stalker killed?"

What color was in that already pale face drained. "Are you accusing me of being the Sequined Stalker?" Her eyes darted around the room.

"I want to know where you were on those dates. Start with last Tuesday," Sullivan ordered. "It wasn't so long ago."

Her hands went to her face. "I don't know. How would anybody know?"

"Do you own an ice pick?"

Her eyes looked as if they might pop from their sockets. "Probably. I mean I guess so."

Sullivan walked over, put his hands on the arms of her chair, boxing her in. He leaned close enough to breathe on her. "Vivian," he said.

She seemed to suck into herself. Sullivan could smell the fear on her, the odor of ripe lemons.

"Your husband was going to leave you. He wanted Vivian. You've known this for a long time . . ."

"How do you know about my personal life?" Her voice cracked.

Sullivan just looked at her. "Mrs. Richards, I know everything about you. You've known about your husband and Vivian for a long time. Plenty of time to set this up. Did you kill all those other doctors to cover up the real killing last night? The perfect opportunity presented itself. The lake trip didn't work out."

"What?" she gasped.

Sullivan honed in on her. "Your husband called up last night, but he didn't say he'd had too much to drink. He told you something else. Killing that many people, six in all now, calls for the death penalty for sure. Death by lethal injection. Death, just like your husband and all those others got. Absolutely no mercy from any jury with that many deaths. No insanity pleas, either. Not with such planning."

"No," she screamed, cracking like a dropped mirror. "I'm not the Sequined Stalker. No! I'm not." She sobbed into her hands.

"What are you, then?" Sullivan pressed hard, remaining in position.

"Howard was going to leave. I couldn't stand it. I had to stop him." She looked up, her mascara-streaked cheeks shining. "Please, can't you understand?" She had started to shake, her entire body trembling like the ground before an earthquake. "I had to stop him."

"You stopped him with an ice pick." Sullivan straightened.

"Yes," she panted. "I knew the Sequined Stalker would be blamed."

"You're under arrest," Sullivan said. He didn't know if

he was empowered to make such a statement, but said it anyway, knowing how official and final the words sounded.

Looking nervous, Castro stood. "Let's go downtown so you can make your statement."

"Can I get my purse?" she asked Sullivan.

He shook his head. "Don't think you'll need it."

"What about those people in my living room?"

"We'll ask them to leave on the way out, then lock up," Sullivan answered.

She walked out of the room just ahead of Sullivan and Castro. Castro leaned close to Sullivan. "Now we're back to square one. We still aren't any closer to the Sequin."

"We'll get her, too," Sullivan answered.

"I must say, you never accused Mrs. Richards of anything. You just asked the right questions, pretending you had the answers. Telling her things. You gave her a choice. The Sequin or just your husband."

Sullivan grinned. "After she makes her official statement, I might tell her the Sequin kills with a hatpin, not an ice pick."

16

Sullivan and Castro hurried to Chandler's office on the second floor of the Dallas Police and Courts Building. Gilbert and Day sat side by side, Day's expression impassive. Gilbert's face was tight with restraint, smoldering eyes focused on the wall. Sullivan knew Gilbert felt his position had been usurped by outsiders and only Chandler's presence kept his emotions in check.

Chandler greeted them with a broad smile. "You guys did a great job. We've got Mrs. Richards' full confession down. It's amazing really. No use of coercion at all."

Sullivan tightened his lips and shook his head. "She was ready to get it off her chest. I got lucky." He saw Castro look the other way. "When I see a homicide, especially when something's slightly out of sync, I look first to home."

"A good idea, since seventy-five percent of the victims murdered in the U.S. last year were related to their assailants." Chandler leaned back in his chair, hooking his arms around his head. "You know the statistic that if a perp isn't caught within the first forty-eight hours after a crime, the odds increase rapidly that it will never be solved. Under these circumstances, this case could have easily slipped by us. The city manager will be pleased you've already earned your keep. However, we're no closer to the Sequin. I keep expecting her to call. There's not another convention for a month.''

"I talked to Carole Wheeler early this morning," Gilbert allowed. "She hasn't heard anything yet. She's sticking by the phone so as not to miss the call, if it comes. I'm going to drop off some lunch to her."

Chandler studied Gilbert a second. "Friends, are you?"

Gilbert shrugged and nodded. "Yeah." His word was flippant.

"Well, watch what you say to members of the press," Chandler cautioned. "They'll print anything they can get hold of. Can't blame them. It's their job."

Day cracked his knuckles, drawing attention. "Well, all we've got left now is Joyce Morrow. It's Wednesday, the day she said 'the cock will crow.' Whatever that is. As usual, a team will be on her all day. Gilbert and I will be on the stakeout at her house tonight, just to see what's happening." He looked expectantly at Sullivan. "You two gonna be with us?"

Sullivan nodded, wondering when he'd ever have any free time to be with Evelyn. She had been the biggest factor in his decision to work on this case.

Chandler leaned forward, his swivel chair slapping at his back. "I talked to the chief of Narcotics about Joyce Morrow's strange behavior. She's not a suspect of theirs in any undercover operations." Chandler bridged his hands. "Now, the teams working the two boutiques have finished. Came up with nothing on the purses. You two keep at it with the Neiman-Marcus list." He directed his command to Sullivan and Castro.

The four walked out of Chandler's office and broke into pairs. While Castro waited, Sullivan hooked into a telephone booth on the ground floor of the Dallas Police and Courts Building. He figured Carole deserved a head start with the scoop about Loraine Richards which Chandler would release later to the press. Since Chandler knew Gilbert and Carole were friends, he might think the lieutenant tipped her. Gilbert would get the reaming he deserved for giving insider information about Evelyn's profile to the reporter at Carole's rival paper. Sullivan sensed Gilbert wasn't delivering lunch out of consideration. Ever the showboat, the lieutenant wanted to be on hand when the Sequin called and be the first to inform Chandler. Sullivan folded back the telephone booth door and locked eyes with Castro. He told him about the call.

Castro made a face. "I'm glad you're on *my* side."

Sullivan's lips curved downward as he lifted his shoulders. "Gilbert takes things too seriously. It's only life."

Castro hurried down the sidewalk to catch Sullivan. "What if it gets Carole in trouble with Chandler?"

"You heard what Chandler said about the press. It's their job to print anything they can get hold of."

In the car, Sullivan lit a cigarette and looked at Castro. "Know something? Both of us need a break. You could work on the purse list by yourself and I'll take the afternoon off."

"When's my break?"

"Tomorrow."

"I don't know the streets in Dallas," Castro said. "I'd be wandering around everywhere."

Sullivan smiled. "I'll get you a city map."

With a bag of sandwiches in hand, Gilbert walked through the newsroom. Row after row of desks were manned by frantic reporters clattering away on typewriters and word processors as if their lives depended on each word. Wire teletypes spit out rolls of paper. Laboring over copy, editors sat in glass cubicles that partitioned them from the activity and noise but allowed a full view of the action.

The environment was more chaotic than the police station. He threaded through the maze to Carole Wheeler's desk, where she sat hunched over a stack of papers.

Carole looked up, feigning surprise at his appearance. Actually she had watched him from the moment he entered the area. She hoped her colleagues took notice of her handsome visitor. "Wayne, thanks for bringing lunch. I'm glued to this telephone."

When he'd called with the offer, Carole recruited her roommate to temporarily cover the monitored telephone. Dressed in an old work skirt and shirt, Carole drove home to change clothes as fast as her VW bug would take her. She threw on a green skirt and yellow blouse, twisting a rainbow-colored scarf around her neck in such a way that the ends hung like streamers. In front of the mirror, she put her arms out straight and spun like a top, thinking she looked exactly like a maypole. When she returned to the newsroom, Dorothy Virginia said she looked like an explosion. Out of breath, Carole thanked her stand-in for the compliment and relieved her.

Gilbert glanced around, then turned his attention to Carole. "So this is where it all happens. Like to have a dollar for all the interviews I've given to the press, but always on my turf. This is just like on television." He set the sack on Carole's desk, then gave her a big smile. "You know, on the way over here I was thinking . . . you've written all those articles about the Sequin, even named her. Great handle, you gave her."

Carole smiled, pleased with the praise, especially its origin. She was bursting to discuss Mrs. Loraine Richards with him, but didn't want to interrupt.

Gilbert's lips twisted, as if he were deep in thought. "You've written about Sullivan coming to town, his background, but maybe you've overlooked an important part . . . the task force, those who run it, the behind-the-scenes people. The city ought to have a flavor of this. I could help you."

Carole blinked, anticipating working with Wayne Gilbert. Long talks that lasted into the night. "That's a great idea, Wayne."

"Had a call yet?" Gilbert asked, opening the sack.

Carole shook her head, eyeing what he'd brought. Italian meatball torpedoes and a plastic container of cilantro garnish that smelled like a soured mop. She jumped up and helped him arrange the spread on the greasy sack. "Just like a picnic. Here, let me get you a chair," Carole said, grabbing one from an empty desk and dragging it close.

"I have a feeling you'll be hearing from the Sequin soon," Gilbert said, biting into his sandwich and trying to keep the filling between the bread. "You'll let me know right away?"

"Sure," Carole answered, Sullivan's call fresh in her mind. "So tell me about everything."

Gilbert's eyes darted around the room. "Nothing new. Just waiting for all the reports to come back from Forensics."

She felt a prick of hurt, but tried to rationalize. His job demanded circumspect behavior. He had some feeling for her or he wouldn't be here. She was making headway. "We need something to drink." She dug in her tote bag and coins spilled on the floor, rolling across the room. People turned to look. "Just leave them there," Carole said, scooping up enough for the drink machine. She had a picture of Gilbert on all fours, raking up change. "I'll be right back."

Returning from the snack room, drinks in hand, Carole saw Dorothy Virginia approaching her desk. Gilbert turned in his chair to watch her roommate. Carole hurried, hating for the two to meet, yet given no choice but to make introductions.

Dorothy was a petite blonde with skin like a bisque doll and enormous eyes. Soft and appealing as a fawn's. Her

hair lay around her oval face in little wisps, falling un-
evenly across her high forehead.

"Wayne, this is my roommate, Dorothy Virginia."
Carole set the bottles on her desk to keep from dropping
them.

Gilbert took Dorothy's hand in his, then placed his other
one on top of the pile, like the game kids played to see
who was either "it" or out. "Well, aren't you pretty?"
Gilbert said, switching on the charm. Carole stared at him.
No matter the circumstances, the man couldn't help himself, a born Lothario.

"Why, thank you," Dorothy answered in a southern
drawl, syllables flowing like syrup. "I'm liking Texas more
and more every day. I moved here from Mississippi five
months ago." She made a meal of the words.

Gilbert cocked his head to one side, eyes twinkling.
"Five months? That's about when the Sequined Stalker
started. Maybe I'll have to arrest you."

Dorothy giggled. Carole thought Gilbert's lame attempt
at humor unbecoming. "That's about the time I moved
here, too," Carole stated.

"Well, I never suspected you," Gilbert said, eyes still
on the roommate.

"Then, that's insulting." Carole sat cross-legged,
painted fingernails arched on her knee, eyes raised to the
ceiling.

Dorothy Virginia squeaked. "Oh, she's so much fun to
live with. So smart and quick. Already has her story done
about the copycat Sequin Killer. Got to be going to work
on my little ole society column. Toodle." She blew them
a kiss.

Carole felt her face flush when Wayne turned slowly to
stare at her. "Where'd you get the story?" he asked.

Carole bit her lips, pushing her fingers under her thighs.
"Can't tell you that." Her job had its principles, too.

She thought he was going to frown, but he caught himself and tried a smile. "Aw, come on, Carole."

She shook her head. "Can't do it."

She saw a flash of irritation in his eyes. "This is me you're talking to. Who told you?"

"Wayne, journalists have gone to jail over this."

"Hawk Sullivan tipped you. He's pulled the rug out from under me enough." Gilbert touched her shoulder. "Carole, you can't print that story just yet. Just hold off until Capt'n Chandler makes a statement. For me? Okay?" He lifted his eyebrows. "Say, I was about to ask you to go out Saturday night. Meet Day and his wife and some of the group at the Palm for dinner. Okay?"

Carole firmed her jaw. "Is my hold on the story dependent on it?"

Gilbert opened his palms. "Well . . . I wouldn't want to look like a fool."

"You already do to me." Carole was seeing Wayne Gilbert in a new light and didn't like what was exposed. She leaped to her feet. "Why don't you just boogie on out of here."

Gilbert's features turned sharp, jaw pulsing. "You and Sullivan got something going?"

Carole glared at him. Let him think what he liked. "Maybe. What's it to you?"

Gilbert gave her a huff, turning to leave. "Nothin', babe."

Boiling, she watched him swagger away. She wadded the sack into a ball, wound up like a major-league pitcher and hit Gilbert on the back of the head.

Gilbert reached back with his hand as if swatting a fly from his ear and kept going.

"Who was that?" a male reporter yelled across the room.

"A fucking policeman," Carole yelled back, and sank to her knees, picking up change.

Sullivan watched Castro drive away, then rang Evelyn's doorbell. When she appeared in the threshold, he realized

that the picture of her he carried in his mind wasn't half
as good as the original. Evelyn wore a denim skirt and
blouse, her feet in college-girl loafers. Little makeup. Hair
cascading to her shoulders. She always dressed down as if
her beauty embarrassed her. That, her hard-mindedness
and her determination were an intriguing combination.

"What's put that big grin on your face?" she asked,
finding his smile contagious.

"You, of course," he answered, stepping in.

Evelyn looked at him. "And what else?"

"Solving a case."

She caught her breath, eyes widening. "The Sequin?
You got her?"

"No, but we got Dr. Richards' wife."

"Tell me everything about it," Evelyn said as they
walked to the den.

Sullivan knew she loved even minute details, and he
enjoyed recounting a case. So he turned loose on the subject, expounding like a guest speaker who had hit his
stride, his audience of one rapt in concentration. He concluded with his call to Carole. "So this calls for a celebration. I'm taking the afternoon off. How about some
lunch? I'll fix it or take you somewhere."

"Mary's gone to a funeral. You could have the whole
kitchen to yourself." Evelyn pushed up from the sofa.
"Why don't you open a bottle of white wine and we'll see
what's in the kitchen to work with. Maybe not much. She
didn't go to the grocery store this morning and neither did
I. I had to sign some AFEs this morning at the office.
Then, as you know, I went to SMU."

"What's an AFE?" Sullivan asked, uncorking the
chilled wine.

"Authorization for expenditure. Cougar Oil is drilling
a well in North Dakota. Quinn left this morning."

"That's interesting." He didn't mean the AFEs. "Here's
your wine." He handed her a stem glass and followed her

into the kitchen. "Come across anything new with your professor?"

Evelyn opened the refrigerator door. "No, and it irritates me that I can't get any kind of handle on the profile that could help. I keep feeling I'm on the verge of grasping something, but whenever I try, whatever it is moves back in my mind, just out of reach. It's frustrating, like having a touch of Alzheimer's."

Sullivan chuckled. "I think you're a few years away from that. Don't force it. If something's there, it'll come floating out when you least expect it. I've had that happen plenty of times. What's in the refrigerator?"

Evelyn looked apologetic. "Nothing much. Just some staples. Eggs, milk, cheese. Some greens, a little wilted. Tomatoes, onions. Maybe we'd better go somewhere."

Sullivan held up his hand. "Perfect. You've just named the ingredients of a cheese soufflé and a salad to go with it."

"It takes a real talent to make something out of nothing," Evelyn said, sliding onto the tall kitchen stool. She watched him beat the eggs with a whisk, his sleeves rolled up over strong forearms. Sipping her wine, she thought about her life when Hawk returned to San Diego. It would be dull, like going back to black and white when you're used to color. Maybe she could think of a way to keep him in Dallas. That wouldn't be easy. No one could lead Hawk Sullivan in a direction he didn't wish to go. Plus, he loved the ocean and his home. "What do you think is going to happen with Joyce Morrow tonight?"

Sullivan grated cheese into his mixture. "Maybe nothing. The whole thing could be an exercise in futility."

"You don't think she's the Sequin?"

"I don't rule out anything. There are over a million people in this city, probably more than half of them women. One of those is the Sequin. I just have to find her." Sullivan looked up from his culinary chores and smiled as if singling out the killer was a simple task. "Seems our conversation is always centered on this subject. Let's take time out and talk like normal people. I'll just put this in the oven."

In the den, Sullivan opened the cabinet and put on a Mozart cassette. He saw a full selection of Willie Nelson tapes, one or two of Julio Iglesia. "So you're a closet country and western addict."

Wineglass in hand, Evelyn lay on the couch, propped up by a stack of pillows. Her hair was splayed out as if she were under water. Sullivan sat on the end of the couch. She pushed her feet under his thigh, wriggling her toes. Just as he turned to her, the phone rang.

Evelyn jerked up, then paused. "Maybe I won't answer."

Sullivan cut his eyes in her direction. "You're too curious not to. Maybe you'd better. Could be for me."

Evelyn went to her desk and picked up the receiver. "Hello?"

"Evelyn Casey?" a raspy voice asked.

Evelyn felt her heart do a quick flip-flop. Lifting her eyebrows, she caught Sullivan's attention. "Who is this?"

"I think you know," the voice said.

Evelyn motioned toward the kitchen. Sullivan hurried in to pick up the extension.

"So you're working on my personality profile . . ." The voice paused for drama. "I'll tell you something you don't know . . ." Again, a pause.

Evelyn thought quickly. "You didn't kill the last victim . . . Dr. Richards." That should throw the Sequin off balance, usurp her element of surprise. Silence. "You called to talk to me, so talk," Evelyn said.

"How"—the voice quavered slightly—"did you know?"

"We know quite a lot about you," Evelyn goaded the caller. While she had the opportunity she decided to slap the Sequin with the questions she had rehearsed with Carole. "You had a miserable childhood, didn't you? Got punched around a lot, huh? You were little and couldn't fight back. Now you're trying to take it out on somebody else who wasn't responsible. What good does that do you? You're smart. Try to reason with yourself. The killing doesn't really satisfy you . . ."

"Shut up," the voice broke in. "You don't know anything about that or me. You never will. You aren't smart enough to figure me out . . . Just because you helped Hawk Sullivan catch that man doesn't mean you can even come close to anything about me. You don't know where to look. So stop while you're ahead. I'm warning you, stay out of this."

The voice was silent for a beat, then Evelyn heard a low guttural chuckle. The Sequin had changed mental gears. Evelyn pressed the receiver harder to her ear, waiting for more to come.

"You dress better than Carole Wheeler, but I must say with all your money you could do better." The voice described what Evelyn had worn at the Hyatt.

It was Evelyn's turn to be shaken. She clutched the receiver until her knuckles turned white. "You need help. You're sick. Think about it. Turn yourself in before it's too late. You'll get the proper help."

The voice cackled. "You're the one who's going to need help if you don't stay out of this." The line went dead.

Evelyn held the receiver close and stared at it as if some explanation would come from the instrument, then gently replaced it on the cradle.

"Jesus Christ," Sullivan said, lumbering into the den. "Why didn't you tell her you'd stop or had given up. Get yourself off the hook. I had to fight not to tell her myself, but coming from you . . ."

"Because I'm going to find something that will trip her." Evelyn looked up at Sullivan looming over her.

"You're not going to stop and neither am I. We can't have any normal relationship until this is over."

Sullivan picked up the phone and called Captain Chandler. When he came on the line, Sullivan explained what had happened.

"I'm going to put you on hold," Chandler said. "I'll check with the officer who's monitoring Joyce Morrow's line."

Sullivan lit a cigarette, eyes on Evelyn as she doodled on a pad at her desk. He couldn't imagine what she might discover that would trip the killer when a battery of trained homicide officers was batting zero.

"Sullivan." Chandler was back on the line. "The call didn't come from Joyce Morrow's residence. However, I got patched in to the surveillance team on her and they said she just made a call from Crank Case's gym. Went into his office. They saw her through the glass. Talked less than three minutes."

"About right," Sullivan said. "Maybe something will pop tonight."

Sullivan hung up and looked at the top of Evelyn's head. The soufflé was probably ruined and so was the afternoon.

The sun was slipping beyond the horizon, its last rays casting a golden crust across Joyce Morrow's wooded property. Sullivan and Castro sat in the back of Gilbert's car, which was parked behind some trees in a vacant lot down the street from the wrestler's property. In front, Gilbert and Day said little. Carole Wheeler's article in her paper's special edition, which Sullivan had read, lay between them.

Two men worked on the street by an open manhole. A linesman was hooked to a telephone pole. A taxi drove by, then a repair truck from the gas company. A delivery van doodled along, stopping now and then as if the driver were lost. A tow truck bumbled by, pulling a car. Everyone was in place. Narcotics was out en masse, since Chandler had felt compelled to inform them of Joyce Morrow's strange packages.

When darkness fell, cars and pickups started arriving at Joyce Morrow's. Soon her yard was filled as if a party was in progress. There were dim lights in the thick trees behind her house, and hoots and shouts could be heard clear down the street.

"Maybe she's having a bar-be-cue or something," Day ventured.

"Something's going on," Gilbert said. "Probably nothing to do with us, but we can't pull out till it's over." He glanced back at Sullivan as if the whole thing were his fault.

When the arrivals at Joyce Morrow's slowed to a halt, Gilbert's radio crackled. He picked it up.

"We're going in," a voice said.

"No," Gilbert yelled. He turned to Day. "It's the goddamn narcs. They're going to blow the whole fucking operation."

Day grabbed the dashboard. "Stop 'em."

Gilbert fumbled with the radio, unable to get a response, except from Central. "Put me on their frequency," he demanded.

"Channel's closed," Central informed him.

"Get Capt'n Chandler to get hold of Narcotics. This is our operation. Repeat, Homicide's operation." Gilbert slammed down the microphone. "Shit! Shit! The sons of bitches are going to blow Joyce Morrow right out of our hands."

The four leaned forward, watching the swarm of men converge on the property. Dark figures eased around the house, then disappeared in the trees. Sullivan grabbed the back seat. The scene was a disaster.

They waited, eyes glued to the scene. After a few minutes two visitors ran out of the curtain of darkness and jumped into a pickup. Gunning the vehicle, they bounced

over rough terrain, heading for the main entry gate. Two
police cars, blue lights revolving on top, pulled up and
blocked their exit.

"Jesus," Sullivan said, nose almost pressed to the window. "Let's go see what's happening."

They hit the ground running, Gilbert in the lead, sprint-
ing like a trim racehorse. He slowed by the police cars
and flashed his badge. "We're going in."

The quartet ran through the trees and stopped in the
lighted clearing where chaos reigned. The wind whipped
money in the air and bills glided around, falling finally
like snowflakes. A round pen had been dug in an old barn,
and two fighting cocks, outfitted with metal spurs, were
pitted in a death fight. Other roosters, released from pens,
squawked as they scrambled fruitlessly to gain altitude,
feathers flying everywhere.

The crowd had been rounded up into a cluster, Joyce
Morrow and Crank Case in handcuffs. Officers herded the
group to the front of the house. Gilbert walked up to the
officer in charge.

"What the hell?" he asked, perspiration rolling down
his temples.

"Cock fight." The narcotics officers laughed. "Cock
instead of coke. These crazy sons of bitches drugged
these birds just long enough for them to be brought out
here in birthday packages with holes punched in the
boxes. Joyce Morrow's kept them in cages until the big
fight tonight."

Sullivan stepped up. "I guess anybody low enough to
put razors on game cocks and let them fight until one kills
the other wouldn't mind stooping to drugging the birds.
What's the penalty?"

The narc eyed him. "I just called in about it. Falls under the cruelty-to-animals law, a Class A misdemeanor,
punishable by up to one year in jail and a two-thousand-
dollar fine." He shook his head. "Ain't this the pits.

Wait'll the press gets hold of this." He stomped dust off his feet and walked off.

Gilbert whipped around to Sullivan. "I guess you'll be calling the kook you sleep with so she can get her story in ahead of time. You're nothing but an over-the-hill fuckup. A woman had to do your last job."

Sullivan's eyes narrowed as he reached forward to grab Gilbert by the lapels. Before he made contact, Castro was between them. With one fluid judo maneuver, Castro grounded Gilbert, pinning him to the ground.

"You better cool it, fancy man." Castro was breathing on Gilbert's face.

Day threw up his hands. "Hey! Hey! Everybody stop it. This is out of hand." He reached down and pulled Gilbert to his feet.

Sullivan glared at Gilbert. "You better be damn certain of yourself before you take me on. I don't give a shit what you think of me, but I'm going to tell you what I think of you."

Under control, Gilbert smirked. "Yeah? I can hardly wait."

Sullivan punched him on the chest as he talked. "I think you're about as sharp as any officer I ever saw. If you get a harness on that attitude, you're going places. If not, you're still going places, the wrong ones. You're the kind I'd like to have on my side *anytime*, once you get that ego and disposition in the right notch." He turned. "Let's go, Castro."

"Hey, wait," Day said. "We're out in the middle of nowhere."

"We'll catch a ride with some of the guys out front," Sullivan said, lumbering away from the pair.

Castro caught up with Sullivan. "Didn't mean to take it away from you, but I thought it was better me than you, if one of us got thrown off the case. I know it means a lot to you . . . the case. Tough about losing Joyce Morrow.

If the killing stops now, we'll never know if she was the Sequin or not.''

Walking toward the patrol cars, blue lights slashing across his face, Sullivan looked straight ahead. ''Joyce Morrow wasn't the Sequin or she wouldn't be out here with a crowd doing something illegal that could jeopardize her main mission . . . to kill. It takes priority in the Sequin's life. She's getting uptight. A mistake is coming. We'll get her.''

17

The roar in my head grows louder. Thoughts rumble like the sound of an approaching subway, then flash by without stopping. Get help? Evelyn Casey tells *me* to get help? She's the one who needs help. And that article the reporter wrote wrongly accusing *me*. She continues to call me the Sequined Stalker. It must stop. But, Evelyn Casey *knew* the signature was not mine. How did she know? Is she so smart? How dare that doctor's wife attempt to lay blame where it did not belong. Only I do that with expertise. I concentrate. But, of course. The woman's technique was different, something that clued them. I laugh.

They are all like Doctor. Evelyn Casey thinking she's so smart, telling me to get help. The reporter calling me names and falsely accusing me. The wife, a fledgling, a cheap imitation. I'm about to show them the real maestro. I've planned long and carefully.

I am standing on the stairs. I turn to Doctor's den. I can still hear him talking to Momma. It was just after my sixteenth birthday that nobody celebrated, Momma too

drunk, Doctor too busy, indifferent. I asked Doctor for a
car like everybody else had. He said I didn't deserve one.
I told him I wanted to go to med school when I graduated,
thinking it would please Him, make Him like me. He
laughed. *Laughed.*

"Weird, I'm telling you. Something's got to be done,"
Doctor is saying.

"Listen, I gave birth to a wonderful child. Tore myself
up doing it and look how you talk."

"Ever try to talk to that wonderful child? No, of course
not. Too damn drunk. You ought to try it sometime. Just
say hello and catch the weird smile the kid gives you.
Stays in the bedroom all day, all night. Christ knows what
goes on in there, besides wearing your clothes sometimes."

"My darling is smart. You can see it in the eyes."

"Hah! Flunking out of school, hasn't gotten better than
Ds in years. You wouldn't know about that, though. They
call me. Teachers, counselors. The principal called me last
week."

"Did you tell the principal it's because of a mean father
who never pays attention to his child or wife?"

"No friends except your brother's kid. No attention
span, sits in class staring into space. The principal suggested psychiatric help . . ."

"You're not taking my child to any head-shrinker."

"I'll do what I damn well please. Maybe it will help.
Maybe not."

"Over my dead body. Those psychiatrists just fuck up
people."

"This kid is already fucked up, with some thanks to
you."

"Me? It's all your fault."

I showed Doctor how fucked up I was. I got a job after
school and on Saturdays at the hospital. I knew they hired
me because of Him, but didn't care. I got a real feel for
the place, the office, the labs, operating rooms, especially

pathology. Learned a lot. I turned a minimum wage into something profitable. It is amazing how careless people are, leaving drawers and lockers unlocked, purses on desks. I took only small amounts, but it added up. I smiled at everyone, was on time and willing to do anyone a favor. Bought my own car.

I watched Doctor in his own element. Jerk didn't even know I studied him. To Doctor I was some piece of shit that didn't exist, invisible, which was perfect. He was an even bigger fool than I thought, King Shit, ordering people around, furious when his orders weren't carried out exactly. So furious his hateful face turned red. Fucker might drop dead of a heart attack before I can kill Him.

I turn around when I hear Poo bumbling along, knocking into the wall. Blind now. Eyes milky and skimmed over. Can't spy on me anymore. Cuz will be back soon. It's time to do something. I scoop up Poo and go down to the cellar. A cobweb catches on my face and I bat it away. I switch on the lights, go to the oubliette, pull the heavy wood cover back and look down in the dark hole where I put Sheffield. I throw Poo down in the darkness and hear him hit bottom with a squeak. It wasn't enough to hurt Poo. Not near enough. I have to do more. I pull the cover back over the hole and climb the creaking stairs. I will say Poo ran off when I let him out.

Upstairs, I look in my closet to decide what to wear to my appointment. The dark suit I wore to Doctor's funeral is still hanging there. He pulled the ultimate trick before I could get Him and dropped dead, like I feared. Just left me hanging in a void with no chance to complete what was destined. *Big heart-doctor*. I was twenty then. Eighteen when Momma was buried. Before He died, Doctor took me to a psychiatrist. Not took, dragged. I wouldn't talk, wouldn't cooperate, couldn't make me. Then I decided to tell some lies to see if the shrink knew. Bastard did. Told Doctor he couldn't help. *Help*. That's what I'm going to get. Just what everybody suggests.

I call a psychiatrist picked out of the yellow pages. Imagine. Was booked up until November. He missed out. Hah! Call another and got an appointment because of a cancellation. *Death by cancellation*. A good title for his life story.

I put on a thick layer of makeup and apply false eyelashes. Looking at myself in the mirror, I add my short curly red wig. I select a dress like Momma used to wear. A silk suit, russet-colored that matches my hair. I pull on panty hose and step into patent-leather heels that go with my purse. I add my hat, a straw creation, then touch my thumb to the hatpin, testing. The prick gives me a thrill like no other. It will give Doctor even more. Hold on, Doctor, I am coming.

Downstairs, I look around as I do each time I go after Doctor. I always have the feeling I might not return, my journey eternal. That is silly, though. It always works. I always come back. Alone, like after Momma and Doctor were gone. Place so quiet. I glance at the phone and get excited. I'll show my Extreme Power to the reporter and the police who are listening. I laugh and dial. *They can do absolutely nothing about what they hear. I am the one with power.*

"Carole Wheeler's desk, please." Polite. I tap my painted nails on the table. Anxious.

"Carole Wheeler." Flippant.

"You accused me of something I didn't do." Matter-of-fact.

"It's you!" Taken aback.

I check my watch. "You also called me by that *name*. I told you not to." Adamant.

"Listen, we know you didn't do it. Haven't you read the latest edition? The doctor's wife confessed." News flash. "You were at the Hyatt that night it happened. What were you doing there?" Inquisitive. Playing for time.

"Watching you and your friend who thinks she can find out about me." I laugh. "I've already told you who I am.

My name, wrapped up in words, and something important about me. You're all too dumb to figure it out." A puzzle to titillate.

"You told me your name?" Redundant.

"In a sense." Clever. "Now I will tell you more. I am on my way right now and everyone is helpless to stop me. You will hear about the Doctor before the day is over." *Power.*

I hang up and drive to the psychiatrist's address I knew was a free-standing building, an old renovated house that doctors like to use as offices. No traps, like in multistoried buildings. I know from experience that a patient arrives at a psychiatrist's ten minutes before the hour, waits in the reception room, then is shown in on the hour. After the fifty-minute session, the patient leaves by a side door so as not to be seen by the next patient in the reception area. Perfect. Doctor showed me the way.

I don't park in the lot by the house, but leave my car a block away and walk. The nearer I get, the louder the buzz.

Ummmmmmmmmmm Ummmmmmmmm. The chant in time with my footsteps. *Um yea um yea um yea um yea.* I pick up my pace, getting close. Almost there.

I have to make the voices stop. I can't be distracted. Have to concentrate. I open the door and walk in, switch a smile on my face. "Afternoon," I say to the reception-ist. "I'm Harriet Knight."

"Yes, will you please fill out this sheet."

I take the paper and the clipboard, refuse the pen. I sit down and with a gloved hand and a pen from my purse, write a fictitious address, phone number and Social Security number. I fill in the medical history, answer stupid questions and return the paper to the fat woman behind the glass.

"Dr. Strauss will see you in just a few minutes."

I thank her and take my place, looking around the room. Typical, no imagination, furniture probably his wife's castoffs when she redecorated their house. Old dog-eared magazines. You'd think with the prices doctors charge, the patients could be treated to some decent reading material. Stingy Doctor. Wouldn't buy a car. I finally got it all. Everything but Doctor.

I hear a bell and look at the receptionist. She nods, accentuating the double chin. "You can go in now."

I stand. The time has come. I am calm. No voices. I take a deep breath, excitement coursing through me. I open the door and enter Dr. Stephen Strauss' inner sanctum.

He rises from his desk. The slant of the sun from the blinds turns his face into a study of lines. Except for the beard, he looks like Doctor. He is coming toward me, grinning, the mouth a red slit nestled in all that hair. He says something that doesn't register, but rather echoes and reverberates in my head. I smile, my eyes on his chest, a big wide target. My hand moves to my hat. Long, sturdy pin gripped, I wrench it free and jab with all my strength into the spot where all life begins and ends.

His eyes widen with shock. He drops to the floor with the force of a dead walrus. *Got you, Doctor. Easy.* I open the side door and walk out, bathed with sunlight. I am free.

18

The Crime Scene Unit had finished with Dr. Stephen Strauss' office. Completing his job, the medical examiner released the body for autopsy. The men's eyes followed the body bag as it was carried out by two assistants straining from the corpse's weight.

Captain Chandler sighed and rubbed his forehead, his expression solemn. "Operating this way, the Sequin will cut a wide swath through this city before she's finished. Headlines again." He shook his head. "Even told Carole Wheeler she was on the way to kill somebody and there was nothing we could do about it. The Sequin is getting a thrill out of this."

Before the Crime Scene Unit removed the clipboard, Sullivan had studied the handwriting, an eerie sensation gripping him as if the Sequin had actually touched him. He felt somehow closer to her, staring at the words that were hers. Chandler had immediately dispatched a unit to the address which, as they strongly suspected, was fake.

Sullivan glanced at the receptionist, who was sprawled on the leather couch. Gilbert laid a wet towel on her forehead. With his head, Gilbert motioned Sullivan over.

"Why don't you talk to her? You've got the best knack for it," Gilbert said genuinely, with no trace of sarcasm.

Sullivan knew the words must have cost the lieutenant something. They exchanged looks, then Sullivan focused on the receptionist. Sobbing, large bosom heaving, she turned to face the wall, as if trying to block out the scene.

"I've already told everything. I can't believe I actually saw her. She was here, not a foot from me," she croaked.

"Anything . . . peculiar about her that you can remember?" Sullivan pressed.

The receptionist pointed to Day. "I already told him. I thought the hat and gloves were peculiar, too formal, but we get some strange people in here. The next patient was waiting—Mr. Hibbert. He's got this phobia about death. Thinks about it all the time. Dying and dead people . . ."

"How do you know that?" Sullivan interrupted.

The receptionist turned back, like a fish flopping on its side. "I read the files sometimes."

Gilbert eyed Sullivan, a small smile on his lips.

"When Mr. Hibbert's appointment time came and I didn't hear the doctor ring, I just told him to go on in, thinking Dr. Strauss had forgotten. He does that sometimes. God!" She threw up her hands. "You should have heard Mr. Hibbert hollering after he went in. This is gonna really set him back. Set me back a notch."

Set Dr. Strauss back more than a notch, Sullivan thought. "What about the woman's voice? Try to remember exactly how it sounded."

The receptionist snapped her eyes closed, concentrating hard. "Pleasant, maybe a little hoarse-like. What's that movie star? Humphry Bogart's wife." Her eyes jerked open. "Lauren Bacall . . . like that, sort of."

Captain Chandler walked over to the couch. "I think this is about wrapped up here. Let's go downtown and listen to those recordings we monitored from Carole Wheeler's phone. See if we can find anything planted in there like the Sequin claims.''

"I'll give you a lift," Gilbert said to Sullivan. "After we finish I can drop you off to join Castro.''

Sullivan accepted Gilbert's offer as a peace offering and walked with him to the car. Castro had already left to hit the salesclerks at Neiman-Marcus with questions. Finished with the list of customers who'd purchased the shell bags, he was left with dogging clerks who'd sold the item for cash, hoping to jostle their memories.

On the way downtown, the two discussed the case and potential trouble ahead. No doctor was safe in accepting a new patient. Sullivan raised the question that if a doctor was called to an emergency situation, would he feel safe in going? What were the ethics involved if a doctor refused a legitimate patient who died or suffered severe consequences from lack of treatment?

Gilbert switched the subject, asking Sullivan about the hostages in South America he had rescued after nixing the idea of paying ransom. Sullivan told him about the caper, the trek he led across the border into Bolivia. Days like those paid for days like these, Sullivan thought, then shrugged, saying he got lucky. He knew Gilbert snatched side glances of him, thinking he was too engrossed in the story to notice. Sullivan thought he saw a speck of something he'd call respect in Gilbert's eyes.

"Like that old saying," Gilbert said, pulling into the parking lot adjoining the Police and Courts Building. "The harder somebody works, the luckier they get.''

They joined Day in Chandler's office, where a recorder had been set up on the desk. While it was fresh in their minds, Sullivan and Evelyn had written down everything the Sequin had said. He passed the paper around for the officers to read.

"I just don't see anything in there," Chandler said, brow looking as if it might be permanently furrowed. Flak from city officials was taking its toll. The captain's appearance reminded Sullivan of every President after a year in office. "Now the Sequin claims she's told her name, in a sense, and something else about her. She called Carole Wheeler again this morning after the killing. So I have these recordings to play over and over until we come up with something."

He pressed a button and the raspy voice at full volume filled the room. The men leaned back to listen. He played each recording twice, then for good measure, a third time.

"Anything?" The captain looked from man to man.

Gilbert's eyes narrowed in concentration. "The bitch is clever. Maybe she's putting us on. Nothing in there at all."

Sullivan dug at his temple with his thumb. "I don't know. It's a serial killer's nature, male, that is, to think they're smarter than anyone, invincible. Living on the edge gives them a kick. I think something's there. She's enjoying us playing with a puzzle. Run that first one again."

The captain hit the button and they listened, straining forward. The voice told Carole Wheeler not to call her a monster, and after Carole Wheeler asked what she'd call herself, the Sequin replied that everything was in the eye of the beholder. Twice she said that she was attuned, and she criticized the reporter's clothes. Then she asked about Evelyn Casey, Sullivan, and wanted to know who the Mexican dude was. A cop? Carole's boyfriend?

When the recording finished, Day shook his head. "I don't know. Attuned? That sticks out. A tune?" He cracked his knuckles. "Maybe she has something to do with music. You tune an instrument. That could be the something she said she told about herself. But her name?" He sighed. "I don't know."

Gilbert toyed with the word "monster" that the killer so objected to being called. "That really gets her. Could be it hits too close to home. Monster. Muenster. Could be that's her name or she's from there. Muenster, Texas, almost a suburb.''

Sullivan lit a cigarette, then remembered he was in Chandler's office. ''Okay,'' Chandler said, pulling the ashtray out of his drawer.

Sullivan took a long drag, rapt in thought. ''Everything is in the eye of the beholder, she said. That could mean we're looking at something, but not really seeing it for what it is. An illusion, so to speak.'' Sullivan felt something stir deep inside. Call it intuition. Call it nothing. Still, he had the sensation he'd hit on something. An illusion? What could it be? ''You know Carole got a call the day I got here, before her line was bugged. She told me what the Sequin said, but things were so new then it didn't quite register with me. Something about how she didn't like the handle 'the Sequined Stalker' . . . wanted a better name.'' He bolted upright. ''She suggested a better name for herself.'' He shook his head. ''I can't think of it. We'd better call Carole right away, see if she can remember.''

Chandler grabbed the receiver and dialed the *Dallas Morning News*. He asked for Carole Wheeler, then waited. Her line rang repeatedly before somebody finally answered.

''Carole Wheeler, is she there?'' he asked.

Chandler lifted his eyebrows. ''Have her call Captain Chandler when she comes back. She knows the number.'' He hung up, eyes moving from man to man. ''She's gone to lunch. We'll have to wait.''

Wearing a beige linen suit the saleslady called smart, an adjective Evelyn disliked when applied to clothes, she gave her 450 SL Mercedes to the valet at the Mansion, Dallas' most chic restaurant. Carole had said she wanted to 'do lunch' there. Laughing at the term, Evelyn had set today for the treat. She missed the place where food was as elegant as the decor.

Stationed by gleaming brass poles, the long canopy
sheltered the way into the entrance. Evelyn strolled underneath to the heavy double doors which were immediately opened by the smiling French maître d'. A mammoth
urn holding fresh flowers that were flown in daily sat on
a round table in the marble entry. Overhead, a palace-size
crystal-encrusted chandelier cast a muted glow.

"Ah, Mrs. Casey," he said, bowing slightly. "It's nice
to see you again. Your table and guest are both waiting."

Evelyn was shown to the first banquette on the left, the
choice seating in the opulent dining room. Carole had lined
up sunflower seeds in neat rows on the snowy tablecloth
and was methodically popping them into her mouth. The
Frenchman eyed Carole as Evelyn slipped in beside her.
He adjusted the table before them, then nodded to the
woman who sat in the adjoining banquette, her elbows
almost touching Carole's.

Carole wore a black dress with billowing sleeves,
diamond-shaped insets of green edging the neck and cuffs.
A gold mesh butterfly that looked as if it had just landed
in her hair was attached to a comb that held back one side
of her carrot curls. As if ready for flight, the creation
moved when Carole bobbed her head.

Evelyn unfolded her napkin and placed it in her lap. "If
you order any health food here, I'm not picking up the
check. Let's order something really sinful, full of calories
and cholesterol. I'm famished. I stayed up most of the
night working on the profile and slept late this morning. I
was up when Hawk and Castro came in last night and they
told me about the cockfight raid and his . . . brush, I
guess you'd call it, with Wayne Gilbert." Evelyn was
bursting to tell someone about the new theory that had
surfaced just before she drifted into sleep. When she
awakened, the plausibility of her idea grew stronger. She
ran to the guesthouse, but Sullivan and Castro were gone.
"The narcs stepping in like that and arresting Joyce Morrow . . . we might never know if she was, in fact, the

Sequin. Unless, of course, the killer hits again. But I've got something . . .''

"We know she's not the Sequin." Carole lifted her orange eyebrows, silver bracelets clanging on her arms. "You haven't heard, then. The Sequin called me this morning, told me she was off to kill again, then did it and called back."

The news that hadn't hit the papers shocked Evelyn. "Tell me about it. Who did she kill?" Evelyn looked up at the waiter who had arrived at the table, menus in hand. "I think I'd like a glass of white wine first. Carole?"

"If I have to eat things that might kill me, then at least let me have a sensible drink. A Perrier," Carole said to the waiter. "And don't let them put any limes in it."

Carole told Evelyn what had happened that morning. Her eyes darted around the room. "Look at that ladies' luncheon over there. Some of them have on hats. Maybe one's the Sequin." Cheeks flushing, she glanced at the lone woman next to them who also wore a hat, then quickly turned to Evelyn and lowered her voice. "God, it could be anybody. Maybe the police won't ever catch her."

Evelyn picked up her wine and took a sip. Deep in thought, she set the stem down, making patterns on the tablecloth. "Carole, I've come up with an idea." She glanced at the woman next to them who was busily cutting a piece of veal. She twirled the bite in a brown sauce, then popped it in her mouth. Evelyn looked squarely at Carole. "What if everybody is looking in the wrong direction? What if the Sequin is a man?"

Carole gulped her Perrier, eyes rolling in their sockets. "Jesus! Where'd you come up with that?"

"Every pattern, every trait is more a man's. I was thumbing through a book that got me thinking. If a woman murders, it's usually a shooting or poison. Everything about this has been different."

Carole picked up her fork and tapped it on the table. "I don't know." She shook her head. "Maybe." She exhaled. "What kind of man? A man who dresses up like a woman, a good enough imitation to fool other men?"

Evelyn picked up the menu. "Maybe it's far out, but I'm going out to SMU after lunch and talk with my professor about it. I can't wait to spring the idea on Hawk when he comes home." She lowered the menu. "You know serial killers are clever, devious, almost all have a high IQ. I mean, it's the ultimate guise, having the police running around looking for the wrong kind of suspect entirely. This has got to give the killer a hell of a kick. The more I think about it, the more positive I am that I'm on the right track." She could feel the enthusiasm bubbling inside. What a coup if she was on target.

The waiter came back to take their lunch order. Carole studied the menu as if memorizing every word. "Go ahead," she said to Evelyn, "I'm trying to decide. After lunch Dorothy and I are going shopping. You'll have to meet her sometime." She made a face. "My dear roommate thinks I need a new look. I don't want to feel fat when I'm trying on clothes. Gotta order light."

"I'll have the veal," Evelyn said, glancing at the woman next to them. She had finished her lunch and was ordering dessert. Evelyn wondered if someone had stood her up.

Pointing to the listing on the menu, Carole said: "I'll have the Sunrise Salad, but could you have them leave off the salami strips? Just have the chef add a few bacon crumbles. And I want it made with Boston lettuce, not romaine." She smiled, snapping shut the heavy leather menu.

Evelyn laughed to herself. Carole had never ordered a dish without somehow changing it. She rested her forearms on the table, looking at Carole. "What about writing a story about my theory? It might shake things up. Really rattle the killer if I'm right."

Carole grinned. "Wouldn't hurt your reputation any, either."

"Or yours, if you were the first to write such an article."

Carole looked off into space. "I'll have to convince my editor to let me go so far out on a limb."

"Will you talk to him today?" Evelyn pressed.

"He's at home, sick. I could call him after I finish with Dorothy. Maybe go out to his house. I'm basically finished for the day. I wrote my story about the doctor this morning. Course nothing's in from Forensics, so I couldn't say it's the Sequin's work, just hint."

Evelyn ordered another glass of wine to go with lunch. "I'm celebrating. This might be a real turn in the case. More leads to look into. Men buying women's clothes. A type who could impersonate a woman and get away with it." Maybe she could help Sullivan stop the killer cold. Then they could put away the case and turn the key on it.

Carole rimmed the top of her glass with her finger. "You know, Wayne called me this morning and said he'd been a butt. Wanted to take me to dinner tonight. I accepted, but everything's gone out of it for me now. My mother always said that a leopard never changed his spots."

Their lunch was served and they tucked into the meal, speculating about Evelyn's theory. Evelyn noticed that the woman next to them was on her second cup of coffee, in no hurry to leave. She wondered why anyone would go to the trouble of dressing and lunch alone. She'd rather grab a sandwich at home. Maybe the woman was an out-of-towner who wanted to see the Mansion while her husband attended a business meeting. Evelyn always played that game with strangers, giving them a past and a present.

Evelyn and Carole shook their heads when the dessert cart was pulled close. The check was presented and Evelyn signed.

"I have to go to the rest room before I take off shopping. Where is it?" Carole asked.

"I'll go with you," Evelyn said, getting up when the waiter pulled out the table.

They climbed the winding staircase that rimmed the entry to the second floor. The rooms for private parties were dark. Evelyn pushed open the heavy door to the ladies' room and held it for Carole.

"Won't be a second," Carole said, lifting her skirt and entering the last marble stall.

Evelyn stood before the mirror, pushing her hair into place. She applied lipstick, then blotted on a paper towel. Washing her hands, she glanced at the mirror and saw the door open. The image of the woman who sat next to them appeared. Eyes on Evelyn, she walked toward her, her stride rapid.

Evelyn straightened and turned to the woman. Their eyes locked. The woman reached up to her hat.

For an instant Evelyn felt an unexplainable flash of fear.

Three gabbing women pushed through the swinging door and crowded around the lavatory.

The woman adjusted her hat, took an atomizer from her purse, sprayed on perfume and left.

Evelyn looked after her as the door closed. A strange feeling settled over her like the sensation just after a near car collision.

19

Gilbert braked before the entrance to Neiman-Marcus in Northpark Shopping Center, one of the two branches of the main store. Sullivan stubbed out his cigarette. "Thanks for the lift."

Gilbert shrugged. "I'll keep trying to get hold of Carole. There's got to be something in that first call from the Sequin. I hope Carole can remember exactly what she heard." He leaned forward, straining toward the windshield. "Oh, no."

Sullivan followed Gilbert's line of sight. "Who's that?" A man fat enough to be on display at the circus labored toward them, an umbrella hooked over an arm the size of a tree trunk.

"The crazy psychic we called in," Gilbert answered, racing the motor. "I don't want to talk to him. A fucking pest. Catch you later, Sullivan."

Sullivan watched Gilbert drive away, fumes from the exhaust stinging his nose. He turned to face the mountain of a man behind him. The face looked like a lump of dough, two raisins for eyes. Strings of hair fell from a partially bald head to his shoulders. One ear was double-pierced, a diamond stud in one hole, a gold loop in the other. Rings on all fingers, the man's fingernails were long and curved under like a Baghdad saber.

"Afternoon, sir." The man bowed his head slightly. "I see Lieutenant Gilbert was in a hurry. Are you a member of the constabulary?"

Some way to put it, Sullivan thought, and nodded.

"I don't recall seeing you when I was downtown to consult," the psychic said.

"Well, I'm new. Out of San Diego." Sullivan glanced around the man, wanting to hurry. Cars zipped by them, looking for parking spaces.

"Like a consultant also, I take it. I hope they pay some attention to *you.*" He looked offended. "Oh, let me introduce myself. I'm Willard Wallace."

He looked like a Willard, Sullivan mused, holding out his hand. The psychic took hold of the tips of Sullivan's fingers in a limp grip. Sullivan had the urge to jerk free. "Nice to meet you, Mr. Wallace. Excuse me, but I've got to meet someone in here."

"It's very crowded today. I was just in finishing my Christmas shopping."

In August? Another kook, Sullivan thought. He tried to step around the mound, but the man moved, blocking his path.

"You see, my chart says travel. So I had to finish before the season approaches so as not to get caught short. I'm called away often on cases. A few weeks ago I located a boy who had been kidnapped in Maine."

Sullivan managed to dodge around the man, turned and walked backward a few steps. "Nice to meet you."

"Homicide should listen to me. I'm certain the killer they are looking for is a man, not a woman. I had this vision."

Sullivan stopped and edged back to the man, lights going off in his head. "When did this come to you?"

"After the third killing, when the scene was fresh. I walked into the hotel room where it happened. I have a strong sense of smell. The room was filled with the scent of evil. It's always there after a murder. It was the smell of a man, not a woman. There's a clear distinction."

Sullivan blinked, scrutinizing the psychic. He might be wrong, but he was in earnest with his beliefs. The phrase "the eye of the beholder" headlined in his mind. Could it be? "Willard, I'm glad I ran into you. This gives me a new slant." Sullivan turned to leave.

"It is a man," Willard repeated. "A small, clever one. You'll see." He stepped off the curb and bumbled across the parking lot.

Sullivan hurried through the luxury store until he spotted Castro at the purse counter talking to a salesclerk. Sullivan tapped Castro on the shoulder.

"Anything?"

"I'm trying to wrap up this one cash sale. I'm waiting on salesperson number four-one-zero-five-five. Name's Mickey Harlow, they say, and he's on a break." Castro hit his forehead. "This is a bitch of a job. I sure hope it pays off." Castro checked his watch. "He'll be back in thirty minutes. A break, for Christ sakes. Wouldn't a policeman like to take one."

Sullivan realized Castro missed Olga and his nerves were ragged. He, too, hoped they could soon wrap up the case, but didn't like to think what the finale might bring. "Let's step out in the mall so I can have a cigarette and catch you up on some things."

They charged through the store and out to the enclosed area where a large fountain spat water high into the air. Gigantic potted plants were stationed at the corners of the pool, wood-slatted benches placed at careful intervals. Tourists and locals ambled by, gawking in store windows.

A clown handing out balloons to children scurried around, tap-dancing.

Sullivan lit a cigarette and filled in the blanks unknown to Castro. "Maybe the psychic has something. I keep coming back to those recordings."

"The eye of the beholder," Castro repeated. "The beholder sees something that's not really there, only what they expect to see." Castro twisted his lips. "Could be something, but the name? What could it be? You think it's something the Sequin said in her first call to Carole."

"Possibly. You heard the same as I did when Carole told us the Sequin didn't like the name, suggested a better one. Think."

"That's what I'm doing, man. Why don't you try Carole again or Evelyn? She was there, too. She's got a hell of a memory. Quinn Stewart was there also."

Sullivan heaved up and walked across to a phone booth. He dialed Evelyn and got no answer. Another reporter answered Carole's line and said she was still at lunch. Sullivan glanced at his watch, then motioned to Castro.

Back at the purse counter, Castro asked for Mickey Harlow. The attractive young blonde said she was Mickey Harlow. Castro and Sullivan exchanged glances. Castro had assumed Mickey Harlow was a man just as everyone assumed the Sequined Stalker was a woman.

"According to these records, you sold a Judith Leiber shell purse back in April," Castro said, after showing her his credentials.

"Homicide? Gee, it must be important, but that was so long ago. I'm like trying to remember."

"Those purses are so expensive, surely you don't sell a lot of them," Sullivan charged in. "Especially somebody doling out that much cash. Eight hundred bucks."

"Plus tax," the salesclerk added. "I could buy a nice purse with the tax money."

"Think about it hard," Sullivan pressed.

The woman frowned. "Usually women charge big purchases like that."

Sullivan lifted his hand. "Wait a second. You're on the wrong track. I didn't say it was a woman. Maybe it was a man. Think."

"That's it!" She brightened. "It *was* a man. I remember now."

Sullivan felt like jumping over the counter. "What do you remember about him now that you've got the connection?"

"Well, let's see," she said, looking around as if she expected some help to come from the store. "He goes, 'I'd like to see that purse,' and I go, 'The one shaped like a Buddha?' He was pointing at the case, kinda snitty-like, tapping on the glass. 'No,' he goes, 'the shell.' I'm like trying to be helpful."

"What did he look like?" Castro asked to get her back on track.

"He was like effeminate, said the purse was a gift. I thought it was for him, though. Maybe like one of those cross-dressers, you know."

"Short, tall, fat, young, what else?" Sullivan questioned.

"Kinda short, maybe five seven. Thin. Probably early thirties." She smiled and looked proud of herself. "I really remember something now."

"Go on," Sullivan urged.

"The man's eyes were permanently tattooed with eyeliner. Lots of women do that now so they don't have to put on eyeliner every day. I thought it was weird for a man to have it done. I was sure he hadn't just drawn the liner on with a pencil."

Sullivan was familiar with the new procedure performed by plastic surgeons and dermatologists. A male patient might not be hard to trace. He thanked the clerk and told her she'd been a real help.

Castro and Sullivan drove at breakneck speed to the

Police and Courts Building, parked in the lot and hurried to Chandler's office. Sullivan explained the new situation to the captain, adding his own speculations.

Chandler leaned back in the chair as if slapped. "This takes some mental adjustment. I don't know. Could be we'd be wasting time off on some wild tangent. Dr. Strauss' receptionist actually *saw* the Sequin, the only person who has except the room service waiter. Neither one had the slightest feeling the killer wasn't a woman. She picked up all those doctors, too."

Sullivan stared at Chandler. "We haven't got anything else to go on."

Chandler blinked, rubbing his chin. "Unfortunately you're right. Carole Wheeler still hasn't returned my phone call. I've tried her several times." Chandler stood. "Okay, I'll get the task force assembled. Every plastic surgeon and dermatologist in the city is listed in the latest yellow pages under their separate heading. We'll call until somebody makes a hit."

After Chandler went out to the squad room to round up the task force, Sullivan used his phone to call Evelyn. The line continued to be busy. Finally, irritated, Sullivan dialed the operator and asked her to interrupt the call for an emergency.

"Yes, sir," Mary said.

"I need to speak to Mrs. Casey right away."

"She's out at SMU."

"Do you know her professor's name?"

"No, sir. She had lots of them."

"Tell her to call me here at the police station when she comes in. She'll know to ask for Homicide."

Sullivan hung up and called Carole Wheeler, who was still not in. He was about to dial Quinn Stewart at Cougar Oil to see if by chance he recalled what Carole Wheeler had said, but remembered Stewart was in North Dakota overseeing a well that was being drilled. He was tempted to get the number of where Stewart was staying from his office and try him in North Dakota, but decided he was overreacting. Chances were Stewart wouldn't remember, anyway. He'd reach Evelyn or Carole soon. He left Chandler's and arrowed to the squad room.

The speed with which Chandler, Gilbert and Day had organized the task force was amazing. A long row of desks was manned by team members using the phones like campaign workers the day before an election. Yellow pages had been ripped from the phone books, quickly Xeroxed and divided among the industrious group. The captain and his two lieutenants worked alongside the others.

Gilbert handed Sullivan and Castro each a list and pointed to two vacant desks. "Everybody's got to lend a hand. Get on it."

Sullivan gave him a two-finger salute and hooked into his chair. Seated just ahead of Sullivan, Castro picked up the phone and dialed the first name on his list.

Business, as usual, continued in the squad room. Officers in other divisions hustled in and out, curiously eyeing the task force. A uniformed man approached Gilbert and asked what was happening, saying he'd never seen such a concentrated group. Gilbert waved him off without looking up.

Sullivan looked at his list, more than half the names crossed off now. He lit a cigarette, glancing at the team hunched over their respective desks, speaking rapidly into receivers, hanging up, redialing. A study in organization and harmony. Anyone criticizing police officers needed only one glimpse behind the scenes for a change of opinion. He continued calling, ashes spilling over his trousers.

Over an hour had passed when one of the women officers, hand clasped over the receiver, yelled out. "Hey! Got one."

There was a mass exodus to her desk, chairs overturned, people scrambling close to catch one side of the conversation.

The young woman's cheeks flushed as she spoke.

"Homicide wants the information on your male patient, name, address and phone."

"What? You *have* to give out the information. This is emergency police business." Again, she clasped her hand over the receiver and looked up at Captain Chandler. "It's a nurse. She won't give me the information. Says it's privileged."

Chandler grabbed the receiver. "Whose office have you got?" he asked the female officer.

"Dr. William Harper's," she answered.

Chandler addressed himself to the nurse. "This is Captain Roger Chandler. Dallas Homicide. Let me speak to Dr. Harper. This is an emergency." He listened, then slammed down the receiver. "Asshole!"

"What is it?" Gilbert pushed forward.

Chandler's eyes were blazing. "The doctor's doing a face-lift at Baylor. I'd like to give that nurse one. Gilbert, go get a subpoena from one of the judges. Hurry." He turned to the rest of the team. "Everybody get back on the phones until we're finished with every name on the list. There could still be some more male patients."

On his way out, Gilbert winked at Sullivan. "The subpoena could take a while."

Sullivan grabbed his and Castro's lists and handed them to Day. "Finish these for us." He motioned to Castro. "Come on."

As Sullivan and Castro dodged through the squad room, Chandler spotted their exit. "Hey," he yelled. "Where are you two going?"

Sullivan never looked back.

20

Sullivan pulled up to the emergency entrance at Baylor Hospital, left room for ambulances to park, put his credentials on the dash and locked the car when Castro got out. He glanced around the sprawling medical complex, then dashed through the double glass swinging doors. A strong medicinal odor hit him. The emergency waiting room was packed with patients. An agonizing shout from one of the curtained cubicles punctuated the already noisy area.

Following a sign that pointed to the operating area, Sullivan and Castro barreled through the bowels of the hospital. They pushed through swinging doors and slowed in a hall lined with gurneys. They sidled up to a station attended by a hatchet-faced nurse.

Castro flashed his credentials. "What operating room is Dr. William Harper using?"

"You can't go in there," the nurse barked.

Homicide might intimidate some, but not this one. Sullivan looked at her "That wasn't his question."

"B-One," she allowed.

"When will he be finished?" Sullivan asked, leaning on the counter.

"What is this? What's going on?" the nurse wanted to know.

"Emergency police business," Sullivan snapped. "When will he be finished? We have to see him right away."

The nurse picked up a clipboard, taking her time. "Maybe thirty minutes. It's his last operation for the day."

Sullivan glanced around. "We'll wait."

"Not here, you won't."

Sullivan now knew two nurses he could strangle. "Just tell us where, then, and send Dr. Harper in as soon as he's finished."

Like someone thumbing a ride, she pointed down the hall. "Waiting room down there for families of surgical patients."

Sullivan stopped to use the pay phone. After making several calls, he and Castro went to the small waiting area.

"Day said they had finished with all the lists. Didn't come up with any more male candidates. Dr. Harper's patient has got to be our man."

Castro looked skeptical. "If the Sequin is a man."

The waiting room was smokier than an AA meeting and the people twice as fidgety. "My kind of place," Sullivan said, sinking down on a cracked plastic couch. Castro leaned against the wall, folding his arms across his chest.

Sullivan lit a cigarette, high from excitement. He had a gut feeling Dr. Harper's male patient was a lead strong enough to unravel the case. A tattooed man, albeit eyeliner, had bought a shell purse. In Dr. Harper's files might be the name and address of the serial killer. To think of the Sequined Stalker as a male did take some mental adjustment. Sullivan glanced at Castro's profile. The man had good instincts. Some doubt suddenly dampened Sullivan's exhilaration. He could end up looking like a royal fool diverting attention in the wrong direction. Joyce Morrow was a prime example. Still, his own intuition wasn't to be shortchanged.

Sullivan checked his watch every few minutes. Time seemed to be stuck. He smoked two more cigarettes, as anxious as the waiting families. Each time a surgically clad doctor appeared in the doorway, Sullivan lifted off the couch, expecting the plastic surgeon. As visitors were assured their loved ones were in satisfactory condition, the room thinned. Finally, only Sullivan and Castro remained.

A small man in operating greens, mask dangling around his neck, stood in the hall, peering in. "I'm Dr. Harper. I was told somebody was looking for me."

Sullivan scrambled to his feet as Castro presented his credentials. The diminutive man gazed at the papers, then glanced up sharply. "What is this?" Color drained from his face, eyes widened in fear. "Has something happened to my family?"

Sullivan lifted his hand. "No, no. Nothing like that. Sorry if we alarmed you."

The surgeon exhaled slightly, then tightened with a sudden irritation at the scare. "So what is it?"

"You've no doubt heard of the Sequined Stalker," Sullivan stated.

The doctor nodded.

"We have reason to believe this killer might have been a patient of yours. A man who had you tattoo that permanent eyeliner," Sullivan continued. "We need his name and address from your files." Sullivan explained how they had uncovered the patient. "Your nurse won't give us the information."

"This is out of line for me to give out patients' names . . ."

"One of the homicide lieutenants is working on a subpoena right now. We'll get that name, but it'll delay us. Maybe long enough for the killer to hit another doctor. There was another murder this morning." Sullivan put a note of urgency in his voice.

Dr. Harper frowned. "I don't understand. I thought the Sequined Stalker was a woman."

"So did we, all along, but some new information makes us consider that the killer could be a man . . . your patient. You just might be lucky to be alive. Some of your colleagues weren't so fortunate. I'm asking for your help. We need it now." Sullivan pressed closer, dwarfing the man.

Dr. Harper looked hesitant, then checked his watch. "My nurse will have gone by now." He dropped his arms to his sides. "Okay, let me change and I'll meet you at my office in fifteen minutes. Twenty-sixty Swiss Avenue. Not far from here. You know the street?"

Sullivan nodded, anticipation popping through him. "Thanks, we'll be waiting."

After parking her VW bug in the lot across from the Dallas Morning News Building, Carole locked the car, eyeing her purchases in the back seat. She hoped no one would break in. She and her roommate jaywalked to the opposite side of the street, hurrying toward the entrance.

In the newsroom, Carole spotted a young woman sitting in a straight chair pulled close to her desk. As Carole approached, she saw the woman more clearly. Arms crossed demurely over her lap, the woman was dressed in a simple white blouse and navy skirt, low-heel matching shoes. Her hair was cut pixie style, points of blond punctuating her round face. Eyes, set wide apart, were a smoky gray-violet that seemed to be looking at Carole from behind a curtain of fog.

She stood and flashed a badge at Carole. "Marie Aaron. Homicide task force. Carole Wheeler?"

Carole nodded, wondering if this was the officer Wayne Gilbert had been dating.

"I'd better get to my desk and work on the column," Dorothy whispered to Carole.

"See you," Carole answered as her roommate swished by the desk.

"The captain's been trying to get hold of you," the female officer said.

Carole glanced at the stack of messages on her desk. "Maybe I'd better return his call."

"I take it you haven't talked to Hawk Sullivan yet?" Marie Aaron asked, a note of excitement in her voice.

"No," Carole answered, alerted. "Is something up?"

The officer nodded. "I'm really not at liberty to tell you about it. I was sent to get you. You're going to have some scoop." She rose, clutching a navy leather tote bag. "Ready?"

"You bet," Carole answered, feeling her heart pumping. Maybe this could be the Pulitzer knocking.

As the two walked out of the newsroom, Carole raised one arm, fist clenched, in her roommate's direction. "Charge," she said to herself.

Sullivan and Castro waited in the empty hall just outside Dr. Harper's locked office. When they heard the elevator around the corner, they turned and looked in that direction. True to his word, Dr. William Harper appeared, his footsteps loud on the marble corridor and echoing in the distance.

He produced a set of keys, fumbled through the assortment, then jammed one in his lock. "This really disturbs me. I was thinking on the way over . . . if you go and hassle my patient and he's not your man, he could sue me. I'm taking a real risk, just on your word."

"The risk is even bigger if he *is* our man and you had the power to give him to us and didn't," Sullivan answered, trying to keep his impatience in check.

The doctor opened the door and switched on the lights. Sullivan glanced around, thinking the little surgeon did some tall operating to afford such an office. The waiting room was spacious, furnished in ultramodern decor befitting an elegant penthouse. Globs of color dabbed on canvas passed as paintings. Sullivan felt as if he were adrift in a desert of earth-toned suedes and leathers.

"The files are back here." He motioned down a carpeted hall. "I can't remember the patient's name, but I have a system where I can find him by the type of service I performed."

They followed the doctor, passing his private office and a row of examination rooms, including a small surgical area, complete with an operating table. "I operate in the office, too. Rhinoplasty and minor procedures. The permanent tattooing is one of them." He studied the labels on the file cabinets, then opened a certain one, fingering the folders.

Sullivan stood close, jangling change in his pocket. He had the urge to throw the bantam-weight doctor aside and look for himself. To draw his attention from the anxiety of watching the doctor, Sullivan counted the pictures lining the wall. He noticed Castro watching him and looked the other way. For someone who performed delicate operations, the doctor lacked the same deftness in locating files.

Dr. Harper pulled a file from the drawer, spilling the contents of several other folders. "Here it is. Name's Christopher Byrd. Age thirty-two. No home address. Gave his place of business for an address and phone. The My O My Club."

"I know the place from the old days," Sullivan said, turning the man's name over in his head. "Christopher Byrd," he spoke aloud, wondering if he'd just uttered the killer's name. "It's a nightclub where female impersonators perform. It all connects. He's it." Sullivan turned and looked at Castro. "We've almost got the Sequin."

The doctor hunkered down to pick up the files. "I guess I'm lucky to be here."

Sullivan stood there, trying to decide the best approach to Christopher Byrd. The busted operation at Joyce Morrow's scared him. Not that he didn't trust Homicide's precision, but the more people involved, the riskier the situation became. He couldn't allow Christopher Byrd to slip through his fingers. He wasn't trying to grandstand, but figured he and Castro could handle the confrontation alone.

"I want to use your phone," Sullivan said to the doctor, who had straightened and was stuffing folders in the file cabinet.

The doctor led them into his private office, a replica of the reception room, and indicated the telephone on his desk. Sullivan saw the doctor's eyes go to the picture of an attractive woman and two small blond children, knowing the surgeon was thanking some higher being for his life.

From the number in Christopher Byrd's file, Sullivan dialed the My O My Club. An effeminate male voice answered, "My O My," emphasis on the *O*.

"What time does the floor show go on?" Sullivan asked. He had no way of knowing if Byrd was a performer, but strongly suspected he was.

"It's continuous, luv, after five. One *divine* act after the other."

"You take reservations?"

"Certainly."

"We especially wanted to catch an act somebody told us about . . . said he was really great . . . can't think of the name exactly . . . starts with a C . . . Christian . . ."

"Christopher Byrd. He's 'mahvelous.' Don't miss him. He goes on in an hour. What's the name for the reservation? How many?"

"Jones, H. Jones. Two people."

Sullivan hung up, tapping his fingers on the receiver. He snatched it up again and dialed Evelyn. Mary said she still wasn't home. Sullivan checked his watch, wondering why she was so late. Laboring away with her professor on a profile that had lost its significance now. Still, the exercise had been good for Evelyn. He paused for a moment, then dialed Carole. He wouldn't mention what he'd discovered, but wanted to hear what she remembered from the first call when the Sequin suggested a better name. That might really wrap up things.

"Carole Wheeler's extension."

"Is she there?"

"Who's this?" a cautious southern voice asked.

"Hawk Sullivan, a friend."

"Oh, sure, Mr. Sullivan. This is Dorothy Virginia, Carole's roommate. I'm working late and was grabbing Carole's calls for her. I thought maybe the Sequined Stalker would call and I'd get to talk. Carole went off with some female police officer from Homicide. Any message?"

Sullivan supposed Chandler had sent for Carole, wanting to hear about the first call. "No message." He hung up. Gilbert would find the office closed for the night when he arrived with the subpoena, if he'd convinced a judge to work that fast. Sullivan stood and locked eyes with Castro. "Let's go. It's show time."

21

Pulling around to her garage in the early evening twilight, Evelyn was surprised and disappointed that Sullivan's car wasn't parked in front. She supposed the doctor's murder that morning had Homicide tied in knots. Anxious to spring her theory on Sullivan, which the professor had readily agreed was more than plausible, Evelyn hurried to the kitchen door. She planned to start a surprise dinner for Sullivan's arrival. She imagined them, settled in the den, wineglasses in hand, exploring the new slant that the Sequin might be a male. Sullivan would probably be skeptical, even brusque with her, but she felt armed with enough ammunition to convince him to at least consider the possibility. If she had the case figured correctly, a national reputation was in hand.

Before she could put her purse on the counter, the doorbell rang. She was charged with excitement. He was here. She hurried down the hall and paused to check herself in the mirror, pushing back her hair.

"Mrs. Casey," Mary yelled, peeping around her room door. "Mr. Sullivan's been calling . . ."

"He's here," Evelyn called, striding to the front door. She grabbed the brass knob, unlatching the bolt, and was taken aback to find a young woman on her doorstep.

"Mrs. Casey, I'm Dorothy Virginia, Carole's roommate. I've been looking forward to meeting you. Carole's spoken of you so much."

"Thanks, you, too," Evelyn answered, admiring the attractive blonde. Her small ears were set far back, her eyes alert, full of intelligence. She wore a chic white linen suit emphasized with a high-back collar and cuffs that spoke of money and taste. A good guide for Carole in the shopping world.

"Carole's tried and tried to call you. The line's been busy, busy."

Evelyn glanced back at Mary, who had edged down the hall, pretending to dust a table. "That's certainly possible." Evelyn grinned.

"Carole is so excited. She sent me to get you. Her editor is sick today and she's gone to his house. Wants you to meet her there and give the editor some of the profile and background stuff you and she discussed at lunch today. They are going to break a big story tomorrow morning. Carole got another call from the Sequined Stalker and she accused the killer of being a man." The woman's eyes widened. "Guess what? The killer admitted it. You were right."

Evelyn drew in a deep breath, flushed with a heady sense of triumph. She broke into a smile. "What a turn of events."

She returned Evelyn's smile. "Carole's pretty thrilled. I'm sure you are, too. Big headlines tomorrow." She gestured with her hand. "We'd better get going. Carole's working like a jackhammer and she's waiting for you to help her add the authentic part. Her editor's going to work as she goes along."

Stationing her bag under her arm, Evelyn turned back

to Mary. "I'm going with Carole Wheeler's roommate out to her editor's. Tell Mr. Sullivan. I'll be back as soon as I can."

"He wanted you to call him. Said you'd know to ask for Homicide," Mary said.

"You can buzz him when we get to Carole's editor's house," the roommate said. "We've got a lot of traffic to beat at this time. Better get going. He lives out north of town. Everybody's getting off work and heading that way," she urged.

"Okay," Evelyn said, closing the door behind her.

She walked with the blonde through the shadows of the giant oaks to a new Cadillac. The moon filtering through the trees made weird patterns on the woman's face as she looked at Evelyn across the car's roof. She opened the door and was suddenly illuminated in the darkness. Pinpoints of light seemed to fly like sparks from her eyes that never left Evelyn.

She slid into the car, adjusting her skirt, then hooked the seat belt. Hesitantly Evelyn touched the door handle. For some reason, an uneasy feeling gripped her. She had a strange sensation she had seen the face before, but couldn't place when or where.

"Ready? Carole's waiting. You know how frantic she is about things."

Evelyn edged into the car and slammed the door. It must have been the picture. Carole had dropped her roommate's picture out of her purse and she barely glanced at it before handing it back. The image had simply stuck in her mind. Evelyn tried to relax.

The blonde gunned away and after maneuvering through Highland Park, edged into the traffic on Central Expressway snaking north. She lit a cigarette and offered Evelyn one. Shaking her head, Evelyn looked at the woman's trim legs, small foot in an expensive shoe pressing on the accelerator. Lighted storefronts, billboards and buildings flashed by, melding in a swirl. Evelyn felt as she had as a child, when the carousel started going faster and faster, faces and forms streaming together so that she had to watch closely to sort them out. Finally the entire circle turned everything into a dizzy blur.

"I'm still stunned that the Sequined Stalker is a man," the blonde said, flicking the long gray roll at the ashtray. "Everybody will be when it hits the papers. I guess it will make the police look pretty stupid. Carole said you brought it up at lunch just today. Had you been thinking about the possibility for a while?"

"No," Evelyn answered, wondering why she felt so uncomfortable in the woman's presence. With the insider information the woman possessed, she had to be who she said she was. "I just hit on the idea last night."

"I understand you shot that serial killer who murdered your sister. Must have been awful to kill somebody." The blonde turned briefly to Evelyn, passing headlights flashing on her face. Her eyes danced with interest.

Evelyn clutched her purse closer. "Not good. It was a bad experience, but something that had to be done. He almost got away."

"Serial killers are supposed to be a special breed, very clever. I guess that one was no match for you and Hawk Sullivan. Maybe the Sequined Stalker has more genius. He already proved it . . . having everyone looking for a woman. A real master of illusion." She gripped her wheel tighter and turned on the off-ramp, heading down a dark street. "I don't think he will ever be caught, do you?"

"Eventually most serial killers have been caught, simply because they think they can't be. There's a misconception among some people that serial killers actually want to be caught. That old 'stop me before I do it again' theory. In reality, they want to go on forever with the killings. I can tell you one thing," Evelyn said, looking out at the dark wooded area they were driving through. "If the killer knows anything about Hawk Sullivan, he'd better be careful. Sometimes I think the man has almost supernatural instincts, to say nothing about his experience.'' Evelyn glanced at the blonde, lights from the dashboard glowing on her face. ''Where is Carole's editor's house? We're almost running out of real estate.''

''We're close. Just up ahead.'' She slowed and turned onto a gravel road that wound through a copse of trees.

The secluded old Victorian house glowed with lights shining through lace curtains. Twin cupolas were joined by a gingerbread balcony. In the back, an open turret stood like a sentinel.

The blonde braked and opened her door. ''Quaint place, huh? That's what I thought when I dropped Carole off.''

Evelyn looked out at the setting. ''I feel like we just dropped back into another century.'' She got out, following the woman up the wooden stairs. A swing suspended by chains from the porch ceiling creaked as it moved with the wind.

''The editor is sort of a kook. He and Carole are a pair.'' She rang the bell, touched the door, which was slightly ajar, then pushed it open. ''Let's go on in. They're in the back den.''

Closing the door behind them, the blonde looked at Evelyn with eyes that appeared shrouded. A slash of fear suddenly struck Evelyn. Carole had joked about her roommate's thick southern accent. This person had no trace of one.

The foyer of the My O My Club was packed. A tuxedoed maître d' escorted customers into the show room. Posters of entertainers on gold easels were displayed in red velvet insets around the walls. Sullivan and Castro eased through the crowd studying the almost life-size photographs of Christopher Byrd dressed and posed like Marilyn Monroe, Rita Hayworth, Hedy Lamarr and Jean Harlow. Bearing a strong resemblance to Jackie Kennedy, a picture showed the impersonator dressed in a suit and hat. There were other advertisements, but Christopher Byrd was the establishment's unmistakable star.

When their turn came, Sullivan and Castro were ush-ered through the gold Ionic columns into the opulent show room and given a table the size of a large round serving tray. Men, obviously aspiring performers, were dressed as cocktail waitresses.

"Hi, I'm Diana," the one assigned to Sullivan and Cas-tro said in a breathy tone.

Sullivan looked the apparition up and down. "Two Cokes. Leave them in the bottle."

"You could have at least ordered beers," Castro said.

Sullivan lit a cigarette, glancing around. The room was a sea of red velvet and gold light fixtures. A large mirrored bar wrapped around one wall, a stage, complete with or-chestra pit, dominating the other. "I feel like a whore in church. Soon as Christopher Byrd gets offstage, we're go-ing back to the dressing rooms. Jesus! What a spot."

Sullivan and Castro were served, none too politely. The musicians tuned up and, as the lights dimmed, broke into a medley of Broadway show tunes. In the dimness, Sulli-van watched the glow of the tip of his cigarette. He knew Evelyn would be anxious about his absence. He would call as soon as possible. The idea of wrapping up the case before the night was over zipped back and forth in his mind, Christopher Byrd the center of every thought. He was afraid to even entertain the notion that he might be speeding down a dead end.

When the velvet curtain went up, Sullivan turned side-ways in his chair, barely deigning to watch the act. A man dressed and wigged like Phyllis Diller wobbled on the stage in high heels, telling jokes. Even though the imitator's delivery was better than good, Sullivan lacked the capacity to be impressed, anxious as he was for the act that was billed next. The audience roared at the off-color stories. Sullivan bent the swizzle stick until it broke.

Finally the entertainer segued into a song and a soft-shoe shuffle for a finale. After several bows, the female impersonator flounced off the stage and the curtain fell.

Sullivan straightened and turned his full attention to the stage, anticipation high at seeing the person who might possibly be the Sequined Stalker.

The audience waited in silence, then grew restless, conversations breaking out as the interval grew longer. Sullivan fidgeted in his seat, exchanging glances with Castro. Someone started a slow-clap, then was joined by others, the rhythm quickening.

The emcee walked between the curtains and held up his hands. The crowd grew quiet. Taking hold of the mike, he said: "Ladies and gentlemen, due to illness, Christopher Byrd won't be appearing tonight, but we have many more fabulous acts, as you'll see." Before the crowd could protest, the curtains were drawn and a bevy of Ziegfeld-like chorus girls strolled down a glittered stairway.

Sullivan threw a ten-dollar bill on the table. "Let's get out of here and go talk to the manager."

He and Castro weaved through the tables and asked the maître d' to show them to the manager's office.

"What's the trouble?" the man asked, arrogance in his posture. "Can't I help you?"

Sullivan flashed his ID. "You want to deal with this?"

The man looked ruffled. "Follow me."

He led them down a narrow corridor and knocked on a door. "Jake. Couple a guys here want to talk to you."

"Tell 'em to wait in the lobby. I'm busy right now," a scratchy voice called out.

Sullivan nudged the maître d'.

"Jake, these you better see now." He hurried down the hall to greet new arrivals pushing through the foyer.

The door opened with a jerk, and a weasel of a man stood in the opening, his bald head rimmed with a fuzz of electrified hair. His ferret eyes darted from one man to the other. "What's this?"

"Homicide," Sullivan said, showing his papers, dog-eared now.

Like a top, the manager spun around in place, threw up his

hands and footed it to his desk. "So come in, interrupt. If it ain't Vice, it's the narcs. I run a clean place here. Ain't nobody killed anybody except for the audience on a few comedians." He plopped down in a swivel chair and rubbed a hand over his glistening crown. "What's this about?"

"We'd like Christopher Byrd's home address," Sullivan said evenly.

"Little bastard called in sick again. This is happening too often. Fucking prima donna's believing his own publicity. I'll show him who the star is." Jake leaned foward, beady eyes too close to a nose that looked like it needed to be lanced. "What d' ya want to see him for? He kill somebody? Mean enough to, like all these flighty characters."

Sullivan leaned on the desk, fingers splayed. "Look, I'm in a hurry. This is official police business. I'm going to say this in English so you'll understand. *Get me his address.*" Sullivan glared at the little man.

"Okay, okay!" He pushed back from his desk and opened a ledger. He copied the address and phone number on a scratch pad, tore it off and handed the paper to Sullivan.

Sullivan wasn't familiar with the street, but he had the city map in the glove compartment. He looked up at the manager. "You're going with us to Christopher Byrd's."

Jake touched his chest with all ten fingers. "Me? I can't leave here."

"I can't leave you here to call Christopher Byrd and tell him we're on the way, either," Sullivan barked.

"I wouldn't call that snit and warn him if the devil was personally on the way. Count on it." Smiling as if a pact had been reached, Jake showed them his stained and partially rotten teeth.

"I don't count on anything. Did Christopher Byrd perform here Tuesday night a week ago?" Sullivan asked, still leaning forward.

"How do I know without looking it up?" the man said, then hesitated. "So okay, I'll look it up." He filed through another ledger, running his finger down a column of names. "Naw. Was off that night."

"You know anything about Byrd's background?" Sullivan asked.

"A snob. Well off. Father was a doctor. Byrd was always saying he didn't have to work 'cause the old man left him so much money. Always wore a little pinkie ring with his family crest on it."

Sullivan moved behind the desk, crowding the manager, and picked up the phone. He dialed Evelyn's number and was relieved not to get a busy signal. Mary answered on the second ring.

"Mary, has Mrs. Casey come home?"

"Come and went."

"Went where?"

"With Carole Wheeler's roommate. She came to get Mrs. Casey to take her to some editor's about a story. Mrs. Casey said tell you she'd be back as soon as she could. That was a while ago. 'Bout six."

"Thanks, Mary." Sullivan hung up, puzzled.

He dialed the paper and asked for Carole's extension, hoping to catch them there. "Carole Wheeler's line," a southern voice dripped.

"Is this Carole's roommate?"

"Yes. Mr. Sullivan? I recognize your voice. Carole still hasn't come back from when she went off with that police officer."

Sullivan felt an alarm go off in his head. "Evelyn Casey's maid said you went there and picked up Evelyn to take her to see Carole's editor about a story." As he spoke the words, Sullivan prayed they were the facts.

"I've been right here. I don't even know where Evelyn Casey lives."

Sullivan slammed down the receiver, his face hot, body cold. Twin symptoms of fear. He faced Castro, finding it hard to speak the words. "The Sequin has Evelyn and Carole."

22

Floating through curtains of mist, Evelyn slowly opened her eyes. Disoriented, she glanced around, events she hoped were only dreams fogging her mind. In a world of slow motion, she felt groggy as if waking from an uneasy sleep. Turning, she realized she was constrained in a sitting position, unable to move her hands or feet. When she tried to open her mouth, nothing happened. A tight band of something numbed her lips, rendering speech impossible.

Adrenaline surging, she strained against her bonds. The room was so dim she couldn't see what immobilized her feet and secured her hands behind her back. The last thing she remembered was entering the strange house with Carole's roommate. Was the woman actually Carole's roommate? Then a shattering thought struck her. Was she being held by the Sequined Stalker? Had she been mistaken about the killer being a man? Had she been injected with some drug or had she been knocked out by a blow to the head?

"So you thought you could work up another accurate

personality profile," a voice mocked. "A real expert, aren't you?"

Evelyn jumped, heart hammering. She couldn't tell if the raspy voice was masculine or feminine. Her eyes slowly adjusted to the darkness.

Evelyn saw a figure, leaning from the waist, edge close to her. Straightening, the person paced back and forth. "Got yourself in trouble, didn't you? Something you can't get out of. Hawk Sullivan won't be able to get you out of this, either. You didn't get the chance to tell him about your little theory. He and the police will continue looking for someone they won't find." The silhouette cackled. "The Doctor killer is safe. Safe forever. But not you. And you brought it all on yourself by meddling where you shouldn't have. If you'd just stayed out of something that didn't concern you, I would have left you alone. Evelyn Casey, you changed the course of your own destiny. You'll have to pay." The voice grew even more raspy and filled with fury. *"Pay."* The raw hatred in the word sent a chill through Evelyn.

Suddenly the room was quiet. Evelyn sat in total darkness, her mind screaming with questions for which she could find no answers. The only time she had mentioned her theory was to Carole at lunch. Evelyn thought of the woman at the next table and remembered the strange sensation she experienced when face-to-face with the woman in the rest room. Why did her theory that the Sequin was a man suddenly spur the killer into action if it wasn't on target?

She desperately tried to think of some solution to the deadly situation, but could find no ray of hope. She was completely and utterly helpless and at the mercy of a maniac. She couldn't even plead or try to reason.

Evelyn heard footsteps, then the sound grew faint and muffled. She thought her heart might burst from fear. Where had the person gone? What was coming next? She made a sound deep in her throat. Someone returned the communication with the same noise.

Suddenly the room turned into a blaze of lights, the glare stabbing Evelyn's eyes. She closed her eyes and squeezed them tight, then looked around. Carole Wheeler was tied in a chair. Across her mouth was a swatch of electrical tape, hands and feet bound with the same material. Her eyes were wide enough to pop from their sockets. Tears rivered down her cheeks. Evelyn wondered how Carole had been lured to the house. She lifted her eyebrows, hoping to encourage Carole not to give up. There was a small chance some miracle might happen.

Evelyn tried to memorize her surroundings. The room was enormous, the wide burnished floor covered with a palace-size oriental carpet. Light played on old lacquer boxes. The fireplace, tall enough for someone to walk in, was edged with green-mottled marble. The mantel held ornate bronze urns, cherubs wrapped around the lids. Two rosewood couches were separated by an oversize table, a lake of smoked glass. There was other light, soft and melting into shadows. The silk-shaded lamps beside the sofas increased the play of light and shadow that mottled the green walls. In one corner, a full set of armor stood guard, a sharp sword drawn. Evelyn half expected the metal suit to charge forward, brandishing the weapon.

The lights went off and Evelyn heard someone walk into the room, speaking in that same rasp. "I should introduce myself, but I'm sure you've already guessed. Well, what will I do with you?" Fright mushroomed in Evelyn. As carefully as this murderer plotted, there must be a plan. The psycho was merely toying with their emotions, smart enough to have taken away their only weapons, words. If only she could speak, goad, taunt the killer, she might break the Sequin psychologically.

"Now, let's see. I could tape your noses. Cut out your air completely. You'd smother in a matter of minutes. No! That's too quick. You should suffer. I have all the time in the world to wait. I want to come up with something really . . ." A pause. "Excruciating.

"I know," the voice continued. "Are you ladies afraid of the dark? Most people are, especially if they can't move and don't know what will happen next. I have a place to put you where you'll either die of fright or you'll last and last, fighting to stay alive until you starve or suffocate. No one will ever find you. Monstrous way to go."

Evelyn strained to decipher the sudden noises. A chair moved. Someone grunted with effort. She listened to footsteps disappear down the hallway. A door opened with a scrape and she heard steps creak from the weight as the killer descended to someplace below where only echoes were audible. Fear stabbed her as sharply as a knife prick.

In a few minutes the figure was back, leaning close. "Your friend is settled now. Your turn." Evelyn felt evil hot breath on her face. "You know what an oubliette is?"

The word scared Evelyn even more. It sounded like some instrument. Then she remembered that an oubliette was something like a secret dungeon with an entrance only through the top, a well dug into the ground.

"Well, do you? Nod if you do."

Evelyn blinked and nodded.

"No, you don't. This one is a tomb." The person was untying the rope that held Evelyn to the chair, picking her up. She was thrown over a shoulder.

Evelyn felt the muscled back. Strong. Head hanging toward the floor, she looked sideways, dizzy, the dark house upside down. She hoped to faint. Die. Anything to escape what faced her.

The air turned damp and musty as she was transported down into a cellar. The steps creaked. She prayed the killer would fall. Head bashed. Killed with one blow. The Sequin kept walking, now and then pushing her further over the strong shoulder, balance like a tightrope walker.

Cobwebs grazed Evelyn's face. She heard mice scurrying for cover. She was hoisted off the shoulder and rolled

closer to the dark pit in the dirt floor. She was shoved
closer. She could just make out the wooden top that fit
over the hole. She was dragged until her feet were dangling down the pit, then pushed from behind.

Her body dangled, half in and half out, balanced like a
seesaw. Suddenly she went straight down over the side,
falling through space. Nothing but darkness.

Speeding down Central Expressway, Sullivan rejected the
thought of calling for help on the car radio. He was too
afraid to trust anyone else with Evelyn and Carole's rescue. There was no margin for error. If the police rushed
in, sirens blaring, the Sequin might panic. He was dealing
with someone far too clever and had to act accordingly.

In the passenger seat, Castro gripped the dashboard.
The manager, Jake, jostling in the back seat, shouted that
he was going to sue the city. Sullivan hadn't wanted to
bring the man along, but was afraid he might be in cahoots
with Christopher Byrd and tip him. When they arrived at
Byrd's, he intended to gag the manager and put him in the
trunk.

As Sullivan barreled through the night, he weighed the
situation again. Was he taking too much risk by acting
solo? So much time had elapsed since Evelyn and Carole
had been whisked off by someone that might not even be
Christopher Byrd. *If* Byrd had them, no telling what
awaited at his house. He might need some backup. Wayne
Gilbert was competent and clever enough to improvise in
any situation.

Steering with one hand, Sullivan grabbed the radio,
called headquarters and asked for Gilbert. The police operator told Sullivan the lieutenant was not there, but she
could patch him into Gilbert's mobile phone.

"Watch it," Castro yelled as Sullivan roared up too
close to a car.

Sullivan pulled around the vehicle and accelerated, listening to the crackle on the line. Finally Gilbert came on

and Sullivan explained everything that had transpired. "I'm on the expressway, heading out to Byrd's address. Just passed LBJ Freeway."

"I'm even closer to the place." Gilbert's voice seemed tinny. "I can make it there quicker than you can."

"Silent approach," Sullivan ordered. "You know what we might be dealing with. Play it cool."

"Gotcha," Gilbert answered.

Sullivan still felt uneasy, but decided he'd made the best decision. Suddenly Sullivan saw that the solid string of car lights on the curving expressway was not moving as it had been. Vehicles were slowing. He was forced to brake, move forward slowly, then brake again. Up ahead, Sullivan saw the trouble.

"Look," Castro said, pointing at the windshield. "A big truck has broken down. God! It's one of those wide loads. It's hauling a house on a flatbed. All the traffic's balled up."

The driver of the car in front of Sullivan suddenly slammed on the brakes. Sullivan rear-ended it. Then a car behind Sullivan slammed into him. They were snarled in a sea of vehicles, hopelessly stuck. Drivers jumped out of cars, yelling and waving their hands.

"I'm certainly going to sue now," Jake screeched. "I've got a hell of a whiplash. You crazy bastards."

With no choice but to call for help, Sullivan grabbed the car radio and couldn't get a response. The crash had damaged the mechanism. He opened the door and hauled out. "Let's go, Castro."

"You can't leave me here," Jake shouted.

Sullivan climbed on the trunk of the car in front, Castro following suit. In a race against time, they ran over hoods and tops of cars, moving down the expressway toward the cutoff to Christopher Byrd's house.

23

Evelyn's fall to the bottom of the pit had been broken by Carole's body. She hadn't hit her squarely, but jolted down on her back, knocking them both to the dirt floor. Evelyn heard a low moan, but had no way of knowing if Carole was hurt. With no way to comfort her, Evelyn edged toward Carole and laid her head on her shoulder. Carole responded by pushing her head against Evelyn's. Carole shook like a palsy victim.

The darkness was so complete Evelyn felt as if she had her eyes closed. She tried to keep in mind what Sullivan once said: panic reduces chances of survival. As long as someone was alive, and willing to fight, there was always a possibility of mastering the situation. The point was not to give up hope. All was lost when that happened.

Evelyn touched the curved wall behind her, fingertips running over the rough bricks. In the old days, these cylinders dug into the earth were used for storage of certain foods, a pulley lifting the goods up and down. Barefoot, Evelyn pushed up and felt the walls, pacing off the round area which she figured was the size of a small powder room. There were no ropes or pulleys attached to the walls. She remembered hearing of old houses with tornado shelters, possibly the original purpose of this oubliette. Involuntarily she glanced up as if to see, wondering about the depth of the brick cylinder. There was no way to gauge the fall.

Making a guttural noise, Carole scrambled closer to Evelyn. Evelyn realized she was afraid when their bodies lost contact. Evelyn dropped to her knees when her foot touched something soft. She moved her hand and wanted to scream. Something furry lay on the dirt floor. Was the place infested with some kind of animals? She jerked back, repulsed, heart pouding.

Trying to calm herself, Evelyn took deep breaths, exhaling and inhaling through her nose. She wondered how much air was left in the cylinder, how it felt to suffocate. Did you grow drowsy, then simply lose consciousness? She tried to push such thoughts from her mind.

She stretched her legs, flexing her toes. Something sharp jabbed her skin. Pulling back, Evelyn felt a rush of pain, then a thick warmth puddling down her foot. Blood! Some object drew blood. She scooted carefully, until positoned so that she could feel with her hands. Moving with care, she touched something that felt like a skeleton, many of the bones jagged and sharp.

An idea flashed in her head. If she could buy them enough air time by moving the cover off the top of the oubliette, she might be able to grasp one of the bones in her hand and pick at the tape on her wrists until she worked free. She moved close to Carole, trying to communicate.

Making sounds deep in her throat, Evelyn touched her head to Carole's shoulder, then with a pushing motion urged her to stand. Receiving the message, Carole complied. Evelyn leaned against Carole, forcing her back to her knees. They went through the exercise twice. On the third try, while Carole was on her knees, Evelyn moved onto her shoulders. Almost losing her balance, Evelyn angled her feet and stationed them around Carole's neck. As Carole strained and rose, Evelyn tried to relieve some of the pressure by leaning against the brick wall.

Carole weaved under the weight, making small whimpering sounds. Evelyn stretched, trying to feel the wooden lid with her head. Suddenly Carole collapsed, bringing them both to the floor.

Evelyn pushed up, urging Carole into position, and they started the exercise again. This time, Evelyn felt several bricks that were slightly out of line with the wall. She edged the toes of one foot, then the ball of her foot on the small ledge, keeping her other foot on Carole's shoulder. In that precarious position, she strained upward, her head just touching the lid. Knowing she had only one chance, Evelyn lurched upward like a torpedo launched from its pad.

Evelyn's head struck the lid and she felt the cover move out of position slightly as she tumbled downward, striking the dirt with a resounding thud. Glancing up, a sharp pain coursing across her skull, she saw a dim crescent above. Carole wiggled close, making a squeaking sound, her head near Evelyn's. That small vent would provide enough air while they worked on the tape.

Evelyn edged over to the pile of bones, hands tied behind her back, fingers running over shapes, testing sharpness. She selected the one she thought best. Holding the bone upward, she started to dig at the tape that bound her wrists. The job was going to be long and tedious, probably impossible, but it brought hope.

On the gravel rural road, Wayne Gilbert slowed when he saw the mailbox, 13 BENT TREE painted on the side. Christopher Byrd's address. With headlights out, Gilbert eased down the secluded driveway, barely touching the accelerator. He knew it had cost Sullivan a great deal to have to call him, the anxiety the man felt, the crushing disappointment not to be able to finish the job himself. A sense of pride that Sullivan had singled him out swelled in Gilbert.

Stopping the car away from the house, Gilbert switched off the ignition and eased out in the cover provided by the trees. Doubts about not calling for a backup crept into his mind. He had wanted sole recognition for catching the Sequined Stalker. He edged through the brush, circling the house blazing with lights. Gun drawn, he checked out Byrd's garage and the thick underbrush in the backyard. Stealthily he moved around the house's perimeter, looking in windows.

Gilbert stopped at the kitchen window, almost holding his breath. A small man in pajamas and robe finished a sandwich, rinsed his plate, then slugged down a glass of milk and yawned. Harmless. Maybe Sullivan was wheezed up over nothing. Still, somebody had lured Evelyn Casey and Carole to some unknown place. The innocent-looking man before him might have nothing to do with the case, even though he was a female impersonator. Having tattooed eyeliner, a likely professional requirement, and buying a purse like the killer carried wasn't a crime. He stuffed the gun back in the shoulder holster. He'd question Christopher Byrd, take him downtown for further grilling while a search warrant was prepared, then have the place combed.

The man left the kitchen and Gilbert lost sight of him. He moved down the side of the house, catching glimpses in the window as Christopher Byrd proceeded toward the front area. Byrd turned on the television set in the living room and settled in a chair.

Gilbert walked up the front steps and knocked on the door, watching Byrd through the glass panel. Seeing Gilbert, Byrd got up and hurried to answer the knock.

"Who is it?" Byrd asked, leaning toward the door.

Gilbert held up his badge. If the suspect tried to run, he could shoot through the glass.

Byrd unlatched the spindly lock. With such lack of security, the man obviously wasn't nervous about isolated places.

Byrd peeped around the door's edge. "Can I help you? What seems to be the problem?"

Gilbert smiled so as not to alert him. "Probably nothing. Just like to ask you a few questions. Are you Christopher Byrd?"

Nodding, Byrd peered up and down his driveway, then looked at Gilbert, opening the door wider. "Well, come on in." His voice was calm, not one of apprehension. "I can't imagine what you'd want to talk to me about." He gestured toward the living room. "Has something happened down at the club?"

Gilbert shook his head and followed the man.

Byrd sat on the couch and crossed his legs, running his thumb and forefinger down the pajama leg's sharp crease. Gilbert stood before the mantel, trying to evaluate the suspect. Unruffled. Cool. Maybe too much so. Homicide always struck a note of fear, guilty or not.

Gilbert eyed the man. "Mr. Byrd, where were you this morning?"

Byrd looked insulted. "Right here. I've been sick all day with a cold and a migraine. My cousin is a nurse. Came by and gave me a shot. I've been knocked out all day. I just got up." He twisted the gold ring on his little finger.

"Any witnesses to that?"

"Being sick doesn't call for a crowd," Byrd snapped.

Gilbert had developed a distinct dislike for the arrogant little man. "Can you tell me where you were a week ago last Tuesday?"

Byrd frowned. "Not right off. Probably working at the club. You could check. If I wasn't there, I was here. I don't go out much when I have a free night. What's this all about?"

"You have any medical background, Mr. Byrd?"

"I'm an entertainer. Always have been."

Gilbert surveyed the room, Byrd now watching him closely. "Mind if I look around the premises?" If the man agreed, it would save the time it took to get a warrant.

Byrd hit the floor. "You have a warrant?"

"I can get one."

"Well, I suggest you do just that and come back."

Gilbert moved away from the mantel. "Mr. Byrd, I'm going to have to ask you to come down to headquarters."

Byrd's eyes looked angry enough to have arrows flying from the pupils. "Are you arresting me?"

"No," Gilbert answered. "But I will if you don't come along voluntarily."

Byrd returned Gilbert's stare. "On what charge?"

"Suspicion of murder." Gilbert saw the words make headway in Byrd's mind. For the first time he looked nervous.

Byrd jammed his hands in his pockets. "This is ridiculous. I'm going to call a lawyer."

Gilbert nodded. "Feel free."

Byrd threw up his hands and started out of the room. "Never mind! I don't need any lawyer. Let me get dressed and get my wallet from the bedroom and I'll go with you."

"I'll have to go with you to the bedroom, Mr. Byrd," Gilbert said, moving close to the suspect. He kept his hand in position, ready to draw the gun if necessary. He still felt that Byrd was just a punk but he didn't want to take chances while Carole and the Casey woman were in jeopardy. Sullivan would figure he'd taken Byrd downtown when he found the house empty. Gilbert wasn't about to entertain Byrd until Sullivan arrived.

Gilbert stayed close to Byrd as they climbed the stairs. He followed Byrd into a bedroom that looked like it belonged in another century. The whole house unsettled Gilbert; the atmosphere was creepy, like a movie set for a haunted house.

"Mr. Byrd, you bought a shell-shaped purse at Neiman-Marcus." Gilbert lifted his eyebrows, gauging the reaction. "I'd like to see it."

Byrd pursed his lips, as if thinking. "Yes, I did, but I don't have it. It was a present."

"Who for?"

"Robin Anderson, my cousin, the nurse. She's not in any trouble, is she?"

She just might be, Gilbert thought, suddenly alerted by a lead that might be more promising than Byrd. He intended to talk to Byrd's cousin immediately. "Where does this cousin of yours live?" Gilbert relaxed his grip on the gun and moved his hand.

"Just down the road, about a mile." Byrd edged to the closet, Gilbert on his heels.

"We'll just stop in, then. Take her downtown for questioning, too."

"Okay! Okay!" Byrd fumbled in the closet, then half turned to Gilbert. "Ready?"

Gilbert blinked at his sudden recollection of the fresh creases in Byrd's pajamas when he'd said he'd been asleep all day. That thought and the consequences of his mistake hit him at the same time.

Byrd lunged at Gilbert's chest, sending the hatpin home.

Gilbert's eyes widened in shock. With a leaden arm, he reached for the gun as he crumpled to the floor. His body twitched, then relaxed.

"No, you weren't ready," Byrd said, standing over the corpse.

Christopher Byrd hurried to the bathroom for tissues. He couldn't let the smart-ass cop bleed on his floor. He placed wads of Kleenex around Gilbert until the bleeding subsided.

Christopher went back into the bathroom, flushed the Kleenex down the toilet and looked at his image multiplied in the mirrored room, thousands of Christopher Byrds. He had to save them all. It was time to stay calm, think, show his real genius. So many questions assailed him, making planning difficult. How did They know to send someone to his house? *How?* Did the purse lead them here? If one cop came, others would follow.

Christopher paced back and forth, watching his army in

the mirrors. Leading them to victory required some strategic moves. Moves that had to be made quickly. Suddenly his face lit up in triumph. He turned slowly to catch the full view.

He ran to the phone in the bedroom, stepping around the cop's body. Picking up the receiver, he dialed his cousin. The phone rang and rang. Answer, *bitch*, his mind screamed.

Finally she picked up the line and offered a lazy "Hello."

"Robin, listen, Cuz, I need to talk to you right away. Are you alone?"

"Yes, Chris. I was asleep."

"I'll be over in a few minutes. Don't answer the phone again until I get there."

"Chris, is something wrong?"

He smiled, unable to resist. "Dead wrong."

Christopher slammed down the receiver and dashed to his closet. Rummaging through the pile of clothes, he retrieved the shell purse. It had to be the key. He put on a coat and jammed the purse in his pocket.

He grabbed the cop's arms and dragged him into the hall, bumping the body down the stairs. At the front door, Christopher strained and heaved the dead weight over his shoulder. Weaving and staggering down the driveway, Christopher reached the police car. He laid the body aside, opened the door, then pulled the cop in, careful not to let the bloodied shirt touch anything. He would wipe off fingerprints later.

Turning the key left in the ignition, Christopher backed around, then sped toward Robin's, a short distance away. After he killed Robin and planted the cop to make the scene appear to be a murder-suicide he would run home. Then wait for what came next. He had orchestrated the scenario perfectly.

24

After reaching the cutoff ramp, Sullivan and Castro stood on the side of the dark road, trying to flag motorists. Sullivan knew there was no point in flashing papers no one could read, and he didn't have a badge to display. Car after car passed, headlights shining in their faces. Sullivan turned to watch taillights receding in the darkness. Overhead, the sliver of moon was shrouded with ominous clouds. Sullivan felt himself shudder. He had to get to Christopher Byrd's house before it was too late, if it wasn't already.

"Well, come on. We can't stand here any longer," Sullivan said, breaking into a trot, Castro following.

They ran several miles. Sullivan felt a stitch in his side, but never slowed. He tried not to think what might have happened to Evelyn and Carole. The optimist in him wanted to believe that Christopher Byrd had the women and that Gilbert had arrived at his house in time to rescue them. Sweat poured down his forehead, blurring his vision.

The road veered sharply to the right, and up ahead in the darkness glowed a service station. "Let it be open," Sullivan said to himself. His luck had already been sour enough. He saw a man walk to the front door, apparently locking up for the evening. Leaving the lights on, the man checked the gas tanks, then headed toward a pickup parked by the building's side.

Quickening his pace, Sullivan lifted his hand and called out, "Wait!"

The man glanced their way and bolted for the truck, jerking open the door.

"Police, stop!" Sullivan shouted.

The man hesitated, looking from the oncoming duo to his truck. He made a tentative step into the truck's cab, then reached under the seat. Sullivan was beside him, holding his papers.

"We got stuck in traffic, had to leave our car. This is an emergency. We need a lift to Thirteen Bent Tree Road," Sullivan said, huffing for breath.

The attendant eyeballed the two as if he wasn't convinced of their identity. He scratched his head.

"Listen, man," Castro said. "We'll run you in for obstruction if you don't get a move on. Let's go." He buzzed around to the other side and grabbed the door handle.

Sullivan slid under the wheel and stationed himself in the middle. The attendant got in and turned on the ignition. "Okay, you better be for real. I've been robbed three times and I don't carry any money."

The truck bumbled over the rutted gravel road, the driver eyeing Sullivan and Castro at every opportunity, obviously uneasy with his decision. When they came to the mailbox on the road marking Byrd's address, Sullivan told the attendant to stop.

Thanking the man, they hauled out and moved cautiously down the tree-lined driveway, a lane curving through thick overbrush. Rounding a group of trees, they saw Christopher Byrd's brightly lit house looming before them. Sullivan's heart lurched when he saw no sign of Gilbert's car. Somewhere in the distance an owl hooted. Sullivan knew nothing short of death would have prevented Gilbert from coming. He had to have been there and left.

Leaning forward, they crept over the yard and edged against the house. Sullivan strained toward the window, smelling his own sweat mixed with the odor of fear.

In pajamas and a robe, Christopher Byrd sat in a chair reading, a lap robe thrown over his legs. A mug, steam drifting up, sat on the side table along with a giant box of Kleenex. Wadded tissues littered the floor by the chair. Outside the window, Sullivan drank in the sight of the man, wondering if he was looking at the killer. He wiped his forehead on his sleeve, trying to figure the situation.

"What the hell do you make of this?" Castro questioned in a quiet voice.

"Don't know," Sullivan answered, easing away from the house.

They made their way around to the front porch, tiptoed up the stairs, and when Christopher Byrd was in sight through the glass door, Sullivan knocked.

He watched Byrd look up from his book, puzzled. Frowning, he threw the lap robe aside and padded to the door, his hand over his eyes, peering through the glass. "Who is it?" His voice was hoarse.

"Police," Sullivan answered, holding up the papers.

Wiping his nose, Byrd jammed the tissue in the robe's pocket and unbolted the lock. "Can I help you?" he asked in a nasal tone.

"We'd like to ask you a few questions," Sullivan stated, studying the small man whose face was flushed. "Are you Christopher Byrd?"

The feverish man nodded, rounding his shoulders as if chilled. "Come on in if you aren't afraid of catching something."

Sullivan and Castro followed Byrd into the living room,

where he nestled back into his place, pulling up the lap robe. Down the hall, a grandfather clock bonged out the hour. The man seemed unruffled by their presence.

"Did one of our men come by here?" Sullivan asked, standing close to the fireplace. He was trying to survey the place without giving the impression of doing just that. If the man denied Gilbert had come, something was amiss.

Byrd sniffed. "I was just about to say, this is becoming a habit . . . police dropping by at all hours." He gave them a weak smile. "All due to that blasted expensive purse I bought. The officer was asking about it. I told him that I bought it as a gift for my cousin, Robin. A little celebration present. She was made head nurse at Presbyterian Hospital."

With that piece of information, Sullivan and Castro exchanged glances and listened as the man continued.

"The officer went flying out of here after I gave him Robin's address. She doesn't live but a mile or so down the road. He wouldn't even answer my questions." Byrd blinked. "What is this? I think I'm entitled to know. I tried to call Robin to see if she was in trouble and there wasn't any answer. Can you tell me if she's in trouble or what?"

"No, I can't. Official police business." Sullivan stared at the man he'd desperately struggled to locate. He noticed the rim of lighter color skin on Byrd's little finger, protected skin. Sullivan felt his pulse accelerate. Now that he was face-to-face with Christopher Byrd, the innocuous little man seemed an unlikely candidate, but the cousin could be another matter. Maybe they had been on the wrong trail all along, but it strangely led in the right direction. He tried to think rationally, keeping emotions aside. "We need to talk to your cousin also. You have a car, I imagine. I want you to drive us there." Sullivan wondered what kind of scene Gilbert had encountered at the cousin's. Sullivan wasn't leaving Christopher Byrd alone. It puzzled him that Gilbert had.

"Me?" Byrd leaned forward, a frown stitched on his forehead. "I'm sick and groggy. Robin gave me a shot that knocked me out all day. I had just gotten up when the other cop came."

"Driving a mile down the road won't hurt you. I have to insist," Sullivan barked, anxious to get moving.

"I'll go change, then," Byrd answered, rising slowly.

"You'll go just like you are. Get the keys," Sullivan ordered. "You drive."

Sullivan and Castro followed Byrd into the kitchen. The little man pulled a key ring from a rack. "Car's in back. This way."

As they pulled out of Byrd's winding driveway and headed down the dark lane, Sullivan asked his cousin's last name.

"Anderson. Robin Anderson," the man answered, concentrating on the road.

Eyes on the driver, Sullivan turned the name over in his head. Were they on the brink of facing the Sequin? Maybe Gilbert had already found Evelyn and Carole safe, had the killer in custody. Hitching in his breath, Sullivan prayed his optimism wasn't false. If Byrd and his cousin were scratched as suspects, Sullivan had nowhere else to look, no line to pursue. The more time passed, the more grave the situation grew. "What's your cousin like?" Sullivan asked, gripping the dashboard. "Can't you step on it?"

Accelerating, Christopher Byrd glanced at Sullivan. "Don't get me wrong, Robin's my cousin, but she's strange. Always has been. I always tried to include her in my circle of friends, but she never really fit. A real loner. Not very dependable except at her work. Loved the hospital. She was the one who talked me into getting the eyeliner tattoo, like she has. It saves time with my profession, make up, you know."

"Okay, okay," Sullivan said, suddenly irritated with Byrd's prattle.

A mile down the road, Byrd turned in a driveway and pointed. "There's my cousin's house."

A freak electrical storm had whipped up the skies, zig-zags of lightning turning the night into a strange purple hue. In the blinding flash, Sullivan saw Gilbert's car parked in front of the two-story clapboard house, a quaint over-grown cottage. He strained forward, nose almost pressed to the windshield, heart hammering in his chest.

"Stop right here," Sullivan ordered as Byrd pulled alongside the unmarked car.

Castro bolted from the back seat and opened the driver's door. "Get out," he said to Byrd.

Sullivan barreled out, pulling his .357 Magnum from the shoulder holster. "Easy, now. Quiet."

Sullivan led the way up Robin Anderson's front steps. Lights were on in the house, curtains drawn, blocking any view. Castro nudged Byrd forward. Sullivan gently turned the doorknob, finding it unlocked. He eased it open and peered around the crack.

"Jesus," he yelled, slamming the door wide open.

Castro and Byrd moved in behind him, glaring at the spectacle before them. Gilbert lay sprawled on Robin An-derson's living room floor, a giant splotch of red staining his shirt. A robed woman slumped against the couch, a hatpin protruding from her chest.

Byrd shrieked. "Robin! My God! What's happened here?" Shaking, he turned to Castro. "I can't believe this!"

Sullivan raced to Gilbert, touching his neck. "He's gone." He moved to the couch, peering down at the athletic-looking blond woman, hair closely cropped, who in life had been attractive. "Her, too. Looks like a murder-suicide." He whipped around to Castro. "Call Homicide. Quick."

Sullivan ran through Robin Anderson's house, searching each room, slamming doors, calling Evelyn. In the bed-room, he rummaged through the dead woman's closet and saw the shell purse on a shelf.

He hurried away and looked in every conceivable hiding place, ransacking the spidery attic. Back down stairs, he hurtled through the kitchen door into the darkness. Intermittent lightning slashes turned the dense foliage into a surrealistic bluish setting, then with its quick retreat, rendered the area completely black. Sullivan felt like a blind man.

Sullivan fought his way through an old garage, striking matches, holding them until his fingers burned. He fumbled around in a toolshed, banging his head and nicking his arm on a rusty saw. Calling Evelyn's name, he ran under the trees, knowing his search was futile.

Suddenly he heard the sirens and saw the blue lights flashing. Three cars screeched to a halt before Robin Anderson's house, men converging on the scene. Sullivan galloped toward the back door and ran through the lighted kitchen.

In the living room, Captain Chandler, Lieutenant Day and four other officers stood around the bodies, their faces solemn. In a ragged voice, Sullivan briefly explained the situation. Chandler listened, never taking his eyes off Sullivan.

"We finally got her," Chandler stated. "She's the Sequin, all right."

Day glared at the dead woman. "So it was a woman, after all. The Sequin's got the two missing women secured somewhere." He glanced around. "Guarantee you they're here somewhere."

"The Sequin?" Byrd questioned in a squeak. "That killer . . . is my cousin, Robin?" He gripped his stomach. "No!"

"Get the flashlights," Chandler said to his men. "Search every inch of this place."

The Crime Scene Unit and the medical examiner crowded through the door, everyone talking at once. Sullivan pulled Byrd aside and over the excited shouts, asked if he knew any special place where his cousin might have secluded the two women. Sweat boiled off the little man. He shook as he told Sullivan he had no ideas. Sullivan thought the man might be going into shock.

Wiping his forehead, Byrd turned to Captain Chandler. "I'm sick. I have to go home. Please." He nodded to Sullivan. "He knows where I live. If you want to question me tomorrow, I'll be available anytime. I'll be glad to come downtown." He clasped his hand over his mouth. "I'm going to throw up." He dashed to the bathroom.

Chandler glanced at Day. "The man's in the way. When he comes out, tell him to go on home. Let's get that search going. Call the rest of the task force." Chandler walked over to where the ME worked on the body and hunched down beside him.

The ME looked up. "Well, it's finally over."

"It's not over," Chandler answered. "We've got two missing women." He stared at the body. "If only she could talk." His eyes drifted to Gilbert. "A good officer." He shook his head. "A shame."

Sullivan heard a crowd shouting and looked out the window. Police officers were holding back a group of people Sullivan suspected were reporters, who had arrived quickly on the scene by monitoring the police channel. He watched Byrd scurry to his car, dodging the throng, and drive away, taillights disappearing down the driveway. He turned from the window, frantic for the search to get under way. It was possible he had been so overly eager that he had missed something. This time the place would be painstakingly covered.

Sullivan looked down, studying the floor. Evelyn and Carole might not be on the premises, but being held anywhere in a city of over a million people. He tried not to let his mind accept any thoughts that they had been harmed or worse.

Castro eyed Sullivan. "We were wrong about the Sequin being a man, but it brought us here, anyway. We'll find the girls. They've got to be around here.''

Sullivan stood stark still, the term the killer used to Carole Wheeler teasing his mind: "the eye of the beholder." Were things as they seemed? Now he remembered. After leaving a feather at one of the crime scenes, the killer suggested Carole use another label rather than "the Sequined Stalker." The name he'd been searching for finally flashed before him. "Fine-feathered Femme," like fine-feathered friend, the killer said over the phone. *Robin* Anderson. Christopher *Byrd*. Either one fit.

Sullivan jerked toward Castro, telling him the discovery. Castro frowned, then said: "But this woman here . . . the hatpin . . . Gilbert . . . She's got to be the Sequin.''

As if to clear his thoughts, Sullivan shook his head. "Since Byrd was a female impersonator I was sure he was the Sequin." Reacting like an animal, when instinct preceded knowledge, he turned and rushed to catch Chandler.

"We've got to search Byrd's place," Sullivan said, urgency in his voice. "Byrd said his cousin came to his house and gave him a shot that put him out all day. Maybe she stashed the two women at Byrd's and he doesn't know it.''

"Okay, Sullivan. You and Castro beat it to Byrd's and if he agrees voluntarily to the search, go ahead. If he doesn't, Homicide can't dash in and search a place without 'probable cause,' " the captain said, then winked. "I'm sure you two can handle it." He glanced at Day, then looked back at Sullivan. "I can't help what you do now. This case is about to be closed, except for finding the missing women. I'm as frantic as you are about them. As soon as we get the task force searching here I'm going to call the chief of police and the press.''

Sullivan gave the captain a salute, then hurried to the front door, Castro right behind him.

The captain turned to Day. "Frankly I'm glad the killer

turned out to be a woman like we originally thought. The department has already looked bad enough. If it got out that we were looking for the wrong sex, we'd look doubly ridiculous.''

The ME looked up. ''Captain, I'm about finished.''

Outside, Sullivan and Castro dodged the crowd and jumped into Gilbert's unmarked car. The seat was pulled so close to the dashboard Sullivan banged his knee on the steering wheel. Automatically he reached for the lever to adjust the seat, then stopped and looked up. The rearview mirror was also adjusted for a short person. Very short. Gilbert was over six feet tall.

Concentrating on thoughts that wanted to pop out, Sullivan rested his hand on the seat while adjusting the mirror with the other, fingers almost sandwiched between the seats. He felt something in the crevice. He reached further down and grasped the object.

Castro whipped toward him. ''What's holding you, man? Get moving.''

Sullivan opened his hand and displayed the ring on his palm. ''Look a here.'' Light caught the gold family crest and clearly showed the name ''Byrd'' engraved below. Sullivan and Castro stared at each other. Byrd had not only been in Gilbert's car but had driven it. Suddenly the whole picture became clear. Dangerously clear. Byrd was the Sequin and he had the women.

Dropping the ring in his pocket, Sullivan started the engine and headed toward Christopher Byrd's house. He knew he had one chance and one chance only of getting the women safely away from Byrd. It all depended on Byrd.

25

Sullivan killed the engine at the bottom of the driveway. Byrd's house was dark except for one upper-story window. Lightning streaked across the night and split the sky, illuminating angry dark clouds. In the distance thunder rumbled as the threatening storm gained momentum. Sullivan looked up, hoping his planets and stars were aligned just right, all signs favorable.

He turned to Castro. "If we ever played it cool, now is the time. Remember how tricky the bastard is."

Sullivan tried to think as Byrd would, his premise based on the assumption that the women were still alive. He dared not think otherwise. Byrd had been forced into behaving contrary to his nature. Kidnapping the women and killing Gilbert and Robin Anderson were acts of self-preservation. None were victims he'd ordinarily choose.

From his earlier phone conversations with Carole's roommate and Evelyn's housekeeper, Sullivan knew that Byrd had lured Evelyn from her house by disguising himself as Carole's roommate and lured Carole by posing as a female police officer.

Now, if Sullivan and Castro found the women at the house, blame would automatically fall on Robin Anderson, so long as Byrd had not revealed his true identity later to Carole and Evelyn. Unaware of the ring's incriminating evidence, Byrd would likely be relieved to relinquish control of the women, thinking he had wriggled unscathed from the situation and was free to start over another day. But if the women could identify him as their captor, everybody was in trouble.

Sullivan eased open the car door, remembering traits Evelyn had told him were indicative of psychopaths. They faked emotions never felt. Were manipulative, deriving a thrill from control over others. Deceiving others was to psychopaths a sign of superiority. They were devious, controlled, always anxious to place blame on anyone but themselves. He intended to play Byrd for all he was worth. Byrd would be engaged in the same game, locking them into a psychological game of wits.

Sullivan and Castro walked up to Byrd's house. Sullivan banged on the leaded-glass front door. Castro stood so close Sullivan felt breath on his neck. Suddenly the entire house came alive with lights. They watched Christopher Byrd descend the stairway. Still in pajamas and robe, he leaned forward, eyebrows lifted. Sullivan motioned for him to unlock the door.

Byrd complied, then faced the men. "What now? I've been through enough," he answered, playing his charade to the hilt.

Sullivan eased forward. Play it natural, he coached himself. Don't overdo. "I understand how you feel and I hate to bother you, Mr. Byrd, but we'd like to look around your place." His eyes darted around the room. Nerves wired, system charged, Sullivan tried to keep his emotions in tow. This was no time to lose it, he told himself.

Byrd's lips drew back from his teeth. "What on earth

for?'' His voice raised several octaves. ''I'm telling you I had nothing to do with all that's happened. Think what this will do to my reputation. Kin to the Sequined Stalker.''

Castro moved closer. ''Maybe your cousin put those missing women somewhere on your property without your knowledge. You said you were knocked out all day. Couldn't we just take a look? The women weren't found at your cousin's. She had to put them somewhere.''

Byrd's face turned into a mask of stone. ''Do you have a search warrant?''

Sullivan tried to look sympathetic. ''I didn't think we'd need one. You haven't done anything except for your misfortune of being related to Robin Anderson.''

Byrd blinked, swelling with confidence. He took a deep breath. ''Have it your way, but you're going to hear about this. Disturbing me at such a time.'' He turned away. ''I'll show you through the house, then you can look around outside on your own. I'm not going out and get hit by lightning.''

Byrd grabbed the banister and pulled himself upstairs, his motions exaggerated. Sullivan and Castro followed him to the second floor and began their search while Byrd watched, arms across his chest, expression smug. Now and then Sullivan looked up to lock eyes with Byrd. Sullivan could feel the machinery behind those eyes turning, planning. Byrd knew exactly where the women were, was only waiting for Sullivan and Castro to find them.

They explored every room, especially the strange mirrored bedroom where secret spaces could have been built behind panels. They examined the closets, floors and walls, knocking for hollow sounds. An array of clothes to rival Central Casting hung in Byrd's closet. They rummaged through the racks, feeling the area beyond, where easy concealment was possible. Though Sullivan appeared distracted, he kept an eye on Byrd.

''Does this go to the attic?'' Sullivan pointed to a small circular wooden construction.

Mouth drawn as if closed by a drawstring, Christopher Byrd nodded. "I haven't been up there in years. Only the exterminator goes up there when I call him to come out. There are rats and things . . . not even any lights." Byrd shuddered.

Byrd fell in behind Sullivan, Castro bringing up the rear. Sullivan pulled out a flashlight Day had given him. They eased up the rickety steps and Sullivan shoved open the attic door. Cobwebs guarded the entrance. He waved them away, shining the flashlight in the darkened area, the beam moving from object to object. Old trunks, boxes of photographs, a dressmakers' mannequin, sheets half draped over old portraits. Racks of dated clothes and shoes. Discarded furniture. Rocking chairs. Old stained mattresses, ticking torn. Sullivan heard small animals scurrying for cover, their toenails clicking on the wooden floor.

He and Castro spent almost thirty minutes rummaging through the dusty, sweltering area. Sweat rolled off their bodies as if they had basked in a sauna. Byrd coughed and sneezed, urging them to hurry.

Suddenly Sullivan had a sinking feeling Evelyn and Carole weren't on the premises. But where else could he look? Maybe Day's search would prove successful. Maybe Byrd had hidden the women at his cousin's without her knowledge. Maybe Day already had Evelyn and Carole safely in tow. A headache hammered Sullivan's temples. Squeezing his eyes shut, Sullivan's eyeballs ached in their sockets. Then the flashlight dimmed, batteries weakened, and died. "Okay, downstairs. Then outside. You have a flashlight?"

Byrd clenched his teeth. "In the garage. Christ! This is getting ridiculous."

The cooler air that hit them on their descent was a welcome relief. Wiping his face, Sullivan took a deep breath as he and Castro combed the downstairs, paying particular attention to the paneling in the den and living room. Sullivan examined the large fireplace and mantel. He touched the suit of armor that stood guard in the corner, noting the sharp point of the sword. Finishing with the area, Sullivan lumbered down the hall, then spotted a thick door. He stopped, eyes on Byrd.

"This a cellar or what?" Sullivan asked, watching Byrd's reaction.

Lifting his shoulders, Byrd sighed. "Storage place, not used for that ever in my family's lifetime. In the old days people kept food cool down there. A root cellar, too. A well down there, before there was running water. Been capped since I was a child. Robin and I used to play down there. Take a look if you want."

Sullivan hit the outside knob, a mechanism the same as on a cold-storage locker, and heaved open the reinforced door. The cellar was as dark as the attic, but there was a light switch near the door. Sullivan slid his hand along the wall, flicking the switch. A dim bulb came to life, giving enough light to define the stairway and the area below. A musty odor hit Sullivan.

"Let's go down. See what's there. Robin Anderson might have been down there," Sullivan said.

Sullivan eased down the wooden stairway, feeling the boards give slightly under his weight. Byrd was the filling in the sandwich the three of them formed. Eyes adjusting to the dimness, Sullivan glanced around at the dirt-floored space. Nothing but a few decaying wooden crates stacked against the walls. An old ladder, slats hanging loose. Wooden buckets pioneer women used. Rusting ancient tools hanging on the walls.

Sullivan looked down at the lid that capped the oubliette. The cover was slightly ajar from its slot, the surrounding earth almost imperceptibly scraped. Even in the dimness, he saw Byrd's eyes flare up. Sullivan felt a surge of excitement. They were close. Almost there.

Byrd quickly controlled his expression, mouth opening in surprise. "My God! You don't suppose Robin did put the women down there? If they're there we have to get them out right away before anyone else dies." He touched his forehead. "This is a nightmare. I can't believe what Robin's done."

Sullivan squatted, removed the lid and peered into the dark hole. He rummaged in first one pocket, then another for a match. His fingers closed on a book and he pulled it out. With the motion, Byrd's ring fell from Sullivan's pocket.

Lighting a match, Sullivan held it forward. "Can't see a thing."

But Byrd had.

After Sullivan had spoken, strange moans commenced from the depths of the pit. Sullivan leaned down to hear. Byrd lunged at Sullivan, ducked from between the two men and bolted for the stairs.

Sullivan hung across the pit, clutching the rim, fingers digging into the dirt. Startled, Castro moved to help him, then, seeing Sullivan's grip was solid, whipped around and started after Byrd.

With lightning speed Byrd was up the stairs, moving like a gazelle and just as surefooted. Castro bounded up the stairs in pursuit, then his weight cracked one step and the rotten board collapsed. Castro cried out as his ankle dug through the jagged wood. The door above slammed shut, bolt hitting home.

"Jesus," Castro yelled, grasping his wedged ankle, trying to extricate himself without further tearing the flesh.

Sullivan swung to the side of the oubliette, escaping the danger of falling into the pit. He called down into the darkness, heart feeling as if squeezed by a hand. "Evelyn! Carole! Are you down there?"

Again, the urgent muffled noise.

"Wait! Just be quiet, then give me two quick sounds if that's you." He leaned into the pit as Castro hobbled close, blood running down his ankle.

"Ummm, ummm," the sound came echoing back.

Sullivan looked up at Castro. "Got 'em." He turned

back to the pit. "Are you hurt? One sound for yes, two for no."

"Ummm, umm."

Spotting Byrd's ring, Sullivan picked it up and dropped it in his pocket, muttering under his breath. His excitement at finding them had made him careless. He leaned into the pit. "Okay, be calm. We'll get you out." Sullivan pushed up, eyes scanning the room. He raced over, grabbed the ladder and tested his weight on the rickety rungs. Deciding which steps could bear the weight and which to avoid, Sullivan pulled the ladder to the edge of the pit. He ripped off the steps that sagged, throwing the pieces across the room.

"I'm going to ease a ladder down the middle. Stay back close to the walls so you don't get hit." Sullivan glanced up toward the door, wondering what Byrd might pull next. They weren't safe until Byrd was neutralized. Handing his gun to Castro, he said: "Watch that door."

Sullivan guided the ladder down as far as he could reach, but didn't hit bottom. Holding on, he yelled: "Is it close to the bottom if I let go? Touch the ladder and see if I'm safe to turn it loose. One sound for yes. Two for no."

Sullivan felt the ladder move, then heard one groan. He let go and the ladder plunged down, then flopped against the wall. He grabbed a small handsaw from the wall, and swinging over the side of the pit stationed himself on the top rung.

Sullivan edged down, feeling the wood give. Slowly he eased his feet from step to step. Suddenly he felt something against his leg. Reaching down, he touched a head, then ran his fingers through hair. Dropping to the ground, Sullivan felt two bodies crowd him. He struck a match.

The flame flared in the darkness, lighting up two faces that filled Sullivan with joy. He worked on the tape covering their mouths, careful not to tear the skin on their faces. When the women were free, both started talking at once, asking questions about the Sequin. Sullivan hugged them close and said: "Save your breath to cool your first cup of coffee. I've got to get your hands and feet undone so we can get out of here."

Castro yelled down: "Everything okay?"

"Getting better al the time," Evelyn called back. She winced as Sullivan held her wrists. "I was working on the tape with something jagged. I think it was a bone. Kept stabbing myself, but I could tell I was shredding the tape some."

Sullivan held up another match. "Bones, all right. There's a small skeleton. Looks like a dog. Your arms and wrists are cut." He took the small saw and cut the tape binding both women.

They let out sighs of relief, stretching, bending, flexing their shoulders. Carole touched Sullivan as if to make sure he was real. "You should have seen the balancing act." She explained how they jarred the cover from its rim.

"Thank God for that." Sullivan felt a rush of pride at Evelyn's ingenuity. He grabbed Evelyn's waist and started her up the ladder. "Castro, be ready to haul them out. Here they come." As Evelyn moved cautiously up the splintery ladder and reached the top, Sullivan started Carole on the way.

Castro leaned forward, grasping Evelyn's outstretched wrists, and pulled her to the dirt floor. She rolled over and lay there, taking deep breaths.

"I'm up," Carole squeaked. "Get me."

Again, Castro reached down and pulled Carole to safety. Carole crouched by the hole, looking down. "I can't believe we were down there." Tears rolled down her cheeks. "I never thought we'd make it out. I thought we were doomed."

Sullivan called for a hand.

When Sullivan was free, he sat beside the pit and caught his breath, eyes on the door. In a voice stronger than Sullivan would have expected, Evelyn explained what had happened, pausing as Carole attempted to interrupt.

"After I mentioned to Carole at lunch that I thought the Sequin was a man everything broke loose, but the person who eavesdropped was a woman."

Evelyn followed Sullivan's line of vision to the door. "When we were tied up, I couldn't see in the dark. The voice was so strange." She followed Sullivan's line of vision to the door. "Who is it up there?"

"Christopher Byrd. You were right about the Sequin being a man. He's a female impersonator and a real master of disguise," Sullivan answered, then told them what had transpired, excluding the part about the ring. His mistake that fouled the plan fried him.

Carole rubbed tears from her eyes when she heard about Wayne Gilbert. Her cheeks were dirt-streaked. "It's a wonder he didn't kill us, too."

"Enough talk. We can do that later." Sullivan glanced around, then took the gun from Castro. "We're not home free yet. Byrd's loose up there and will do anything to keep us from getting out." Plans of escape zipped through his head. He knew a mind as warped as Byrd's had already spawned some bizarre counterattack. "We've got to get out of here."

Sniffing, Castro jerked his head toward the ceiling. "Fire! The crazy bastard's set the place on fire. Look at that smoke drifting in. We'll suffocate." He pushed up and tried his leg. He groaned. "I don't think I can stand on my leg."

"You better start trying," Sullivan roared.

The faint sound of crackling fire filtered from above. Sullivan bolted up the stairs and pushed on the heavy door. Castro limped along, pulled himself up by the banister and tried to help. Stepping back, Sullivan aimed the gun at the outside lock's location and fired repeatedly. Splinters flew as the wood cracked. He and Castro shouldered into the door that still wouldn't budge.

Choking from the smoke, Sullivan tore off his shirt, ripped off a section and tied the cloth over his face. Castro

followed suit, calling to the women below to do the same.
Again, they heaved into the door and felt it give slightly.
Both kicked in unison, Castro using his good leg.

Sullivan motioned to a support post. He and Castro
grabbed the wood and jerked with all their strength. Nails
yanked from their position. Sullivan twisted the post while
Castro jerked at its roots on the stairway. Sweat poured
off Castro's forehead, pain etched on his face. Finally they
wrenched it free and both grabbed hold, slamming the
butt into the door. Falling from its hinges, the door slapped
forward into the hall. Sullivan motioned for the women to
come forward.

Sullivan had used all the bullets, but hoped the gun
might bluff Byrd. He edged into the flaming hall, fire lap-
ping the walls, then signaled for the others to follow.
Smoke stung his eyes and choked his lungs. He tried not
to breathe as they slunk down the hall. Castro walked between the two women, using them as support.

The front door was in view. Only a few more feet to
freedom. They moved quickly now, choking, glancing
from side to side, filled with fear that Byrd would somehow block their way. The intense smell of gasoline per-
meated the air. Passing the wide opening to the living
room, Sullivan stopped in his tracks for a moment. The
others edged close. Byrd was busy dousing the draperies
with gas. He threw the can aside, lit a match and tossed
it forward. The wall roared into an inferno.

Eyes on the front door, Sullivan motioned for the others
to follow. They walked in a line as if on a tightrope, carefully inching forward. As Sullivan eased almost past the
opening to the living room, his foot hit a gas can, knocking it over. Hearing the noise, Byrd whipped around. Evelyn immediately recognized Byrd as the man who had
wanted to buy them drinks in the Hyatt bar.

Dwarfed by the suit of armor, Christopher Byrd stood
close to the hollow metal shape as if it were an ally. He
was circled by flames licking toward the ceiling. Ears

pricked, eyes exuding evil, he looked like a devil come from hell. Sullivan pointed the gun at Byrd. "Don't move or I'll shoot. I'm coming in to get you."

Byrd cackled. "You don't have any more bullets. I counted." His eyes moved off Sullivan for an instant and flicked to a gun that lay on the mantel. As Byrd reached for the weapon, Sullivan grabbed the gas can and hurled the remaining gas in Byrd's direction. It was enough. Byrd screamed and dug at his eyes.

Byrd lurched back and the sword extended from the suit of armor surged through his chest. Byrd's face registered shock.

"You'll never know who the real Monster was," he rasped, his tone like a death knell. The grin on his face was paralyzing.

The curtains and wooden rods crashed down on the suit of armor into which Byrd had backed, sending the metal body and Byrd slamming to the floor in a blazing funeral pyre.

When they reached a safe distance from the house, the four turned to stare at the blaze, cinders fluttering around them like snow. Sullivan glanced at Evelyn, her hair trailing blond ribbons.

Staring straight ahead, Evelyn said quietly, "By saying we'll never know who the real monster was, Byrd was still laying blame on somebody else. Right to the end. I wonder if it was his father. I'll bet he was a doctor."

"There you go with your psychology again." Sullivan lit a cigarette. It tasted better than he remembered. He blew a smoke ring, then took a deep breath. He hoped Evelyn wasn't damaged from the experience as she had been with the killer she was forced to shoot. "You almost got it. I should have figured it out sooner."

Evelyn turned to him, head cocked to one side. "What makes you so special? What makes you think you should have foreseen what no one else foresaw? Are you blessed with some divine power you haven't informed us of?"

"On occasion." Sullivan shrugged, happy with her attitude.

Just as an unmarked police car pulled up, Carole glanced back at the burning house. "Halloween will never be my favorite holiday again."

Day and Chandler got out of the car, both breaking into wide smiles. In a gesture of triumph, Chandler raised his arm high over his head. "Great! You got 'em. They're safe. We saw the fire." He motioned to Day. "Get on the horn and call off the search. Get the fire department out here." Chandler turned to the burning structure, patterns of light playing on his face. "So the Sequin had 'em here all along. How did the fire start? What happened to what's his name . . . Byrd? Poor little sumbitch get burnt up?"

Sullivan looked at Chandler. "Byrd was the Sequin."

Chandler whipped around. "Whoa, now. Just hold on here." His eyes darted from Evelyn to Carole. "Did Byrd bring you two here?"

"We couldn't see who it was," Evelyn answered.

Chandler looked relieved. He faced Sullivan, suddenly agitated. "Why did you make such a statement? You just grasping at straws to make your point that the Sequin was a man? Trying to make the department look bad? We've got to function in this city. Your hitch is over here. Just stay out of this now. Go on back to San Diego. We've got it all wrapped up. I'm on the way downtown to a press conference."

"Byrd started the fire," Carole blared out, then addressed Sullivan, her reporter's interest obviously piqued. "You said Byrd was the Sequin. What's going on here?"

"Sullivan is wrong," Day broke in. "Robin Anderson is the Sequin. As for the fire, Byrd probably just panicked, afraid he might be implicated," Day said, nodding his head to confirm the statement.

Sullivan fingered the ring in his pocket only he and Castro knew about. He was tempted to let Chandler have his moment of glory with the press, but it went against his grain to allow blame to be placed where it didn't belong. Fingers closed tightly around the ring, Sullivan withdrew his hand from his pocket and slammed his palm into Chandler's as if giving him a "high five." As far as Sullivan was concerned, the captain was on his own to do what he wished.

Sullivan got the captain by the eyes. "It was in Gilbert's car. I'm sure he'd want you to have it." He turned to his group. "Let's go." Sullivan lumbered away, hesitated, then turned around, walking backward. He gave the captain his best smile. "To borrow a line from the Sequin, maybe everything *is* all in the eye of the beholder." Sullivan faced forward and kept going.